DRIFT

ALSO BY MANUEL LUIS MARTINEZ

Crossing

DRIFT

MANUEL LUIS MARTINEZ

PICADOR
NEW YORK

FIC
M38567dr

Picador® is a U.S. registered trademark and is used by St. Martin's Press under license from Pan Books Limited.

www.stmartins.com

Book design by Jonathan Bennett

Hand-lettering by Brian Rea

Library of Congress Cataloging-in-Publication Data

Martinez, Manuel Luis.
    Drift / Manuel Luis Martinez. — 1st ed.
        p.   cm
    ISBN 0-312-30995-3
    1. Mexican American teenagers—Fiction.   2. Mexican American families—
Fiction.   3. Los Angeles (Calif.)—Fiction.   4. San Antonio (Tex.)—Fiction.
5. Loss (Psychology)—Fiction.   6. Teenage boys—Fiction.
7. Grandmothers—Fiction.   I. Title.

    PS3563.A73339 D7   2003
    813'.54—dc21

                                                                    2002038162

First Edition: April 2003

10   9   8   7   6   5   4   3   2   1

For Eli, my brother and friend

ACKNOWLEDGMENTS

I'd like to thank the many friends who read this manuscript and gave me good, solid advice. The book is better for your input. I'd also like to thank my editor extraordinaire, Webster Younce, for his sharp eye and keen insight. Many thanks to my faithful and savvy agent, Matt Williams. I couldn't have written this book without the assistance of the Ford Foundation, the MacDowell Artists Colony, and Breadloaf Writers Conference. Thanks to my family for the love and support. Lastly, thanks, Olivia, for being my inspiration and salvation during a raucous youth. You alone kept it from being misspent.

DRIFT

CHAPTER 1

I spend the whole day alone in this cube, having to raise the red, white, and blue Christian flag when I want to whizz or even just stretch. It's a drag. But it's my own fault since I just got kicked out of high school again. Twice in two years, and Grams decides she has to send me to a religious school, one of those Christian fundamentalist ones, the kind that keeps students in line by making them sit facing the wall and putting wood partitions between them. One thing Grams didn't count on, though, was all the fuck-ups and *caranchos* ending up in the same place, and I know I'll get into trouble I never would've found in public school if she hadn't gotten scared that I was going to wind up dead. After eight hours of this place, I'm ready to roll out and do anything—fight, get high, look for girls—just to forget everything till tomorrow. This "place" is Sunnydale Christian Academy. I know—ridiculous name. Why not just call this motherfucker Happytown? It's embarrassing to tell people when they ask where you go to school. But that's what the place is called and it's as bad as it sounds.

I'm sitting in Principal McNutt's office wearing the baby-blue-and-gray ski sweater that belonged to my father. It's sort of big, but it's the nicest thing I've got and Grams wanted me to look decent my first day, *"como la gente,"* she says. Pops left it at the house the last time he split and hasn't been by to pick it up. It's been a while now.

I'm thinking about that when McNutt says, "Oh, I don't want to forget to give you the contract." She opens her desk, one of those mammoth World War II metal deals that looks like it wants to swallow you, and rummages around for a minute before pulling out a mimeographed sheet. Behind her, next to a big-assed American flag, is a picture of her grinning at ex-prez George Bush. There's some bullshit written on a certificate about a thousand points of light. "Here you go," she says, sliding a page over to me. It reads "Sunnydale Academy Contract of Christian Conduct."

"You got to meet Bush?" I ask her.

"Proudest day of my life."

"Yeah? What was it for?"

"A wonderful ceremony in Houston where he recognized various Texans for civic contributions. He's a wonderful man, a real Christian. Not like that Clinton." She frowns at me like I made her say something wrong. "We're not here to discuss politics." She taps on the paper she's pushed over.

It's a list of activities I'm to "absolutely foreswear from taking part in" and a dress code and list of rules I'm agreeing to abide by in order to enroll: "No worldly music." "No cursing." "No association with unwholesome people." "No smoking, drinking, or drugs." "No unseemly conduct with the opposite sex." "Dress code: no tennis shoes, denim jeans, or shirts without collars and buttons. Preferably, shirts should be white." "No getting up from your desk without raising the flag and getting permission from your teacher." And a load of other shit.

"How do you know what 'worldly' is?" I ask her.

She taps on the contract again. "Please sign."

I sign it and give her the check Grams wrote me this morning. Then she goes into the speech about the devil and how he's everywhere. She's got this big window in her bright white office where she can sit and watch the classroom but you can't see her, like those kids out there might be shoplifting or like she's on the watch out for Satan in case he's stupid enough to roll in flashing horns and tail. And while she's invoking the devil, this crazy-looking dude stands right in front of that one-way mirror and stares into the office like he can tell someone's talking about him. He's got crazy eyes trying to jump from his huge head like Ping-Pong balls ready to pop out of a mouth, black hair so thick and short it looks electrified. This bug-eyed freak just keeps looking in through his own reflection, but McNutt doesn't skip a beat. She keeps talking while she stands and walks to her door, poking her head out. "Ignacio, come in here. I have someone for you to meet."

Bug Eyes walks into the room still smiling insanely. I can tell that this is *the guy*, the guy who's into everything. "Ignacio, show Robert around a little. Be a peer counselor."

"Nacho," he says to me and McNutt. I'm not sure what he means. "Call me Nacho," he says, this time pointing to himself. He is thick, squat, and carries himself confidently, like a Mexican wrestler. I shake his hand, but before we can really start to talk, McNutt tells us we should move into the classroom.

She does her introduction bit while all the students stare at me. There's about forty of them in the high school room. They look mostly like losers, all of them wearing the boring clothes the dress code calls for, boys on one side, girls on the other, in the long, narrow rectangular room. Above each of their cubicles is a stenciled Bible verse on yellow cardboard. This is the "sunny" part of Sunnydale, and McNutt tells me I have to pick out my favorite and do the same thing. The partitions between the desks are cheap wood and painted blue, making the place look almost bright. In the middle of the room, from the ceiling, hangs a three-foot cross. It marks the desk where the teacher sits.

Right away I notice that there are some cuties in the room. Loose, curly perms and all sorts of braids and twists catch my eye. Leave it to girls to figure out a way of looking different even in a place like this. That isn't the case with the other side of the room, though. The guys all look nerdy as hell, all of them but Nacho, that is.

He's different, and I can tell that this guy isn't going to give me the kind of counsel McNutt has in mind. As he walks me to my partition at the end of the men's side of the room, he sounds me out quick for my fuck-up potential. "You party?" he half-whispers to me on the way to my new desk. I nod as I look at the kids who are looking at me. They're craning their necks because they're supposed to be facing the wall. It's a sad sight, all of them looking cowed like they're afraid to peek, only they're so bored they're willing to take the risk.

After school Nacho and his weird brother, Pito, get me high on the way to their house. Pito's got frizzy hair and he's tall, rangy, looking nothing like Nacho except for the nutty grin. He gives me his hand, his sleepy brown eyes opening up for a second. "Wha's up?"

Even though all we do is hang out, it's great, hitting the bong and listening to Nine Inch Nails until their hairdressing mom gets home. She comes in tired looking, puffy red-dyed hair, and saggy, sad eyes. "What's that funny smell, Ignacio?" she asks right off. He shrugs a "Nothing," letting her know he doesn't want to get into it. We split because his mom starts quoting scripture at her two sons. She wants me to understand that her sons' sins aren't her fault. I don't mind her because she tells me that she'll cut my hair whenever I want for free.

Older people always seem to like me pretty fast. What I got going for me is that I'm innocent looking. I'm a skinny motherfucker, and older women, mom-types, are always trying to feed me because my ribs stick out and I have long, gangly arms. They find out my moms is gone, give me a sad look like they want to hug me, and then bam, I'm hooked up for free food and other good shit. That conversation usually goes something like this:

"So, Robert, what does your mother do?"

"My mom died eight years ago, when I was about to turn nine. She caught pneumonia in Mexico and they couldn't do anything for her in the mountains."

"Oh, that's terrible." During this part they look embarrassed and sad at the same time, like it's their fault or maybe they're next. "What was she doing there?"

"She went down on a missions trip for her church. I think they were trying to convert the *indios*, and they didn't have any medicine."

"Well, who takes care of you? Your father?"

"Nah, he's a musician and he's always traveling, but he sends Grams money—that's my grandmother—and she watches me."

"No wonder you're so skinny. *Puro huesito*. Ignacio"—or whoever the friend bringing me home is—"you bring him over for dinner whenever he wants."

My moms isn't really dead. I just prefer saying that because it's easier than getting into the whole damned story about my pops leaving and her having a nervous breakdown and then splitting to Califas with my baby brother, Antony, and leaving me here to look after myself.

Before all that happened, I was sort of looking forward to everything. High school was supposed to be hype; me and my friends could hardly wait. We imagined that it was going to be off the hook with girls and parties. But when my pops left for the last time, things got so rough that I was looking for signs from God, not for sexual healing.

My uncle, a preacher, was always after my pops to quit the music business and come back to God. But my pops never even gave it a shot, even though as a kid he used to be religious. His father was a preacher, too. When pops split, I began to listen to my uncle a lot more carefully. Maybe God could keep my father from loving the road and women so much, from wanting to spend weeks away from home. From needing all that freedom. Freedom from us.

The night before my first day in high school, there was a church rally for the back-to-schoolers. My cousins Enrique and Juan were there, too. My Uncle Augustine, Enrique's pops, put down a mean sermon. He told us about all the shit we'd face and that we were on a mission. He didn't pray that night. He threatened God: "I know you, Lord; I know that these young men and women will not put out prayers that will not be answered. They are yours and you are their Father. They are alone in a world of iniquity, a world of sin, a world of terrible violence and danger. Look on them now, Lord, and protect them—their minds, their bodies, their spirits—from the attacks they will face beginning tomorrow." It didn't exactly make my heart race with anticipation. It sounded more like some hellish battle where a square kid like me was sure to get stomped.

My uncle wasn't even half close. Crockett High was more fucked up than the school Michelle Pfeiffer tries to straighten out in *Dangerous Minds*. On the first day, I walked through the front door to stare up at a big white statue of a mustang on its hind legs, as if to say, "Don't even try it here. We don't fuck around." The thing must have been twenty feet high, impressive until I noticed that he had no sack—no cock, no balls. He was all attitude. You gotta have equipment if you're gonna front like that. The school was the same way. Lots of talk about this and that, but no action. Mostly people were worrying about getting out of that mother-fucker without getting stabbed.

Early on I had this stupid notion that I wanted to be a musician like my pops. It's pathetic now, but I wanted to try to impress the old man, show him we had something in common. Something that connected us, you know, *father and son*. So I tried band at Crockett, but within a week it was obvious that I had zero talent. But at least I could *tell* what sounded right and what sounded wrong. I couldn't stand to be in that practice room with people who played even shittier than me. Most of those motherfuckers didn't know which end of the horn to blow into. The music roiling around that hall made the band teacher clench from his ass to his scalp. Kids would pretend they were blowing notes when they weren't doing shit; some of them didn't even have reeds in the mouthpieces; others just played nonsensical notes, doing their own thing. The drummers were so off, you might've thought they were playing a completely different piece of music. Half the time, they were. Band dude would stop us in the middle of a piece and take a stroll, his face red with fury and disgust, to the back of the room and take a glance at the music stands. "That's not even the piece of music we're playing!" he'd scream. "Jesus, can't you people read? The friggin' title is at the top!" I got the hell out of there as soon as I could.

I decided to go it alone. I didn't really want to talk to anyone around there, anyway. Everyone was either fucking stupid, acting crazy, or trying to be a roughneck. I started skipping my classes. I'd head straight for the library and look for books to read. I figured I'd learn better on my own.

In a couple of months, I went through a lot of Kurt Vonnegut after I picked up *Slaughterhouse-Five* by accident. The librarian, this guy named Mr. Crane who was pretty cool actually, told me that if I liked Vonnegut, I would like Joseph Heller. *Catch-22* was so good, I read it over and over. Hunter Thompson's *Fear and Loathing in Las Vegas* was next. Those three kind of explained my life to me. Those guys see the world filled with monsters and freaks, and the scary shit is that it's the monsters who run things and make life hard for the rest of us. They corrupt everything they touch.

When you're surrounded by crazy shit, just like Yossarian in *Catch-22*, you have to go with it, be just as crazy and absurd. I can relate to that. Life is completely unpredictable, but somehow you have to be able to find some way to deal.

Although I tried to stay out of everyone's way, the teachers couldn't leave me alone. They called my moms and told her I wasn't coming to class. She tried to get tough with me and ask me where I was going, but she wasn't very good at it. I'd promise that I was going to stop screwing around and go to school, but I just couldn't do it. After a couple of months of this, they kicked me out. I didn't care. I was relieved.

But my moms got sicker and my Aunt Naomi came and took her and my little brother, Antony, to L.A. He was still a baby, only a month away from being four. They left almost two years ago. I moved in with my grams because she was the only one who offered when no one else wanted me. I think she felt responsible because her son had split on us.

She lives on the Westside. It's rough, but I'm no stranger to the *barrio*. I grew up here more than any other place.

Living with Grams meant that I had to go to Edgewood High. I'd go to school every day because Grams doesn't play the way my moms did. After Moms fell apart, she didn't have the strength to make sure I went. So I didn't. But Grams has plenty of strength and she makes damn sure I get up. But she couldn't be around at school with me. Every day something had to go down at that place. There was some crazy motherfuckers at that joint. It don't take shit to get into trouble around a place like that. I got busted for having a quarter-ounce bag of weed in my locker and that was it for me. They have a zero-tolerance policy and that means I can't go to high school anywhere in the Edgewood School District for a whole year. That's when Grams called Sunnydale.

But here's what nobody knows: I've decided to make it a go at Sunnydale. I have to keep my grams happy while I institute my plan. See, I'm not going to stick around this place too long. I'm L.A.-bound. I'm gonna get together some money, enough to get over there and lay some on the table in front of my moms. I turned sixteen and I can drive to work now, and I'm gonna show my moms that she needs me around to help her out. When she was here, I couldn't do much. I almost wigged out myself. I know that all the shit I did contributed to her falling apart, but she needs to know that it isn't like that anymore. My shit's wired now. But I gotta bide my time around here until I'm ready.

Tonight Nacho and Pito take me to meet their old man. He runs this cool-assed bar called La Parranda. Pito explains on the drive that it's a dump, but that his pops doesn't care that we're all under-age. That makes it the number-one place to chill. The bar is on Zarzamora Street, just down the way from Church of the Little Flowers, where everyone tries to stage their daughter's *quinceañera*, the Sweet Fifteen for teenage Mexican girls. Normally, I wouldn't be creeping the streets in this area, but Nacho and Pito don't seem worried. They come up here after midnight all the time. Still, Zarzamora is the kind of street even cops hate to patrol because there's *always* some craziness going down. Stand there long enough and you'll see somebody get their head busted and their shit taken—probably you if you're stupid enough to be standing there. The locals keep clear when the sun sets because around this block Zarzamora is always dark. Not a great place for the city to be saving money on streetlights, but the bastards on the city council always screw the westside. Most of the businesses have left the neighbor-hood, too. Now there's only a few bars, a Mexican bakery that closes early to avoid any trouble, and the occasional check-cashing place that'll cash a check with somebody's severed hand still attached to it.

La Parranda is one hundred percent pure dive. We go in through the back door. Nacho's dad lets us hang out around the pool tables and smoke and drink beer. Ten or twelve alcoholic-type burnouts from around the block, harmless really, all of them looking to keep the buzz going no matter the cost, are on their usual seats around the bar. Lots of cowboy hats and flea-market Spurs T-shirts hurting to keep it together around huge beer bellies. There's a few used-up-looking older women, all of them old enough to be my moms. Maybe my *moms's mom*. The women are hanging out, looking for a free drink and maybe a little bleary-eyed attention even if it's from a big, fat, sweaty, drunken slob. It's enough to make you wonder if it wouldn't be better—more merciful—for everybody involved if God didn't just wipe the place out with a great big celestial bowling ball, one of those with the flames on it. But I guess everyone needs a place to hang out, and Nacho's pops is kind of doing the neighborhood a favor by keeping these people from going outside. On the far end of the lounge, across from the bar, is an old jukebox that cranks out Mexican cornball, mostly *cumbias* and a few *polkas*. Good stuff when you're drunk.

What's coolest about Nacho's father is his 1976 Monte Carlo. It's way fucked up. The guy got it from this *vato* who owed him a couple of hundred bucks. It was all rusted and dented, but Nacho's father went and bought some Krylon and spray-painted it black. He put this little Mexican flag on the antenna and he's proud of it, too. That Monte looks like the Mexican batmobile, parked outside the bar ready for action should an emergency arise. You never know.

"What's your name?" his father asks me from behind the bar. He's standing in front of a big bar mirror that's framed by dozens of liquor bottles and red chile pepper Christmas lights.

"I'm Robert."

"That's a good name. *Roberto*." He twirls it around a time or two, like he's almost satisfied with it. He starts shortening it like old-timers always do. "Roberto, Berto, Beto. I used to have a good buddy named Beto. He's dead now." He lays it on thick, pausing a second before he says, "Junkie." He gives me a straight look. "You know him?" I shake my head. "Yeah, a stone-dead junkie. You don't sell that shit, right?" I shake my head again. "Yeah, you better not. I don't need the competition," and then he laughs. I can tell when I'm being fucked with and I laugh, too. "You watch out for my boys. They're motherfucking sons of bitches like their old man." He says it proud and pours me a beer. "Yeah, you watch out. They're the reason I had to leave their momma. Somebody be dead by now if I hadn't." The two or three burnouts sitting closest to us laugh. It's all good, though. Nacho's old man is cool.

Nacho, Pito, and me sit down near the pool table and put down a couple of quarters. While we wait for the table to open, we try to get a good buzz going. We're talking about Sunnydale and Nacho asks me who I think is hot. He wants a list. "I haven't been there but a couple of days, man," I say, not wanting to commit myself. "Besides, they got a careful watch on us."

"Man, sinners and saints all wind up in the same place," he says. "All those pops think they can send their little girls off to be kept away from us dirties. That's why they got us sitting with little walls between us. Like that's going to keep us apart. Shit! McNutt's"—he pronounces it My-Nuts—"got it set up so the only way to talk is to raise the little Christian flag. You need more than a little flag to keep me out of the pussy, dog. I get to them no matter what." He points down at his pecker and makes a few half-hearted gyrations. "They need to be calling me Snatch-o instead of Nacho."

He goes on and on, giving me the list of Sunnydale chicks he's "pounded" and how before he graduates he wants to "do" Sister McNutt. "She's gonna raise *her flag* up my pole before it's over."

Finally we get our turn at the pool table and he turns his attention to trying to beat me out of my last four dollars, which he does because by that time I'm all the way plastered.

Sister McNutt's watching. She's on me about my not being in dress code, about my sneaks and sinfully baggy jeans. She also wants to know why I don't put something more uplifting than "Jesus wept" on my Bible verse poster.

I get my first demerit for getting up to take an unauthorized piss. "Mr. Lomos," Miss Terry says snotty, "another student is in the bathroom. Only one student can be out of the classroom at a time. I'm *sure* that you know that. So how about turning around, marching to your desk, and waiting."

I'm not looking for trouble, I'm really not. The thing is, I had a big-assed glass of Kool-Aid and I'm not going to make it. I can feel the other kids looking up from their desks since this is about as much excitement as you get at this place. So I don't say shit. I just walk past her without even giving her a look. Not like I'm pimping or even showing off. I'm just trying to make a simple, dignified statement. Human rights, that's all, but the class is all whispers like I kicked her desk over.

By the time I get back, Sister McNutt has gotten the news. There's a note on my desk. "Come see me," it says, signed "Sis. McN." As I walk back there, Miss Terry gives me a little smirk. It almost makes me laugh. I knock on Sister McNutt's door. "Come in," she says like she's very tired. I sit down. "Robert, what are you trying to do?"

"Just went to the bathroom, Sister."

She gives me a "Come now" look. "That was stupid and rude. You're getting two demerits for what you just did." She lets it sink in, but I don't say anything. "You will do things the way you're supposed to around here. If you do, you'll be a better person for it." She sounds almost sincere for a minute. "Do you understand?" But that last phrase gives her away. She looks at me from behind her thick glasses. This is her moment. I decide I have to play along for now. I don't want trouble with Grams.

"Sorry, Sister McNutt. I thought I was going to lose it. I've got a bleeding ulcer and sometimes I gotta get to the bathroom really fast." I'm not lying about the ulcer. I've had it since I was about twelve.

"Hmmmm," she says. "I'll let Miss Terry know that you are allowed to go to the bathroom when you need to. But you absolutely must make sure to raise the flag first. There's no negotiating that one. Now, go apologize to her. I don't want the other students to think that rebellion will be tolerated around here. Remember, Robert, rebellion is the root of witchcraft."

I don't let on about any of this with Grams because she's hoping for a lot with me being at Sunnydale. Every day at dinner she wants to know how things went. I think she's looking for clues. Clues that she missed during my disappointing stints in public schools. She feels responsible about me losing it and getting kicked out. I told her it wasn't her fault. It was really nobody's fault. I just didn't want to go anymore. So I quit trying. Only now that I've got a plan, I'm going to keep it together.

CHAPTER 2

Me and Nacho get along because he hates his pops but looks up to him at the same time. That, and Nacho loves to get high. A couple of nights ago, Nacho, Pito, and me drove to La Parranda to get some money from his old man. But Nacho didn't ask him right out. He asked his pops to let him use his apartment to play some poker with me and a couple of other guys. His old man gave him the keys to his hotel room, one of those pay-by-the-week joints. Nacho didn't waste any time ransacking the place looking for money and dope. Inside the closet, in a boot, wrapped up in a blue bandana, we found about a thousand white tablets. The pills had EVANS.DBS written on them and when Nacho read that, he smiled big. "Dexedrine!" There was a gun, too, but we didn't mess with it because we knew the old man would miss it. But we took about fifty tabs apiece of the speed. We could use them at the school and around the neighborhood to trade for pot and cash. I need to get my hands on enough of both, pot to tolerate all this bullshit, money to get to California.

One thing I can say for Nacho is that he's got a good set of girls to hang out with. Some of them go to Sunnydale and some are from the neighborhood. They are always available when we want to ride around. We pick up some weed, buy beer and cheap wine, roll to where they live, and wait. They show up and we head off for the park. Sometimes we go to the Chinese Graveyard, sometimes we go to the haunted railroad tracks. These girls are different from the ones I couldn't get next to at Crockett or Edgewood. These girls are accessible. I don't mean they like to screw, but they don't mind messing around a little and just chilling. They don't scare easy, and they tell you quick when you're acting a fool.

Tonight we pick up Rachel and Elena from some dead party in a part of town I don't recognize. I thought I knew all of San Antonio, but Nacho is taking me into some new territory. We drank a lot last night and the last thing I want to do tonight is repeat that performance. My stomach won't stand for it. But right off the girls give me heat. "I don't care what you say, I'm not drinking," I tell them. They laugh and Rachel says, "Well, you can't just watch us have a good time." From in front, Elena pulls a joint out of her purse. "We got some good pot from my uncle. Me and Rachel smoked some this morning and just sat on the floor and laughed for an hour."

I figure that smoking up is my only out. "I'll smoke some weed, yeah, sure. But I'm not drinking." She passes me the joint and I take a big hit. I hold it in until my lungs are burning hard. I cough up the smoke in a fit, tears rolling down around my nose. "Are you alright?" Elena asks with a laugh, slapping me on the back. I collapse into the backseat, choking to death, my eyes itching. "I can't catch my breath."

"Damn, it isn't crack. Drink some of this, you wimp." Nacho is holding out a can of beer, but as much as my throat and lungs ache, my stomach is even rawer and I shake my head. "I'd rather choke." They think that's real funny.

In less than a minute, my legs loosen, the weight melting away, no mass below my knees. It creeps up to my waist and I feel my stomach relax. "Are you alright?" Nacho asks with a grin that spreads across my entire field of vision. He looks like the Joker, the Latino one, what was his name? Cesar Romero.

I snap back as a smile of sheer insanity floats just inches from my face. I'm wrecked and I have a decision to make here, one I gotta make within seconds, that's gonna determine whether I'm psychotically frightened over the next hour or whether I'm amused and delighted. The sight of Nacho's bared, horse-sized teeth has put a lot of pot-addled motherfuckers on the road to a paralyzing freak-out. I decide to relax, to lose the Joker image and go instead with a softer, more soothing Jester. Nacho isn't a frightening, demon-possessed sociopath and the girls are *not* his witches. Yes, his head *is* big, maybe even gigantic . . . is it . . . is it . . . *growing*? No, it's not. He's harmless. I'll concentrate on his eyes. His *kind* eyes, filled with a gleam, which, although just on the other side of demented, are somehow calculated to please. Yeah. That's it. I can see him clearly for the first time since I met him. I laugh because Nacho's harmless. He's my friend, and he wants to be laughed at. But not like he's the joke. This happens to me when I get high sometimes. It's a good thing, because I see what lies below the surface. Sometimes it's spooky, sometimes it's amusing and entertaining, but most often it's just sad.

"Nacho." I laugh, but I'm laughing a little too much and tears are running down my cheeks because I see my friend's inside on his outside.

"He's fucked up good," Elena says. "Get back in the car, you're making too much noise."

"I'm trying to take a piss," I yell. I've lied to make them stop the car so that I can stand outside for just a minute.

"Hurry up, Robert," Elena says, dragging me back to the LTD.

I back up against the opening of the car, resisting her push. I want to tell her that she is funny, too, and also that I love her very, very much. But I can't talk. Nacho comes around and pushes me inside. I know I'm making an ass out of myself, but even though I'm trying not to, I can't help it. I lie on the backseat laughing until the car goes into motion. Nacho puts on some music and I put my head on Elena's lap and she strokes my hair. My head cradled, her breasts inches from my face, the music washing over me, her long fingernails playing on my scalp. Normally, this would make me think about sex, but right now I'm just feeling happy. I smile, wanting to talk, but I can't be heard over the music, so I shut up, close my eyes, and just live inside the motion of the car. It takes me back to when I was a kid and my pops would tell my moms to get in the car and we'd go on a night drive for no reason, just to take a sweet, long ride. He'd roll down the windows and the air would blow mad-hard back where I was, cool but not cold, exhilarating, and me just a kid with the wind blowing over my body, naked except for my underwear, happy like a little dog as I watched my parents in the front, my pops in control, my moms content, until I got tired and drifted into black, purifying sleep.

I know now that hanging with Nacho is giving me the chance to do shit I've been told is evil ever since I was old enough to understand my uncle preaching in church. My grams and company have always drilled it inside of me that those on the outside of church are sinners, are damned, are dirty—*cochinos*. But she's wrong, not so much about the sinning or the damnation, or even so much about being dirty—but she's wrong because it's a kind of dirtiness she's got no knowledge of. Rolling with Nacho is like being a tourist in some foreign country I've read all kinds of books on. Only when I get there, the place turns out to be totally different from the picture I'd put together from the books. These people, fucked up as they are, are real. I don't want to be bullshitted anymore, by anybody. I'm past that now. That's part of why I like getting high. It peels back the layers of things, like stripping the old paint off a wall, so that I can see it with all its flaws and scratches. It's like having a good, clarifying heatstroke like the one I had a few years ago. I was sitting outside during Field Day where I was supposed to run the hundred-yard dash even though I'm slow as hell. I was on the bleacher, bored, when I suddenly felt like I was going to pass out. By the time I got home, my head was so fried I thought the fucking TV set *was talking specifically to me*. I was delirious, I know, but Peter Jennings had given me permission to enter his world, the *real* world that I'd only been looking at. Riding with Nacho is like that. It's doing, not watching. Night after night of laughing, screaming, dancing, running. Drifting.

My grams works. She works at everything she does. She cleans wealthy white women's houses and takes care of their complaints, but she's never been one to take nonsense. She gives as good as she gets, even now after she broke her hip. She limps along with mad authority on a cherry-wood cane that's all knotted up. She uses it to punctuate her slow dignity in case some sucker ever doubts it. She speaks English, but uses only Spanish in our *barrio*, especially when returning something to a store or making a complaint to a white clerk or manager who is used to pushing meek Mexicans around on our side of town. You should see her, standing there with her cane in hand, her proud, dark Indian face, iron-gray hair pulled back severely in a traditional Mexican bun, and demanding that her terms be met. When I was a kid, I'd stand behind her and watch cocky Anglos melt before my grams's Mexican indomitability. When it became clear that she wasn't going to leave or even speak in English, they'd begin to stammer in broken Spanish until they could no longer talk out their argument and they realized that it was just easier to give in. My grams is smart. She learned this trick from *bolillos* who intimidate *Mejicanos* because they can't debate anything if they don't speak English. Grams flipped the script early on and showed me what you can get done if you don't back down.

She drives a big muted-yellow Buick that Gramps left her when he died. I never knew him. She drives herself everywhere even though she's getting old. She's gotta be near seventy. But even when her back hurts so much it keeps her up all night pretending like she wants to finish knitting something, she gets up tough the next day to go work.

I told her the other day to go see the doctor.

"I don't need no doctor," she said. "Those doctors, their whole job is finding something wrong with you so they can make their money. I don't got nothing wrong with my back that Doan's pills don't cure."

She tells me all the time about growing up a migrant worker. That was a tough gig, let me tell you. Her mom was dead by the time she was eight, and she had five brothers and sisters younger than her who she had to learn to take care of. Imagine that. Eight and already a mom. She never did get to go to school, only picked up a little here and there in the migrant camps once in a while. She always has to ask me to come help her with adding up things, or she'll look up in the middle of paying her bills and say, "Roberto, how do you spell 'thirteen'?"

She's always trying to teach me how to be tough because she knows I need to be.

"You don't ever feel sorry for yourself. Nothing ever been easy for Mexicans. You don't got a choice, boy. The best you hope for is that God lets you see the problems coming so you can get ready."

She's old school. She went through the Depression Mexican-style. That means poor, sick, and getting chased off like a dog by cheating-assed farmers and the like. So I gotta believe her, especially now. I mean about trouble. It comes and it comes. I'm trying to learn how to see it better.

Grams was cool from way back when my folks were still cohabiting. She'd roll up on Saturday mornings and pick me up. That meant Pizza Hut, going to the grocery store, and my one-dollar allowance.

"You save that up and you'll have enough to buy what you want."

She was like that. Don't get the wrong idea, though. I had to work for that dollar. Every week I was in her big backyard, mowing, pulling weeds, helping her plant shit. Then she'd send me to the store to buy some ice cream. I'd take my bath, eat good, and watch *Star Trek* with my treat. Then in the morning, what she calls "early-early," she'd wake me up to get ready for church.

Once when my pops went on tour with some salsa band he'd signed up with, my moms went with him feeling like she needed to be on the scene to make sure he'd come back when it was over. I lived with Grams for what felt like a year. That was the first time my parents left me, but back then at least I'd get a postcard or a phone call once in a while. Grams would always tell me, too, "They'll be back, Roberto, very soon. They'll be back to get you and take you to your house." She has this huge, creaky, heavy gray metal fan on wheeled feet. We would roll it from the bedroom to the living room. It made a terrific noise when it was turned on, like the propellers of an old airplane. Back then, when I was homesick and missed my parents, I would listen to that fan and pretend I was on a plane to wherever they were. I know it's a joke to pretend that anymore, but I still listen to that fan every night to help me get some sleep. I'm an insomniac.

The house is cool. It's small, but it seems bigger on the inside than you'd think when you see it from the outside. It's like a maze in there. Little halls go in different directions with lots of musty closets that are filled with old, mysterious stuff. Pictures of people who are dead but look like they might've been up to something interesting in those black-and-white days.

My grams keeps my gramps's service revolver in one of those closets. I used to jack around with it when she wasn't home. Even now, I find books all the time in those closets. When I was a kid, I found a set of old encyclopedias from just after World War II in a closet. It had this long-assed section on Hitler and the Nazis, big black-and-white portraits of these evil fuckers that kept me reading. I was freaked all day long when I read about Goebbels and how he had gone home and watched his wife give all their kids strychnine before they offed themselves when they knew they'd lost the war. Twisted. The best book I ever found, though, was this Time-Life book all about natural mysteries. It was divided into "Space," "The Animal Kingdom," "The Ocean," and "The Earth." I read about black holes, the Loch Ness Monster, vampire bats, and volcanoes. All the stories had color pics. That book smelled good with its heavy, oily print and thick, bitter, glossy paper.

There was a small public library in Las Palmas shopping center where Grams took me to get my first library card. I was about nine, and she watched as I picked out a book on World War II and another that gave you the lowdown on the lives of the presidents. It was cool to come home from the library with a stack of books and take a nap. I'd go to sleep looking at them sitting on her big desk and thinking, When I wake up, I can grab one of those and start reading. When I was younger than that even, and there was a book fair at school, Grams'd give me five bucks and I'd spend all weekend long figuring out how to get the most books for my money from the book sheet the teacher would give us on Friday. Man, it was torture waiting for Monday to roll around. It was better than Christmas.

Next door there live two little girls and they're usually playing in their yard. They're new to the neighborhood. I never see the mother around during the day. She works. The old man is always there but usually in the house. I think he's an alky. The yard's all fucked up, grass overgrown and choked with weeds. The house needs painting. It's a raunchy-looking yellow, peeling and puckering all over. But the dad doesn't do shit except yell all the fucking time. The little girls don't seem to mind it, though. Or at least they do their best to ignore him when they can. But they do alright so long as he keeps inside and doesn't bother them. They're friendly. The older one is about eight. Her name is Tina. The other one is named Ruthie, but she's only about five and she says her name "Roo-T." Sometimes, for kicks, I have conversations with them. I like to watch them because they get along so well when they play. They never fight. I feel sorry for them because no one pays attention to anything they do. One day the older one knocked on my door and asked me if she could have some water. I thought it was strange and I asked her where her moms was. She told me she was at work and that her daddy wasn't opening the door. It made me good and mad, that goddamn drunk not opening the door for those little girls. I gave them a glass of Kool-Aid to drink. My grams wasn't home and so I let them sit in the house and watch cartoons for a while because it was so hot outside.

"How come you live here now?" the older one, Tina, asked me. "Who takes care of you?"

I thought it was a strange question because no one seemed to be taking care of them. Tina's got these dark black eyes that stare at you. "I just moved here. My mom is sick."

"Why don't you take care of your mommy if she's sick?" she asked like I was lying to her.

"She went home to be with her mommy," I said. I felt weird talking to a little girl about my situation. She seemed to take the hint, though, and the two of them sat there and watched *The Flintstones* until my grams got home.

CHAPTER 3

We're rolling around the northside, looking for some place called Arturo's. It's this club that Nacho says we can get into without ID. I don't really want to go because this place is for old people, but Nacho's hot for some chick he met at the mall and she told him she'd be there tonight. She sold him some ugly sunglasses and he spent an hour trying to look cool for her. He even put the fucking things on right after he bought them. I kept laughing at him standing in front of that Sunglass Hut cubicle, but he didn't pay attention because I was sitting at one of the benches behind him as he talked to this girl. He looked like a clown, wearing those shades and trying to convince her to give him her number. But she did it. "So fuck you, fucker," he said, waving it at me. He didn't even have the smarts not to wave it around in front of her.

I know Arturo's will be lame, but I didn't want to stick around the house with Grams another night. Tonight this new kid, Leo, is riding around with us. He's alright, but he's real quiet. An unsettling kind of quiet, a *Christopher Walken* kind of quiet. He's from L.A. and his parents sent him to the academy to keep him from doing the shit he was doing in Califas.

After half the night, we find the place. It's worse than I thought it would be. I like joints that are shitholes but know that they are shitholes. This place is a shithole that thinks it's not. There's a bunch of older people prancing around in suits and tight dresses. They have a band playing, but they suck. They're trying to do an imitation of Sonny & the Sunliners, playing these old fifties love ballads one minute and then the faggy lead singer going into an Engelbert Humperdinck routine, shaking his fat ass up on the stage. Even the Mexican music sucks. No *cumbia* or *polka*. Just some tired *orchestra* shit.

Nacho finds his girl. I have to admit she looks kind of hot. She's wearing this tight, short black dress, showing off her thinness and her nice legs, long and all shapely. I try not to look at her too much because I'm high and I'm a little paranoid. So Leo and me are sitting at a table watching Nacho dance to the corny music, but he's doing a good job. That motherfucker can dance. Leo's not much of a conversationalist. He's more the cold-blooded starer, with an almost stalker type of intensity. I don't feel much like talking, anyway. So we drink rum and Coke and chill.

"Wanna dance with Diana?" It's Nacho and he's trying to be cool, like, "You fuckers don't threaten me." I say sure and I take her out for a spin, only I'm not too coordinated at that moment and I'm bumping into people. Thing is, this girl's kind of grinding me. Maybe I'm *imagining* it, but my *pingo* knows what's up. I can't lie to him. The way I look at it, I got no choice. I didn't ask to dance with this chick and Nacho took his chances trying to be suave, so I go ahead and lean into it a little bit. The band goes off for a break and by accident the DJ puts on a nice slow groove. I spin her around a little bit and notice that Nacho is watching us, but I don't care and I feel her put her arms around my hips. So I go with it and slide them around and she's holding me loosely so that I can feel her hands gliding down around my ass. I put one of my hands on the back of her head and she puts her face on my shoulder, only she's facing my neck and I can feel her breath, her lips so close that my *pellitos* stand up around the edges of my mouth. *So what's all this about*, but before I can finish the thought, the song goes off and the DJ puts on some old heavy metal song, so I walk her back to the table. Nacho's looking at me funny, but I play it off and just shrug my shoulders. "She's hot, motherfucker." He seems to be satisfied with that. He takes her back on the floor without skipping a beat.

After a few drinks, with nothing else to do, I find myself almost missing my pops, regretting that I've never heard him play at a club. I wonder where he is. I never ask Grams anymore. It makes her feel bad that her son doesn't call very often. He does send some dough, but Grams needs it all to help out with the tuition.

Elena shows up and she says, "Hey," but I'm not in the mood to talk. I sit at the table and drink up, all the while Nacho and even Leo, who's loosened way up, lead the girls around the floor. "Come on, get out there. Diana's a good teacher," Nacho says, grinning. He's good at picking up heavy vibes.

"Nah," I say. I don't want to go out there. I'm bummed now and I feel like going home. "I'm fine right here. This isn't my bag. This stuff is for old folks."

"C'mon, sad boy," Diana says, grabbing me by the hand. She leads me out on the floor again. She's a little drunk now and I get the sense that she's tired of Nacho. Having my arms around her makes me sad and excited. She smells sweet, her breath like the wine we've been drinking at the table. We go around in a circle, and I realize that I am hot for Nacho's girl.

After, we decide to go to the park. First thing Nacho does is roll a joint. He steps outside the car with Leo to smoke it. I'm about to go out, too, but Diana holds me back and whispers, "Why don't we stay here and talk." Nacho doesn't seem to care. He's tripping by now anyway and he's more concerned with whirling Elena and Leo around a merry-go-round, laughing like all hell is breaking loose. "He's a maniac," she says, but not like it's a compliment. "You're already older than him, I can tell just by the way you look at me." She leans over and kisses me. "Watch out," I say, backing off even though I don't feel like it. "Nacho's been talking about you all day since he saw you at the mall. It wouldn't be cool for him to come back and find his boy messing with his dream girl."

Diana acts mad. "I'm nobody's girl. I'm just here to see what's what. I like you better already, but suit yourself." I look back at Nacho and he's acting a fool now, lying on the grass singing and laughing. I look over at Diana. She really is beautiful, light brown hair and smart, playful eyes that make me want to be with her. I reach over and pull her to me again, this time kissing her without thinking about anything but how good her lips taste, how warm her tongue is as I smooth my tongue over her slick teeth. I'm crazy, I know, but I'm into her already.

A couple of weeks later, I find out that Diana's father owns this *barbacoa* joint called Los Reyes Molino. And she tells me that he always needs part-time workers there, especially on the weekends. I'm not that interested, but I agree because it's kind of hard to say no when she's rubbing my belly, lying in my bed. Plus, the sixty bucks for two days' work doesn't sound so bad, either.

I show up at five in the morning feeling hung over. I didn't want to come. I'd changed my mind, but Diana called me up this morning to wake me up. I guess her dad has had too many workers who've blown it off when they feel that morning hammer come down at four A.M. when they try to drag themselves out of bed.

The building is a squat beige deal with an ugly tin roof and a tacky white sign that says LOS REYES MOLINO: BARBACOA, TAMALES Y TORTILLAS. I can't imagine any king wanting to eat that shit, but I don't have too much time to consider the irony. Once inside, Diana's mom, this fat, short woman who seems to be moving constantly and talking at the same time, throws an apron in my direction.

"You Robert?"

She doesn't seem to know who I am. Diana's been sneaking around behind their backs. She's only sixteen and not supposed to be going out, let alone fucking *cholitos* like me. That's why her parents send her to Incarnate Word High School for girls. They've made the mistake of thinking that being around the nuns and the Virgin will make her good.

"Yes, I'm Robert," I say, already getting a vibe that this isn't gonna work out. She makes me nervous flapping her jaws like she is, not bothering to look at me while she busies herself looking around for something to give the new boy to do.

"Yeah, well, *m'ija* told me you're a hard worker, that right?"

"Uh-huh," I say, tying the white apron around my waist.

"Well, we'll see." She gives me a suspicious look, already sizing me up. "You know I take care of my boys so long as they work, but you gotta be busy all the time. You won't believe how busy we're gonna get today. You just wait."

I don't know whether to wait or get busy, but she doesn't give me much time to think about it. "Okay, you take one of those washcloths, dunk it in that water with the bleach in it, and start cleaning the counters."

I take one of the cloths and start shining up the stainless-steel counters, which are streaked with congealed grease. The bleach smells strong and it covers up the whiff of corn that's barely hanging in the air. "Smells good in here," I tell her, but she doesn't say anything and I decide that will be the end of my chitchat for the day. After a while, maybe about fifteen minutes, this other kid comes in the door. He's thin but wiry and he has big teeth that make him look kind of goofy except for the fact that he doesn't look too happy about anything.

"Who are you?" he says none too friendly.

"Who're you?" I say without even looking at him.

"I'm Renaldo, *vato*. And I've been here a long time." He keeps staring at me while he ties on his apron. "Yeah, that's right. Been here for two years. So, who are you? Some goddamn relative?"

"I'm a friend of Diana's."

"That lazy *puta*?" he says with contempt. "I hate that little bitch."

"Watch your mouth," I say, "it doesn't sound like you know her well at all." He gets this look on his face, like he just discovered a Jerry Springer–type secret.

"Oh, you're *that* kind of friend. You bangin' that *nalga*?"

"Hey, *vato*, I told you to watch your mouth," I'm getting ready to clock this motherfucker.

He turns back toward the bucket with the washcloths and I decide to ignore him because I can see that he's a punk, anyway.

After a few more minutes this other guy comes in. I like him better than Renaldo right from the beginning. He's a body-builder type, but you can tell he's cool. He walks in humming some song or something and he says hello to everyone with a smile. He comes up to me and offers me his hand right away. "I'm Jorge. You new?"

"Yeah, I'm Robert." He shakes my hand Chicano style— thumb-grip, to hooked fingers, and ending with the palm-to-palm. But he doesn't do it corny like some of those old-timers who try, only they're so drunk they get it all wrong.

"I gotta do my stuff in the back," he says, "I'll talk to you later." As soon as he splits, Renaldo comes up to me.

He hates Jorge. "That son of a bitch thinks he's strong," he says. "He ain't so fucking strong. He thinks he's bad, always taking off on those body-building contests, trying to win, coming in here bragging about how he placed." He watches him walking across the store. "He don't got shit. I got more muscles than him. Look at this." He lifts his shirt up and shows me his stomach, which I have to admit has no fat, just a pretty defined six-pack. "And this," he says, flexing his shoulders and biceps at the same time. This is getting a little gay, but I nod. "You see, I just don't go showing it off."

I find out that Renaldo lives in the Alizondo Courts, a housing project close to the stockyards, *la matanza*. That place stinks so bad that coming in from town, when you have to pass the yards where you get off the highway to get to the westside, you have to roll up the windows and hold your nose so as not to smell that sick-sweet stench. Fucking slaughterhouse makes you want to throw up. People usually drive fast to get past the yards. But they drive even faster through Alizondo, or Tripa Courts. Motherfuckers get dropped there. It's known as the most violent spot in San Antonio. Me and Grams live on the westside, but I don't go near that place. The courts are surrounded on one side by the stockyards, on the other by a huge length of drainage canals to keep the area from flooding in the rainy season. Renaldo has to walk to work on the weekends, maybe an hour in the dark, cold morning. He tells me he doesn't care; in fact he prides himself on it. "I'm no fucking punk-ass, man. Lots of pussies in the courts, dude, but I'll walk around by myself and shit. I don't need a fucking gang to watch my back like some punk bitch." He flashes a set of knuckles that's got a Phillips screwdriver head attached between the middle two rings. "I'll fuck anyone up with this. I always got my hand in my pocket, too. Once, this *pendejo* tried to jump me on my way home. I punched him in his eye. Motherfucker's walking around like a cyclops now."

Jorge lives on the westside, too, but in the neighborhood, and he goes to Kennedy High School, which is the best in the area. That's part of the reason that Renaldo hates him, I think. Renaldo dropped out of La Techla, the worst high school in the city. But more than that, it's like some westside *East of Eden* setup, the two of them competing for Diana's mom's attention and approval, only Jorge knows he has it, and skinny, shifty Renaldo knows he doesn't. I don't guess that he's got a mom, either, but I'm lucky that I don't have to consider that crazy-assed manic midget my moms.

The three of us make sure everything is ready for opening, sweeping and mopping the cement floor, wiping the counters, counting the register money. And then Diana's mom opens the doors for the people lined up outside in the gray dawn. The crowd never lets up on Saturdays or Sundays. People line up holding their four or five dollars, buying the meat and a couple of dozen tortillas, ready to take the food home for their families to eat together on the only day they can spend with each other since the old man probably works like a dog during the week, and the mom, too. What's behind this *barbacoa* thing is that the family can just hang together, eating some tacos, making that goddamned hard week bearable.

Hardly anyone drives to the *molino*. Most people walk since they live in the neighborhood and most of them don't have their own ride. This is the westside and if you can afford the bus, you're lucky. The cars around here are mostly big-assed, rumbling, beat-up pickups or station wagons, driven by some poor, tired-looking migrant type wearing a sweat-stained cowboy hat. Those guys come in, sometimes in twos, *compadres*, talking in Spanish, laughing every once in a while while they talk shit about the new *pendejo* foreman or some white fuck who took a fall or stepped through a ceiling. They order a pound of this and a pound of that.

Women come in, too. They come in wearing rollers and *chanclas*, the cheapy terry-cloth ones you buy at HEB for two dollars. Those shits come in three colors: baby blue, pretty pink, and vanilla white. The women don't care what they look like at this time in the morning. They're there to pick up some food for their kids and husbands, and anyway, they only live down the block, and who the hell is there to impress?

We work fifteen, sixteen hours straight. No official lunch. Just a few breaks in the back where you can eat anything you want for free. I try everything. Hot pork *carnitas* wrapped in a corn tortilla. Tamales from huge tin cans that hold twelve dozen. *Barbacoa,* always the "all-meat" for me, which I comb through back there, making sure it is the leanest I can get. I stay away from the *menudo.* That shit smells good, like warm corn, but its full of *tripa* and I'm not into eating intestines. There's *pan dulce*, too, and Mexican candy, and sodas and juices. Eating is not going to be a problem, but we do it fast because always there's *pinche* customers waiting.

Diana lied to my ass. She said it was an easy job, just take the money and give the customers the food. But she didn't tell me all of them would be ordering in Spanish and fast Spanish, too. *"Dame dos libras de barbacoa, toda carne. Dos dozenas de tortillas de maiz. Un cuarto de menudo, doz regalitos, y dame un ojo."* They say it quick and I'm trying to process that info, write it down on a little slip of paper and weigh that shit out, and they're holding on to their rolled-up wad of ones looking impatient. There's this *mojado* type who's looking like he wants to fuck with me because he can tell I'm a *pocho. "Andale muchacho, chingado, que tienes?"* I don't like his face, so I give him my "Fuck you, motherfucker" look and slow down. Everybody's in a hurry and I got all this *barbacoa* grease on my face and hands and leaking all over my clothes. They keep the *barbacoa* in two huge metal tins, and when someone orders it, I go scoop it out onto some butcher paper, weigh it, wrap it. The "all meat" isn't as popular as the "regular" because it's more expensive, but I wouldn't want to eat the regular. We're always pulling chunks of cow lips out of that shit. I find big-assed cow teeth in there, too. I put them in my pocket so I can freak out Nacho when he's stoned.

The thing of it is, I don't mind the *barbacoa*. It's the other stuff that the Mexican cooks in the back scrape off of the cow head that makes me want to throw up. Those guys get to the store Friday night and start cooking up the heads. They load them into this huge metal pressure cooker that looks like an atomic bomb or something. It takes a while to load those heavy heads in there and arrange them just right. They take hours to cook and then those guys go to work, scraping all the meat off. They take everything that's edible off, too. First, there's the *lengua*, a six-pound cow tongue that looks like it's ready to take a big lick even though it's been cooked. It grosses me out to have to serve that shit, but these westsiders love it. *"Dame una libra de lengua."* I hate to hear that. It means cutting into the big tongue and it gives me the willies. After a couple of times, I don't even bother doing it. It doesn't matter to me how much a customer orders, I give them the whole damned thing, being careful not to let it slide off the big fork as I plop it into a cardboard basket and wrap it up before it leaks all over the fucking place. A close second as far as nausea factor is *sesos*. A big pile of cold, gray brains sitting in a metal tub. I'm like, what the hell is that shit? Jorge laughs and says, That's *sesos*, you know, brains. "People eat that?" I'm amazed at the idea.

"It's good for your thinking, man."

"Fuck that," I say. "I mean, if I was some sort of starving Aztec son of a bitch, I might eat that, but right now, I wouldn't give it to Grams, and she'll suck a chicken wing till it flies."

But the people order it. I've seen a big meat-eatin' Mexican order a pound of it and say, "Hey, don't wrap it up just yet." And he'll pull out a corn tortilla and spread some of that gray gook on it and munch the brain taco down in three bites flat. I guess my face contorts into a look of disgust, because the guy smiles at me with brain goo on his teeth and he says, "Mmmm, that's damn good."

But *ojos* are the worst. They pop those eyeballs loose from the cowheads and toss 'em in a pan, cow pupils all which a way, staring at nothing and everything at the same time. This dude, Pedro, his job is to sit in front of that pan on a stool with a filet knife and cut the brown pupil away. He takes a fork and pulls out the ocular nerve, also gray and looking like a big mushroom. He's about thirty years old and he's got a fat wife who comes in at about nine in the morning. She goes through the back door and takes home this garbage bag full of the shit that was rejected from the morning's cowheads. "For the dogs," Pedro says when he sees me checking out his hefty wife struggling with about thirty pounds of the most heinous "meat" I've ever seen. It looks like somebody just dismembered a couple of murder victims, or like an autopsy. "Dogs love it. It's good for them," he says, smiling at me.

"Yeah," I say, wondering how long it'll be before his dogs jump his ass for making them eat that nasty slop.

After a few trips back to the cook room, I notice the guys are talking shit about me. They're looking me over, cracking a joke or two, but I try to be cool and join in the conversation during break, but they want to put me to the test. Finally, Pedro looks at me, giving me an "Are you a pussy?" look.

"Ay, Beto," he says, shortening my name, "ay, we got a question for you."

I stand there with a fifteen-pound tin of tamales in my arms. "What's up?"

"We wanna know one thing, *vato*." He looks at his pals to show me that they all really want to know. "Are you a man?"

"What?" I know that he's up to something, but I'm kind of unclear. It's a weird question. I think maybe I'm gonna have to fight someone.

"Are you a man, that's all we want to know. Do you have *huevos* or do you have *huevitos*?" It's a provocative question but I don't think about it too long.

"My balls are big enough," I say, trying to sound sure of it.

"Come here, then," he says. I put down the tin and walk closer to them. They're all smiling at one another. Pedro reaches into the aluminum bin and pulls out a big round eyeball, bigger than a golf ball. He holds it out, looking into my eyes. "Let's see you eat it."

Everyone is looking at me. Brown eyes everywhere, even the eyeball in Pedro's hand is staring up at me, all dull and wrinkly, like maybe it would wink if it still had an eyelid. I take it out of his hand. It's heavier than I thought and it feels like a peeled, boiled egg. "You gotta cut it first, *m'ijito*," Pedro says, goading me. He hands me his dirty filet knife. So I take it and slice the pupil clear off. Then, with my thumb, I dig out the mushroomy nerve, pluck it free, and plop it in my mouth. I chew it a few times, and just about the time I think I'm gonna puke, I swallow the whole damned thing. Those fuckers are all laughing. "Damn, dude, I wouldn't have done that. You're gonna choke on that *ojo*. That was gross, man. *Me dió asco.*" They've had their fun, but fuck 'em, I figure, they'll chill now.

The day passes quick after that and I'm bone tired by five P.M. Now it's time to clean up, and it's nasty work, but I'm so anxious to wash the grease off my body and hair that I rush through it. Diana's mom is impressed, mistaking my speed for initiative. We're done by seven and she gives us a big smile as we leave. "You come tomorrow. Tomorrow's the big day. Pay tomorrow," she says all loud.

Grams is out there waiting for me and I watch Renaldo take off into the dark. It doesn't occur to me to give him a ride. "You look tired," Grams says. *"Apestas de pura graza,"* she says, wrinkling her nose at my greasy, smelling self. "It's not me," I say, trying to defend myself. "It's the meat. I brought us some for dinner." And I hold up the grease-shined paper bag for her to see. "It's the all-meat."

CHAPTER 4

I'm staying with my cousins Enrique and Juan this weekend. Grams has to watch Mrs. Roland, an old lady she takes care of sometimes. Her daughter, who is old too, is visiting her son in Chicago. I don't mind staying alone at the house, but I'd rather not if I don't have to, and since Grams isn't crazy about Enrique spending the night here (he's a horrible boy, Grams always says), I go there. It's cool with me. His pops, being a pastor, has a big-assed house out on the northeast side of town, where the white people live. It's got two stories, about five bedrooms, and their neighborhood has a community center with a pool, tennis courts, and a small golf course. It's clean as hell, and you don't have to watch your back there.

I haven't spent much time with either Juan or Enrique since I started at Sunnydale. Mostly because I've been hanging with Nacho, but also because Juan and Enrique have their own high schools and none of us has gone out of our way to kick it together. We used to have a lot of fun. When my pops and moms were together, we went to Enrique's father's church and we'd see each other all the time. Once we bought boxing gloves and had a tournament every weekend for the summer. We'd pound on our friends from church, and it always came down to me and Enrique in the final championship bout. We'd slug it out till we were both dizzy. Most of the time I won, at least until Enrique started getting his growth and he got big all of a sudden.

Enrique's mother is a pain in the ass about order. She's always putting him on discipline because he didn't clean his bathroom right or because he talked back. Always some bullshit with those two. After my pops and moms split, Enrique started going off about how lucky I was, you know, because no one could tell me what to do. All this *freedom,* so different from the discipline his mom was crazy about. My moms was letting me drive and she couldn't really control me too much. But I didn't feel very lucky. I'd look at his crib and his old man sitting at the dinner table, always being nice, but giving me that pitying look, and I'd think about how lucky Enrique was to have his family together even if it meant having to take a little grief about piss sprinkles on the toilet seat.

Tonight we get some cheap wine, Thunderbird, and after we drink it, I go upstairs. I just want to sleep. Juan and Enrique stay downstairs. Somehow they're hungry. My stomach's feeling like shit and I know better than to have drunk that cheap-assed alcohol. I'm not supposed to drink. The doctor gave me a list of foods I'm not allowed to touch because of my ulcer. Some of the things on the list I don't miss at all, like lettuce, radishes, or corn; some I miss a lot, like pizza, beer, and fried food. It's a perforated one, my ulcer. That means it bleeds.

The more I want to sleep, the less I can. The more I pay attention to my stomach, the worse the pain gets. I know the routine by now. It starts out dull, like I've eaten too much, but the pressure grows till it feels like a little animal, a badger maybe, is trying to claw its way out. The pain gets worse and worse till it's so bad I double over in bed, bringing my knees up to my chest as if that might kill the little fucker in there. On top of the fucking pain, I got no fan in this room! I can't drop off without a goddamn fan. *I know that*. Yet I forgot to bring one. It makes me mad, my big metal fan sitting there at Grams's house in my bedroom *not* being used, while I lay here in pain not being able to sleep.

So instead of dropping off, I start thinking about my moms finding out about my pops having another woman and a baby. I spent that night just like this, unable to sleep, knees up to my chest, miserable. First thing I heard was my moms's voice, shrill, desperate, *desesperada*, as my grams would say. It was strange to hear her voice like that because my moms hardly ever got excited. It was late, three or four in the morning, and I was in the living room half asleep after rolling newspapers all night long. My old man, always on the lookout for some extra money, had got the bright idea of delivering some neighborhood rag once a week, five or six hundred deliveries unless he got tired, in which case he'd throw them in a random Dumpster.

I'd rolled the papers and Moms and Pops had taken off to deliver them, another three hours' work. It being a school night, I stayed home. Antony wasn't born yet, although my moms was already big with him. Then I heard my moms's voice outside the back door. Listening to her voice so scared and angry at the same time, I got a cold lump in my stomach. I knew something was wrong. Really wrong. It's like a storm warning, my stomach. I heard my pops's voice, deep, trying-to-be-rational-like. His voice got lower and more persuasive as hers grew louder and more desperate. I was wide awake then, sitting up on the couch looking at their silhouettes bobbing on the back-door window shades.

Wham. The door jerks open. Moms rages in, heading straight for me. "Your father is cheating on me," she yells. "He's got himself another woman." She's crying now. "Real good, Teresa," my old man says, kind of disgusted, but not looking at her or me, just shaking his head. "Just beautiful." He grabs at her. "Leave me alone," she yells. "C'mon," he says, menacing, forceful. Real ugly, like the shock of seeing two dogs tear at each other. Violence hitting home for real. And wham! They're out the back door just as suddenly as they came crashing in. I'm sick, my stomach stewing; I lie back down and bring my knees up to my chest and stare as the blackness outside starts to turn gray.

"Fuck!" I wake up, but nobody else stirs. Juan and Enrique are knocked out cold. The whole house is quiet and I don't have anybody to talk with to shake the dream. It's still with me hard. I lay there like I did that night all hell broke loose, waiting for someone in the house to come back to life. I need distraction.

More and more, my life takes place at night where I can hide. My cousins and friends always ask me, how do you do that? It's easy. To me it's the daytime that's long and terrible. You see everything too clearly during the day.

When I was a kid, I was scared of the dark. I used to get up like some bizarre sort of creeper and inch my way into the hallway, just wanting to get out of my room where the dark was so dense, like I could eat it with a spoon. What was really spooky, though, was that I was afraid that my pops and moms had left me again, like they did when my moms used to go on the road with him. So I'd stand outside their room and make sure they were in there. I'd stay very still, listening for their breathing.

I remember standing, the moon shining from my room's window and me staring at the silhouette on the wall in front of me. My shadow meant the worst—black stillness, emptiness, just me. I'd stare for a long-assed time, almost to where I couldn't stand up. I was like some vampire guard making sure no one tried to sneak away and leave me. My uncle's church played this movie every Halloween. "This is what you should really be scared of," he'd say. It was called *Distant Thunder*. In it everyone gets raptured and a few unsaved suckers get left behind to face getting their fucking heads cut off because they were too stupid to believe. That movie freaked me out good. It *still* scares me sometimes, although I wouldn't tell Nacho or my cousins that. It's the first thing that jumps into my mind sometimes when I wake up in the middle of the night and find everything dead quiet. Nothing is spookier to me than the idea of everyone in the world that I know disappearing without a clue. Can you imagine the feeling of it dawning on you that they're gone permanently? That you've been left behind?

After my pops left, the darkness took on a different feel, though. It meant home. Day was for school, for having to be with assholes who didn't know shit about me, my moms, or Antony. By eighth grade, I knew school was fucked beyond fucked and I didn't want to have anything to do with it. I took this shitty paper route to help my moms, waking up early to deliver papers to deadbeat neighbors who never wanted to pay up at the end of the month. People will do some crazy shit to keep from paying their little piddly-assed bills. They'll send their kids to the door to tell you they aren't home, or they'll just stare at you from behind the blinds like you can't see them peeping out. Lots of times they'll flat out deny that they owe you. But money was tight, so those few bucks came in handy. Plus, with my moms starting to get sick, she didn't mind when I skipped school. I was useless there anyway. By the time I got to Crockett, I had my routine down. I had an ulcer, my moms was sick, and I didn't give a shit.

I had this old teacher, a little nut named Ms. Arania. She liked to give me hell whenever I came back to school. I used to fall asleep in her class because I couldn't sleep at night. It was math and I was always behind. That old malevolent bag decided to use me as her goat. She took to giving me shit in front of the others. She'd stand there in her wig, barely five feet tall, trying to make me do problems on the board. She was always a sarcastic bitch: "Robert, nice of you to join us today. Let's see if you can enlighten us on how to solve this equation for x."

By that time, Moms was staying up all night crying, losing her hair, and I was taking care of Antony. One day, like a sucker, I try to tell her that I can't come to school because I had to take care of my baby brother. She looks at me and says, "That kid has caused me so many problems already, he should be mine!" Then she says, "Get up there and solve for x." I don't know x from o, but I walk up to the board, all the other kids quiet and embarrassed for me. "Take the chalk," she says, and I do, but I don't write anything because I don't have a clue. She bounces up behind and says, "That's the chalkboard," and as she does, she pushes the back of my head so that my face smashes against the board hard. That's it for me. I swear I don't even think about it. It's like my hands decide to act on their own and sweep all the shit off her desk onto the floor. Then, without saying a word, I split. She's so freaked out, she doesn't say anything till I'm in the hallway. Then she comes out yelling, "You little bastard, you little bastard!" That part's almost funny because she's so short. This black kid I know, Sylvester, is in the hallway just coming out of the bathroom and, hearing her, yells, "Fuck you, bitch!" and jumps back in before she can spot him.

That's how I got kicked out of Crockett—that, along with me missing so much school. Moms didn't even make the meeting with the principal. They didn't give a shit and I was way beyond giving one, either. I learned right there and then that people want you to learn things on their own goddamned terms. They had this counselor there who used to say to me, "You have to come face-to-face with your problem." That was all bullshit, though. That old midget Arania taught me better than that. It wasn't the problem on the board, the one everyone can see, that's the bitch. The real bitch is all the suckers who don't know anything about me and want to pretend that their solution fits anyway.

That's how the dark got to be different for me. Even though it still fucks with me a lot, at least now it isn't about being closed in and suffocated. It opens things up, makes the horizon look far away, like maybe it doesn't even exist. Sometimes, when I'm screwing around, I see myself as a vampire. Like them, the hunted, I creep around at night, and when I'm lucky, it's clear enough so that I can see the lights for miles from my hideout, so far sometimes that I could swear I'm seeing all the way to L.A. Makes me wish I could turn into a bat or mist and just drift away while everyone sleeps.

CHAPTER 5

Nacho's strangest kick is the one about his dead friend Jesse. Mexicans love the dead. Saints everywhere you look, especially kids who die young and pure, still innocent. Jesse was killed the year before I got to Sunnydale. He'd been changing a tire on his mom's Buick on the side of the highway, and trying to be careful, he lit a flare. When the dude bent to the pavement to put it down, a pickup crushed his upper body. He was DOP, dead on pavement.

When we get high, Nacho always gets around to telling us how when he went to the mortuary, Jesse looked like Frankenstein. "His face was all fucked up, just scars and stitches where'd they'd tried to make him look like he did when he was alive." He cries for him sometimes when he gets drunk.

I have my own ghosts to worry about.

When I get home from school today, I see my pops's Thunderbird sitting in Grams's driveway. It's clean, shiny, tinted windows, blood-red, sweet. He got it last year. I still haven't ridden in the damned thing. I'm not excited to see the car. My stomach starts to rumble and feel all tight in the middle, the tiny prisoner inside trying to file his way out slow and steady. I walk into the house like nothing, but I'm fronting for no reason because my pops is in the bedroom knocked out. Grams is in the kitchen making something to eat.

"Tu papa está aquí." She's talking quiet so as not to wake him up. She's in a weird spot because she loves him, but she knows she shouldn't for all the shit he's done.

"Yeah," I say, not wanting to get into Spanish with her. It makes me mad that just because he's come here for a day or two that all of a sudden the rules change. He's The Man, and we all gotta be quiet and talk in a respectful tone, which for Grams means Spanish. For all her toughness, he can always turn her to jelly. He does that to everyone except me.

"Ve y dale un abrazo si está despierto." She's tripping if she thinks I'm going to tiptoe to the bedroom and give him a hug if he's awake. "I'm tired," I say. "I'm gonna watch TV." I just want to get the fuck out before he wakes up. I turn on the tube and pick up the phone.

"Nacho," I say when he answers. "Yo man, come pick me up. Let's burn a couple up at your house."

"Fucker. Didn't you get enough buzz last night? Shit, I can hardly concentrate today." But I can tell that he's game. Then he says what I want to hear, "I'll pick you up in about twenty."

"Cool, but pick me up at the EZ. My old man's around, and I don't wanta be here." Nacho's good about that shit.

"Yo, whatever. I'll see you in twenty."

When I get home late that night, my pops is still watching TV. He's still in his dress clothes, black suit pants and a white dress shirt with the sleeves rolled up Latin-lover style. As late as it is, his hair is still combed, slicked black, his mustache sitting above his mouth ready to punctuate whatever bullshit he has in store for me. He's quiet and I can tell he's going to try and play the father.

"You come in this late all the time?" He mutes the set. "You had me and your grandmother worried. I came all the way down here from Houston to see you and you leave without waking me up." He's gotta be kidding. There's so much shit I'd like to spill right now, but I just say, "Sorry."

"Give me a hug," he says, still sitting down. I go over and he hugs me tight. "You're getting too skinny." Everything he says makes me want to punch him or puke. "What's going on?" I say. "Why are you here?" I don't look at him directly. I look at the muted TV. A *Lucy* rerun is on, the one where she's stuffed cheese in all of Ricky's band instruments.

"I told you, I'm playing in Houston this weekend and I thought it'd be good to drop in on you and your grandmother and make sure everything is going alright." He's been on the road for a couple of months now and this is as close to S.A. as he's been.

"It's all going alright," I say. I walk out to the fridge and grab a Coke just so I can get out of the room for a few seconds.

When I come back, my pops has the TV volume back on, but he's flipped it to a documentary on some South American country. I watch that, pretending to give a damn. "Grams tells me you're in school again. A Christian one. Do you like it?"

"It's fine."

"She's good, your grandmother, watching after you while I work."

"Uh-huh." I'm staying out of this whole goddamned conversation if possible. My stomach is starting in on me again. The pot had killed the churning, but Pops is doing his best to get it going again.

I watch the kids on TV, poor and tattered. Some on crutches. There's been a disaster, a flood or something, and there's nowhere for those kids to go. Fucked up.

"You made friends?"

"A couple."

"Your grandmother says you have one in particular that seems strange."

"He's cool." Now I'm actually trying to follow the program. I want to know if someone is going to step in and do something.

"I don't want to argue with you here. You're getting old enough to know what's right and wrong."

The guy on TV says that someone is "misdirecting the aid" that these kids are supposed to have been getting. Flat out *stealing* the shit. Someone should be strung up by the balls.

"Did you hear me, Robert?" my pops says.

"Yeah," is all I can manage. This stuff about the kids in South America is fucking *tragic*.

"You heard from your mother?"

"Don't ask me about her," I say, snapping back into the conversation. I want to get up and leave the room because I really feel like I'm gonna puke, but my legs don't feel like going. He changes the subject just like he's changing stations on the tube. "You want to go to Houston with me tomorrow, come listen to me play?"

This throws me, mostly because deep down, I'm actually excited to hear him bring it up. "You want me to go?" I say like a little punk. I catch myself, though, and tone down. "Beats going to school." That's how my old man gets me. I remember him playing music back in the day when we were still together. Three memories stick with me.

One in the morning and the men in his band are packing up their instruments. A shabby pink house on Laredo Street, darkest block on the westside. Big living room with wood floors where my pops and the two other men in the band have been rehearsing all night. Starting and stopping, trying to get it right. My pops learned to play by ear at his pops's church, where his old man would lead the congregation in rousing choruses while signaling his ten-year-old kid when to change chords with a hand behind the pulpit. I dig watching them rehearse because I get to stay up late. They're trying to get it right, "Three Kings." My pops is young then, maybe twenty-three, making up songs, trying different harmonies, different arrangements, exploring, hoping to get the music right. They're supposed to bring people to God. They play loud, sound reverberating wildly, bouncing off the walls, rebounding off the floor, crashing off the ceiling, with me and my young moms enjoying it together. She understands music, sings, and plays piano herself. Started playing in church as a young girl. I'm in awe of the way the band's individual voices meld into one three-pitched voice, a musical trinity, holy almost, enthralling. Night after night they practice until the early morning, time becoming irrelevant after the music starts. No one thinks to make me go to bed.

In the next one, I'm struggling. Two steps in a chord are easy, but the third is too spread out for my small fingers to press. I practice the guitar, going to get as good as my old man. He's taught me a basic chord and told me, "With this chord, you can sing almost any song." I practice, getting blisters on my fingers. It doesn't sound right and I call him into my room. "It doesn't sound right. When will I get to play like you?" My pops loses patience. "You have to practice years and years and years. If you don't want to do that, forget it." I forget it.

In the third, there's three men, my pops, and me. I sit at the drum set that belongs to the church. My father talks to the bassist, an old family friend, about a song he has written and whether they can have it ready for their first performance. This band is called Wall of

Jericho. The drummer has a huge trap set, four or five cymbals, two bass drums, wood blocks, two kettle drums, a couple of toms, and a snare. He beats on those things loud. The musicians talk and talk before they launch into a first run of my father's new song. I sit at the church drums and discover that the drumsticks are sitting on top of the snare. Quietly I begin to tap a basic beat. No one pays any mind to me. They continue practicing, starting and stopping, my father giving directions and listening to suggestions from the other guitarist. I become bolder in my drumming, though I'm too slow and don't know basic rhythms or even how to hold the drumsticks. But I beat out my exuberance. I feel a connection with my pops. I'm playing with him. I don't know it, but this will be the last time because my moms and him will split up real soon. I hit that snare and pound out an inappropriate beat on the bass drum, hitting the cymbals, which resound with my joy at being here today. The practice ends and my pops takes me by the side and says, "Don't play the drums next time, you distract me."

The drive down to Houston is not as tough as I thought it was going to be. This morning I was pissed at myself for agreeing to go. I spend a lot of time making damned sure I don't give him any thought, and now here I go and get myself in a situation where I gotta talk to him. Shit like that always happens to me. I'm always the one stuck with the chatty chick when I'm gloomy and don't want to talk. I'm too polite for my own good sometimes. I don't want to break anyone down, not even him. All the way there, my pops keeps the radio on and I lean back in the seat and try to sleep. He's a speed-fiend, passing up people, taking chances, getting into close shaves, all the time muttering stuff like, "Son of a bitch needs some fucking driving lessons," or "I hope you flip that fucker over and die," while behind him some traumatized old lady's heart is beating like hell because some madman in a red flash almost ran her off the road.

We get to Houston during rush hour. I've been pretending to be on the nod for four hours and I'm bored enough to start jacking around with the radio now that we aren't moving. Even this is a problem for him. He had it on some corny-assed oldies station playing shit from the seventies. I'm trying to find something that won't make me feel like I'm stuck in a time warp. "Leave it alone, Robert," he says. "Dad, I can't hang with that stuff," but I stop fiddling with the dial, leaving it on a station that plays Top 40 bullshit as a compromise. He reaches over with a sigh of annoyance and tunes it to some straight-out redneck station. "Don't it make my brown eyes blue," some tired-assed lady is complaining.

The 610 is jammed with people trying to get home. In the middle of all this rotten hubbub, I miss Grams and being there instead of here. Pops buys me a Big Mac and he starts snooping around again like he's got a right to be interested. "Your grandmother says that these new friends are worrying her." The guy is crazy to be asking me anything. "I stay outta trouble," I say. Not like you, I want to add, but when we're talking, I can never say shit like that. I get tongue-tied.

"Well, don't go causing her grief. You can't stay with me, since I'm on the road all the time. And your mom doesn't want—" and he stops. He wants to rephrase the sentence before he tells me flat out that my moms doesn't want me. "I mean, she's sick. So treat your grandmother well." He's trying to sound reasonable. I don't answer him right away, like I can't be bothered. It works because about thirty seconds later, he says, *Me oístes?* He's asking me in Spanish, his language of discipline and obedience, if I heard him. I keep quiet. "Well?" he says forcefully, almost angry.

"Yeah," I say, too chicken to say, "Fuck you, man. Why don't you quit worrying her, with your bitches and your drinking and drugging and never coming around?"

Nobody ever tells him shit as far as I can see. Grams is scared of him, or on the flip, he manages to charm her out of her anger. He's a real trip. Used to keep everybody in the house shut right the fuck up when he lived with us. My old man's the type that when you disagree, he gives you this look sideways like he can't believe how stupid you are and then he says, "Shut the hell up when you don't know what you're talking about." But as long as you agree that he's right and go for a swim in the river of his thought, he's cool as a cucumber. Trouble is, that river is full of some crazy turns, and rapids that jump out at you when you least expect it. You take that ride, and you're likely to drown. My moms found that out the hard way.

Pops always has known how to work it. Whenever my Aunt Naomi came to town to convince my moms to up and leave his ass, he'd come around, like he *knew* he had to put in some serious face-time. He never seemed as charming and concerned, repentant even, as then. He'd call a lot more often, trying to give my moms the line that this was all a phase and that he'd be coming back home soon. Of course, when Aunt Naomi went back to L.A., it was like my pops took off, too. He'd go back to the quick Saturday visit, coming in breathless as hell and always in a hurry, sometimes smelling like barbecue smoke, ready to give us a quick hug, toss my moms a few bucks, come up with some bullshit excuse, and then take off as fast as he'd driven up the driveway.

Moms took that shit hard. She didn't know what to do. She'd tried so much, you know, playing nice, being understanding, hoping all of it was just a phase with him. She tried losing weight, buying new clothes, wearing a poor fakey wig over her thinning hair, all the time doing her best to put on a cheerful face when he was around, then crying all night and all day after he left. She'd go days without eating and sleeping, then she'd be like, "Okay, I'm not gonna let this get me down," and she'd seem to be ready to pull it together.

We'd do things, me and her and Antony, go to a movie, wash the old car, but then just as sudden as it started, it'd be over and I'd come home to find her in bed crying, so sad she couldn't say much more than to *please* leave her alone. That was the hardest because you'd just stand there in the doorway, just out of her sight, feeling small because you couldn't do anything, *anything at all*, to help and your little brother'd be next to you, hanging on your leg maybe, completely unaware of what was going on because he was a baby and you'd look down at him and he'd be slobbering, a smile on his face like he wanted to play, and you'd just smile back even though you felt like crying, but you didn't dare, and even if you did dare, had probably forgotten how to do it. So you'd pick him up and just stand there, listening for something, a break in the crying, that small silence giving you a little hope that maybe she'd dropped off to sleep and you could finally just *move*.

There are more than a thousand people at the civic center. *Tejano* and *Conjunto* music are big now that assholes like Ricky Martin and Marc Antony have made Latino music popular. *Tejano* doesn't sound much like the Afro-Cuban and South American salsa that's hot, but it's close enough, and most white people can't tell the difference between a *cumbia* and *merengue* anyway. *Conjunto* has always been big in cities with lots of Mexicans—Chicago, Houston, San Antonio, Laredo, L.A., Tucson, Phoenix—but the gigs my pops plays at now are pretty big and getting bigger. Lots more people, especially girls. The real artists of their time, like Flaco Jimenez,

Ramon Ayala, Los Tigres del Norte, have actually started getting some recognition.

It's crazy in the hall. The people throng to hear them and I'm watching my father up on that stage, part of the band but clearly the standout, the blue, yellow, and red lights disguising the little flaws on his face and hands, his guitar crooning smooth solos. It's a strange scene there, all these people dancing and drinking, smoke thick and noxious. Men are looking at the women, trying to get them on the floor so that they can get them in the sack. The women, all dressed up, hair fixed, high heels and black hose, play coy, looking around at their friends with a carnal gleam as they get up to dance at any half-decent boozy request. Smells like cigarettes and roses.

I wander around the huge hall, with hundreds of tables with little liquor bottles and the setups clubs are allowed to sell in Texas: soft drinks, plastic cups, and a bucket of ice. You provide your own rum or whiskey. I don't really want to stick around. Too many bad memories for me, plus down deep inside I can't get Grams's warnings out of my head about the devil's music and how it's led my pops down the wrong road.

Pretty soon, though, I spot a cute girl and ask her to dance. She's older, maybe five years. She's alright, lively and tall, black curly hair with bloodred lipstick, smelling heavy with sweet perfume and fresh cigarette smoke. She's got a bright smile to go with her white skin. I can feel her warmth over my chest as she pulls me closer, her rum-and-Coke breath washing over me as she leans in and puts her lips to my ear asking me my name.

"Robert," I say.

"What?" she asks again.

"Robert!" I say louder.

She's drunk and I decide I'm gonna fuck her. I pull her closer and grind her. She doesn't seem to mind. We go on like that for a while, sitting down a couple of times in between songs so she can introduce me to her friends. I don't even get their names, and after a few more dances, I ask her to go outside. She's down. She doesn't even bother to ask me why. No game, no blame.

I don't come back into the hall until I see people splitting. I get rid of the girl. She told me her name is Claudia, but I bet it's a lie. I don't care. It got me out of the show and I didn't have to deal with my old man up on the stage. I don't want to see him playing music. I want to stay outside of it, beyond his reach. I don't want to get infected with whatever spirit moves him, like those mother-fuckers at the dance, just swaying along with the groove. It's like smoke—gets in your hair and clothes and in your nostrils, and then you can't find a way to get clean of it all.

By the time I get to the stage, the lights are on bright and the hall is a mess, a rank collage of spilt beer, food, napkins, and cigarette butts. My pops is putting his stuff away and others are breaking up the equipment and instruments. "What'd you think?" asks Efraim. He's the bandleader. He's fairly well known. Lots of people come out to listen to him and he's happy because he just got the band a recording deal. They're gonna go up to L.A. in a few weeks. He's always talking to my pops about distribution and representation. He likes my old man a lot. "It was good," I say. Efraim's alright. My pops is out of earshot so I tell him, "You got me laid, man. You get these girls all hot and all a brother has to do is move in and blam. Hooked up."

He laughs, "Man, you and your old man. You two are always in the bush."

My father comes over. "*M'ijo,* give me a hand." Efraim's hip to the situation, though, and he doesn't say anything. He goes on about his business. My pops wants to pull the father/son routine where I carry his guitar out to the bus. I don't have much choice, so I carry it.

"Are we staying with the band?" I ask him, hoping that we're not going to stay alone.

"No, I thought it'd be better to get some peace and quiet. We're at the Ramada, damn close to Astroworld. Maybe we can go tomorrow." He can't fool me. He knows that those motherfuckers are going to be up all night partying and he thinks that he can hide that from me. Promising me Astroworld, like I'm some punk kid.

My first real conversation with my dad involved blood. For a long time, I faked my stomach trouble so that I wouldn't have to go to bed. After he left, my moms tried to keep the old system up, the one where I went to bed early. But without my pops there to enforce, trying to keep me in line wore her out. She just didn't have the strength to enforce all that quiet and all those goddamned rules. She'd go to bed, Antony'd go to sleep, and I'd turn on the tube and my light. "What's wrong, *m'ijo?*" She'd always get up. She's a light sleeper. That's where I get it. Her father, my *abuelo,* was an insomniac, too. "You have school tomorrow." I'd tell her my stomach was upset and that I needed to sit up for a while. She'd give me permission and soon Antony started to get into the action. Him just a little baby, awake with me watching *M*A*S*H* until the wee hours. It was cool. Communal rule was better for me, but it messed my moms up.

The problem about my bellyaching was that my stomach started to believe me, too. Soon I really was nauseated all the time. I started throwing up. I'd wake up in the middle of the night with wrenching pain that doubled me over with cramps. After a few months, I graduated to throwing up blood and moaning in the bathroom at three o'clock in the morning. The first time my moms saw blood in the toilet, she nearly passed out. She took me to the hospital and called my pops to meet us there. It made me feel guilty to have everybody worrying so much, but it also made me feel safe to have my moms and pops there. In a way, I felt good that I was bringing them together for a while. I was a strong reminder. Maybe that's why he always seemed a little pissed when he got there.

But one night, when the pain was really terrible, he came in without my moms and he sat next to me. I lay there, not sure of what to say. I never knew what to say to him. But back then, I liked listening to him better, whether it was him telling a joke in a funny voice or explaining how things worked. Your standard little-kid syndrome. But that night, he asked me a question. "What's that book you're reading?" I had a copy of *Slaughterhouse-Five* in my hand. My eighth-grade teacher, a strange dude who wore thick black glasses and wore a whacked crew-cut, had used the opening quote in a handout he gave us and I'd found it funny. I explained the plot to my father, telling him this was the fourth time I was reading it. That shit embarrasses me now, but still, he listened to me read from the best parts, and that was something.

At the hotel, my pops is ready to go to bed. This whole thing really sucks. I'm thinking about waiting for him to go to sleep and then getting the hell out of there, maybe taking his T-bird out for a ride. He's smarter than that, though. He's got the keys on the nightstand right next to him.

"When are you going to L.A.?"

"Two weeks or so," he says.

"You should take me there," I say, but I know he won't. I'd fuck up his game.

"I don't know." I can tell he doesn't like the idea at all. "You have school. You can't afford to get kicked out again. You really need to bear down on things." I shut off. I'm going to have to get there on my own. When he's drifting off, I say, "I'm gonna go get a Coke." He's too tired to argue. I go over and grab some change from the nightstand, taking the keys, too. He's dead to the world when he's like that, and he doesn't even notice.

I walk out and take the stairs down to the parking lot. It's dark as hell except for the headlights from the cars and trucks on the 610. It's near four in the morning and all those people are driving God knows where. I open the car door and get in. I think about where I might drive, but I don't really want to go anywhere by myself. If Nacho were here, or Enrique, or even Juan, we could cruise around. I turn the car on so I can get the air-condition going, get rid of that sticky humidity that always seems to be licking at you when you're in Houston. How do you ever get used to feeling like you're living in someone's stomach?

The glove box is unlocked. There's a tape in there, *Chicago's Greatest Hits,* some snotrags, a map that's torn to shit because it's been folded wrong, a nail file, my pops's shades, the kind Burt Reynolds wore in *Sharky's Machine.* No pictures, no money. I sit back and turn on the radio, shift the seat back, and next thing I know, my pops is rapping on the window. It's morning outside, the parking lot empty except for the red machine, and my pops standing in his dorky shorts with his sandals he bought in Mexico: woven leather, very gay.

He's pissed, and after a quick breakfast at McDonald's, we're on our way back to S.A. He wants to get rid of me so he can catch up to the band in Laredo, their next gig. He wakes me up when we get to Grams's. I'm glad to be back, and he's glad to be back on the road.

CHAPTER 6

Nacho doesn't know that Diana's been calling me. She's been coming by to see me, too. I haven't been encouraging it, mind you, but when she called me the first time, I was like "Yeah, come on by and we can watch some TV or whatever." Thing is, Nacho's in love and he keeps talking about her and how fine she is and how he's gonna put it to her before too long. He doesn't realize I've been hitting it for a month now. I felt guilty for an hour or two and then Diana started telling me how Nacho bores her and how she told him there was no way he was gonna get any *panochita*. So, I love Nacho and all, but if he can't get it, then I shouldn't have to suffer, right? Anyway, I dig this girl a lot. She's sweet. She does nice things for me, like calling me up after a long night and asking me how I feel. When she hears I'm hungover, she comes by and brings me something to eat. Even my grams likes her. "She's nice, but why does she wear so much makeup?"

What I like best is that Diana doesn't mind taking care of me sometimes. One night I was feeling so sick from my stomach that I couldn't get out of bed for real. Even Grams didn't give me a hard time about missing school. I'd been up all night puking. I didn't want to wake Grams because she just gets very, very nervous, and wants to start praying for me and pulling *yerba buena* from her herb garden to make me hot tea that doesn't work when the pain is this bad. Sometimes she even ties a long rag around my stomach, like the coils can keep the pain from spilling out, like it might be able to concentrate it into a small ball, like cud that I can then throw up once and for all.

So, I'd had a rough night and was feeling weak. Well, Diana calls me up and I tell her that I'm feeling bad and that I'll talk to her later. That crazy girl came over without me even asking, and she came in while I was lying there moaning like a kid. She walked in and sat on my bed and said, "My poor Roberto," and she didn't say anything else. She just put my head in her lap and started running her fingers through my scalp even though I was sweaty from the pain and probably smelled like shit. You know what? After a few minutes, I forgot what I must've looked like, and my stomach started to feel better. She didn't even expect me to talk, and before long I fell asleep and she left without waking me up. Things like that make me want to marry her. But then there's Nacho. I admit it bothers me.

Grams has gone to church and I get a pass because I'm sick. I've been lying in bed trying to fall back asleep. Sunday morning is good for that, but I can't do it. I get dressed and walk outside. I sit on the back porch, the bleached-out brown-gray, waterlogged wood planks creaking with age. It's nice out here, the sun not yet hot. Tina and Ruthie are outside, too, and I wave at the little girls. "Hi," Tina yells at me. "C'mere." She's standing next to the fence and Ruthie is right next to her, her small fingers poking through the chain links. I lift off the porch with a groan only I can hear and I walk over.

"My sister's graduating tonight," Tina says. "She's got a white robe and a hat, too."

"Graduating from what?" I ask.

"From kindergarten. You want to come? My mom is going."

"Where is it?" I say thinking that I might want to go and practice my big-brother skills. I try and encourage them when I can.

When Nacho comes over later, we take a drive and smoke up. "That little girl, my neighbor, she's graduating," I say, making conversation.

"Wha?" Nacho says. He's deep into some classic Ozzy.

"Those little girls that live next door, the little one is graduating and they want me to go. I feel bad about not."

He turns toward me and says, "Where?"

"At Saint Paul's."

Nacho's senses cheap entertainment. He turns in the direction of the church.

"I don't want to go," I say, trying to stop him. "I don't dig going into church stoned."

Nacho looks at me with that stupid grin of his. "What, you afraid of being struck down by lightning? You crazy bastard, if it wasn't for weed, I wouldn't be able to *stand* church."

Biblical scenes centering around sacrilegious acts begin to come to mind: Eli and his sons; the characters who went into the temple drunk; or that king—Nebuchadnezzer, maybe—who drunkenly refused to read the writing on the wall. What about those fools, also drunk, who joked Noah and paid by drowning? And the punks who mocked Elisha and got mauled by bears! "Dude, it's not a good idea," I say, changing my mind. But he's set for a show and we're not far from the church.

Walking through the doors, I half expect fire to descend, or a holy finger, the size of a missile, to point me out as a grave sinner. No one pays me any attention when I sit. The little kids are all sitting up on the stage, dressed in white graduation gowns, with four-corner caps covered in white satin, little white tassels dangling. It's a Texas summer night, and everyone's waving white paper fans, trying to keep from sweating through their clothes. High above, from the ceiling, hang fifteen or twenty white fans spinning crazily, circulating the hot air. I sit there, my eyes drawn to the motion of the white fans and the featherlike tassles waving in the distance.

And then the children stand and begin to sing, their tiny high-pitched voices warbling "This Is the Day the Lord Has Made." As I listen, I forget being afraid. The kids are angels, a floating chorus, singing so beautifully. I begin to laugh because of the purity of those child-angels flying around, singing for God.

Of course, I sound like some demented maniac, sitting in the middle of a hot congregation, laughing at a children's choir. A few people turn around and look at me, insulted, getting upset, thinking that I'm cracking on their kids or worse, *that I'm a freak who gets off on coming to church stoned.* "You're being rude," some kid's mother says from the other side of Nacho. He shoots me an amused but suggestive look, "Keep cool," he says through his smile.

I try hard, but the angels are now singing "Father Abraham," a religious hokeypokey. They flail their arms and kick their legs, eventually spinning in circles, the tassels whipping around in a frenzy along with the white ceiling fans and white paper fans. I can't help it anymore. I laugh again, even though it's the last thing I want to do. I am busted, conspicuous, guilty, and the finger of God is pointing me out. The congregation will any minute rise up and haul me out to stone me.

Nacho finally grabs me by the arm and leads me outside to the car. I laugh the whole way out of the church. We haul ass out of the parking lot.

"That was classic," he says, "a real Robert Lomos moment there.

Damn, I thought you were going to have a nervous breakdown. One minute you're laughing, the next you look like you've seen a pack of demons eating your mother's heart." He's a little pissed because he was enjoying himself.

"Man, I just had two really different visions in there."

"What?"

"Like those kids were like angels, uncorrupted. I was seeing something really clearly." I try to find the words to make evil Nacho listen. "Sad that shit will happen to fuck them up."

"Like us, you mean?" He laughs.

"Maybe."

"Man, don't buy into the McNutt theory of the holy bubble and the big bad world, the godly and the worldly. I'll tell you what, you're fucked up because you want to believe in all this stuff but you know you can't."

"Maybe I just want to believe that God has some plan or purpose with all this shit. My grams seems to believe it."

"Yeah, well don't fucking count on it," he says. "Spark another one up," he says, pointing at the glove compartment where he keeps his stash. I roll up a pinner. I don't want to be too stoned right now. We smoke, watching the traffic in the rearview mirror to make sure there's no *chota* following behind.

"You punish yourself too much, man. Take it easy. Don't get too fucked up."

"What do you mean, 'too fucked up'?" I ask.

"C'mon," he says.

"Just because I think it'd be good for all this shit to mean something?"

He shrugs. "Look, let's drop it. Everyone's fucked up. Me, too. I'm no one to talk."

"No," I insist. "Tell me what you mean by '*too* fucked up.' I'm *interested*."

He thinks about it for a minute. He's giving the matter serious consideration, so much that he puts both hands on the steering wheel. "Well, you should be taking it easy, man. I mean, I like to party and drink and get laid and generally to have as good a time as possible. But you, you party and drink like you want to kill yourself. You do what most people do to have fun, to have a bad time, to tweak up the pain. Sometimes you look like you're ready to jump out a fucking window."

"No I don't," I say. "I want to have as good a time as you or anybody else."

"Yeah, maybe. But why do you always wind up making yourself miserable or sick?" He's got a point, but I don't want to give it to him.

"Sometimes you can't get shit out of your head," I say in my defense.

"Look, man," he says, "let's just drop it. Smoking too much *yesca* makes everyone think they're Sigmund Freud and shit."

"Well, those kids," I say, "those kids were beautiful up there. That's all. They made me think. That's not a big deal. No one's getting ready to jump out a window about it."

CHAPTER 7

I'm not the only one losing it. Bad Leo, that Christopher Walken, stalker looking, mean thug with a dead-eye stare, has been acting way crazy lately, always starting fights for no reason, just striking out. We'll be on the riverwalk on a crowded Friday night and he'll see some *cholo* he doesn't like the look of, and he'll reach over and pull his hair like the guy is some punk, and before you know it, the two are swinging and people are scattering, yelling, and if the dude's got partners, they're jumping in, which means we're jumping in, and four minutes later it's over and we're running back to find the car before the cops come. "What did you do that for?"

"Man, I just felt like doing something," he says.

I think Nacho is half in love with him, and he searches him out on the weekends. I'm not much into it. I've suggested that we save Leo the trouble and just kick his ass *for* him so we can find another way of spending Saturday night. But Nacho calls the shots, and we cruise by Leo's house and sit outside and listen to music, drink a few beers, take a spin around the block, and then we smoke a joint and come back and hang out in front of his house some more. We do this all weekend long, waiting for something or someone to happen.

Diana wakes me up on a morning after. She was supposed to call me, spare me from going out with Leo and Nacho, but she didn't. "How'd you get that?" she asks. I lay there, my arms crossed, body straight, making it look like I'm dead. I can't relax even when I do sleep. Any sound wakes me up. "Where'd I get what?" I answer back.

"That." She points at my chin. "It's scraped up. Did you go and get in a fight last night?"

"Never mind that shit," I say, "where were you?" I regret it right away because I'm acting a fool by letting her know I care. I cool it. "I wouldn't've gotten in any scrap if you would've been around. Come in here with me," I say, lifting the sheet.

"I didn't come here for that," she says. It's too late to act cavalier and shit. She knows she can play with me a little bit because I gave up that I missed her last night. "Besides, your face is crusted up and you still have on your jeans."

"Suit yourself," I say, but I get up and start looking to grab my towel just in case I can convince her to fuck. I walk to the bathroom after checking around for Grams. She's gone to work. I look in the mirror. My face does look bad. Aside from a long, bloody scrape across the bottom of my chin, I have a big lump on the side of my head, above my ear. My ribs hurt. That fucking Leo. I shower, rubbing myself down with Zest. I can feel each of my ribs, little mountains and valleys for my fingers to ski. Grams is always trying to feed me now, but I'm not interested in eating. I get out and wrap the towel around myself and hustle out to my room. Diana's unpredictable and I don't want her leaving. She's poking through my shit. She doesn't bother to hide it. She's looking at my picture, the only one I have in the room. "Hey," I say. I sit on the bed, leaning against the wall trying to look seductive. She ignores my pose.

"How come you never tell me about your mother?" she says. "You kind of look like her." She holds up the picture to me like it's evidence. "You look cute in this. Why are you crying?"

"Why don't you come in here with me," I say. I don't want to get into my goofy-assed picture. I only keep it because it's the only one I have. "Put that stupid thing down and get in here. C'mon."

"Maybe," she says, bringing the picture over, "if you tell me about this, I'll think about it." She's pissing me off, so sure that I'll tell her what she wants for the chance of getting her into bed.

"Let me see the goddamn thing," I say, holding my hand out. She comes over and sits down next to me.

"How come you're crying?" she asks. I take the picture and pretend to study it like I'm not too sure what she's talking about. It's a picture my grams took about twelve years ago. In it, my dad, skinny, with a ponytail that was in style back then, is sitting next to my moms. She's not smiling, but she looks pretty, anyway. She's wearing a red dress with black sleeves, very Christmassy. I'm on my pops's knee, but I'm obviously trying to get the fuck off. I'm very pissed looking, ready to blubber. "I'm not crying," I say. "I'm just mad. My pops wouldn't let me open any Christmas presents on Christmas Eve."

"That's cute," she says.

"That's not cute," I say, still studying the picture, but now looking at my moms. Her dress seems wrong for her. Too shiny, too trying-to-be-glamorous. Her face looks pinched up, kind of like she's keeping down, out of sight, what I'm expressing right there on my pops's lap. Just like my pops is a Christmas present that she can't open. He's a mystery, always under wraps.

"How come you tell people your mom is dead?" Diana asks. "She looks nice."

"I told you what the picture is about. You don't get to ask any more questions unless you give something to me." I'm wanting her to at least put her hand under the towel, but instead she gets behind me and puts her arms around my chest and begins to stroke my aching ribs softly. "C'mon," she says, "tell me why you go around telling people your pretty mom is dead." I close my eyes because it feels good.

"She's in California. She got sick and she couldn't hack it around here anymore. My pops did bad shit to her and when he split, she went bonkers."

"That's not nice, talking about your mom that way."

"You asked."

"Well, but why? Did she have a nervous breakdown?"

"I guess," I say. I try to sound bored. "I mean, she lost her hair and she didn't do anything but cry all the time. Finally she stopped sleeping. Before I knew it, she was saying crazy things, talking about killing herself. I'd come home from school and Antony would be outside by himself. A little baby, just a couple of years old and he'd be out there in the backyard wandering around and my moms sitting in the house spaced out."

"How did she wind up in California?"

"My Aunt Naomi came and got her. She got her to file for a divorce and to leave for California. Start over."

"Why didn't you go?"

"How the fuck should I know," I say, although I do.

"Okay, relax, *m'ijo*. I just want to know what makes you so sad."

"I don't act fucking sad," I say. She's starting to get on my nerves.

"Okay, you don't act sad," she says. "Relax." She keeps massaging me, rubbing my shoulders and back now. "Why didn't she take you? Do you ever go visit her or your little brother?"

"Nah," I say. I want to change the subject, only I can't. "I did once, but it didn't work out. She's too goddamn nervous when I'm around and my aunt and my gramma over there, you know, her mom, they decided it'd be best for me to come back to Grams. She wanted me around, that is, my grams."

"What about your mom?"

"I don't know. Maybe if they'd given me a chance. A little longer. Shit was crazy then. But anyway, I came back."

"When was that?"

"Almost two years ago now. I'm going back," I say before I know it.

"You are?" she says and she kisses my neck with her lips round and wet. It feels good and for a second I want her to try to stop me, to make it clear she wants to come with me at least. But she doesn't.

"Why you think I'm working at that fucking *molino* of yours. Not for the *ojos*. I'm saving up," I say, being the tough guy. "I'm gonna get back there and show my moms that shit's straight now." I turn around and I kiss her and she slips her hands under my towel as I lift her blouse up. Before she can protest or act stupid, I run my tongue up toward her brown nipples and I lay her down.

Diana leaves before Grams gets home. Grams comes in tired, holding her hip like she does when it's too cold. She walks in slow, puts her keys down. I'm eating cereal. "You didn't go to school today?"

"No," I say. "I felt sick from my stomach." It's true, but the hangover didn't help either. "I had a friend drop off my home-work, so don't worry."

"You going to be a *burro* yet, just like your old gramma," she says, resigned to it by now.

She looks old, smaller, not as tough. She usually gives me a big-ger fight when I miss school, but the way she's doing today makes we wonder if she's right. "Why don't you sit down. I'll fix you something to eat," I tell her.

"What are you going to fix me to eat," she says, turning on the stove. "Cocoa Puffs?"

"I'll go buy us some hamburgers," I say, and I can tell she doesn't mind the idea. "I'll go to Burger Chef," and before she can change her mind, I grab the keys and head off. Grams and I are eat-ing our burgers when the phone rings. It's Nacho. "Hey, Robert, we need you tonight, man."

"*What?*" I'm not in the mood to see any of those fuckers. "If you think I'm gonna fucking—"

"Leo is in trouble," he interrupts me. "He called and said he needs backup. We need you."

"That asshole nearly got us killed last night. I'm not going any-where, dude. My chin's still dragging and I got a knot on the side of my head you could hang a fucking hat on. I'm tired of that motherfucker always looking for shit."

"Look, man, we need you. Get your ass up and meet us at the store in about fifteen minutes," and he hangs up. There's no argu-ing with that guy sometimes. It's crazy. I know I shouldn't go. My stomach is telling me that this is a situation I should stay out of, if only so I don't have to tell my grams that I'm going out after I missed school because I was sick. Deep in my pit, I can feel my ulcer giving me a warning as loud and clear as any Grams might give me. I finish my burger in two bites. I give Grams a kiss and walk to my room. I put on my jeans and a black T-shirt. I don't want to be seen in the dark. I look in the mirror. I make The Face. *I'm a vampire, a child of the night. Cool, collected, invincible in the dark. I cannot be hurt.*

From under my bed, I pull out a Glad bag. I take two of the Dexys we stole from Nacho's dad. I need to be up right now. I have a knife and I'm about to take it when I decide I'd better not. Lucky for me, Grams has gone in the shower and I knock on the bathroom door and yell through it, "I'll be back in a little while, Grams. I'm going to see Diana."

"What?" she yells, but I'm out the back door before she can ask again. I walk down to Calderon's store. It's dusk already, and the dogs in the neighborhood are getting nervous. They bark at me even though they see me every day. My street looks peaceful in the half-dark, not as ratty. Old small houses, choked with weeds and old tires. Others, trying to look neat and clean in the middle of all that neglect, fence off their little yards like they can keep out other people's tragedy like they might a neighbor's dog. But you can't. Sight and sound creep through the barriers. They come through the holes in your walls like some uninvited mouse stealing in. It's gonna nibble on your food no matter what you do, and one night you find some rat sitting on your chest even though you thought you kept everything locked up tight. I get to Calderon's. It's closed. He's an old guy, like my grams, and he doesn't want trouble. He is not going to keep the store open at night. Too many goddamn thugs in the barrio now.

I'm glad Nacho and Leo aren't there yet. It gives me a few minutes. I sit on the stoop of Calderon's. It's nothing like a store. It's really an old house that he runs his *tiendita* out of. Outside, there's a heavy metal soda dispenser, very old-fashioned. It still takes quarters for a ten-ounce Coke in a glass bottle. It's been spray-painted to shit. Assholes always gotta tag what ain't theirs. I'm studying the pair of tennies hanging on the telephone lines above my head, when the headlights hit me square in the eyes. I shrink back.

It's Nacho. "Where's Leo?" I say.

"He's not here. Can't you see? Get in." He's acting dramatic, like there's a big crisis. The speed is kicking in, though, and I'm feeling better, more energetic. "So what the fuck, man? Am I supposed to guess what the *pedo* is?"

"There's some real bullshit this time."

"Man, that motherfucker walks around like he wants a lifetime supply of broken noses."

We drive to Leo's house. Leo is outside talking to his sister. She's pulling the traditional *Mejicana*-trying-to-talk-sense-to-the-hot-headed-Latino-macho routine. The one where he shakes his head a lot and tells her no, he will not be reasoned with. He is going to kick someone's ass and that's all there is to that. She pleads with him while he stands there being a prick. Most of the time this is all it takes to make a macho feel better, to have a woman notice that he's ready to get violent. Usually he winds up drinking all night and finally collapses into bed, waking up with a hangover and no memory of his bullshit the night before. But Nacho isn't drunk and he isn't interested in talking sense to Leo. He's stoked for a fight. "What's up?" he asks, playing the good buddy come to the rescue.

"Some dudes from around the other side of the block, these fuckers I had trouble with when I was going to South San. In fact, those motherfuckers were the reason I got kicked out. They came by here and tried to take my mom's car." No one asks for any evidence. We just accept it.

The whole time I'm standing there, I'm aware that there's two of me. There's the me who's just watching, thinking the whole time, How stupid, these three morons, these little punks. What in the hell are they going to get mixed up in now? That's the me that lives behind The Face, the guy who worries, the guy who gets scared, the guy who reads and misses his moms and doesn't want to keep fucking up. But the me that is The Face, the Mask, doesn't think about shit. He's all about emotion and acting on it. He lives in my stomach, in that cauldron of acid, and he festers till he says fuck it, it's my turn. The two are knotted up together, linked, and they live together, but they don't like each other much. All I know is that at times like this, the ass kicker, the acid-born protector comes in on cue, right on point.

"We need to fuck them up," Leo says.

"You know where they live? We can break up their shit," Nacho says. Leo nods.

"Well, let's fucking do it," I say. Nacho smiles, grabbing me around the neck.

Leo puts his father's pipebender and a wooden Louisville slugger into the backseat of Nacho's mom's car. Some avenging is going to get done. We're armed with artificial courage, artificial energy, and an artificial cause. We creep up to where the guys live. Leo points at some nondescript house. It could be anybody's house and I guess it is. Outside, in the driveway, is parked an old Monte Carlo. I don't know who lives there and I don't care. I'm flying high now, feeling wired from the energy of what I'm about to do and from the amphetamine.

I step out with Leo and grab the bat. Nacho stays in his mom's LTD, the lights off, the engine running. We hunch over, like little kids playing hide-and-seek, only we're not. We're here to do damage. Leo goes over to the front of the car and I stand at the back. I watch him lift that pipebender above his head and when I see it dip, I strike at the back window with everything I've got, the convulsion of hitting it driving a shock wave that slams inside of my skull like a punch. The vibrations run all through my arms and back. I bash the window again and again before I hear it break. Then I flat out lose it, and in a frenzy slam the car everywhere I can, trying to cave in the roof like it's some kind of *piñata* and I'm going to get some prize if I just break the fucking thing open. I want to destroy it, but seeing the dents pop and snap isn't good enough. *I want to annihilate that fucker.*

Then from the corner of my eye, I see a light blink on and long shadows cutting across its path like a fan blade. They come fast. Something grabs me from behind, and I hear curses as a sharp thunk ricochets through my head. I see stars, honest-to-goodness stars, and then I'm down on the ground being kicked by a dozen-footed beast. It's pissed, frantic, kicking my back, my face, my legs, my ears, and then I lose track. It's just like being rolled over a hill, when you can't tell which way is up, and the rocks and sticks poke you all over and you try to catch yourself, but nothing comes into your hand.

"Motherfuckers!" I hear Leo yelling, but it's no use. I can't see him, and I can't figure out how to get up. My legs won't work and the kicking won't stop. I try to roll over onto my stomach, but my arms keep getting kicked out from under me and all I can hear now is my heart beating with a fear that seems to come from outside me, a jolt delivered by the blows. Then, in a muffled instant, my face is slammed into the pavement, a boot crashing into my mouth from the side at the same time, and I *hear* my shit crunch. I've got rocks in my mouth, little sharp pebbles that I want to spit out. "What the fuck," I hear just before thunder breaks through and crashes into the car with a squeal of tires. Nacho has run his mother's LTD through the yard right into the car we were smashing up. The kicking stops and the crowd jumps back. "Get in, get in!" Nacho yells. I crawl quick, trying to stand up, only I can't and I keep crawling till I half-fall into the backseat. Nacho pulls out of the yard, backing over the mailbox. I hear pop! pop! pop! "They're fucking shooting, dude!" and we haul into the street backward. Somehow Leo has run down the street and he jumps on the front of the car when Nacho slows down for him and we keep on going until we turn down another lane. I open the other back door, and he jumps in as we speed up and out. Nacho is laughing with relief, but I can't. I'm looking at my front teeth. They're lying in little pieces in my palm in a nauseating soup of blood and spit and I suddenly feel so sick and dizzy, but as I heave I find I can't even breathe enough to do it. The pain's too much and I sink into the back into something in between unconsciousness and sleep.

At the hospital, the cop wants to know who did this to me, or better yet, what the hell I did to someone else. Nacho and Leo are gone. They dropped me off at the entrance and took off. "I got jumped," I say. "I was minding my own business, and someone tried to rob me. I didn't see them. It was dark."

"You're going to need some serious stitches on that eye, and your lips are seriously fucked up. I don't even want to tell you about your teeth, and all you can tell me is that it was too dark to see? Looks like you got a real ass-kicking. Why would somebody do that just to rob you?" The cop is smart. I'm in too much pain to give a shit. "I don't know. Leave me alone, alright?" The doctor comes in to tell me that I've got two broken ribs on top of it all. "Lucky," he says, "you could've punctured a lung. Very close." My grams is there, too, but they don't want to let her in until I'm stitched up. "How'd you get here?" the cop wants to know.

"I walked. I only live a few blocks away." He doesn't believe me, but the doctor asks him to go outside. "We're going to try and put you back together now. Don't talk. I'm going to give you some local anesthetic for your teeth and for the stitching." My face goes numb and the pain stops, although I can feel muscles in my cheek throbbing up near my eye. My face jumps every few seconds, making my cut eye flutter. "Try and hold still now," the doctor says. "Stay real still for me." I can see the thread and needle tugging at my skin, lifting it up, and I'm thinking, Damn, that looks painful. They've got an emergency dentist who they call, and while I'm waiting, they let Grams in. *"Dios mio, Dios mio, Dios mio,"* is all she can say, and she puts her hands up to my face, but the doctor stops it. "Mrs. Lomos," he says, holding up both hands, "don't touch him. We've still got some work to do. He's going to be okay, but just try and relax."

I try to say, "I'm okay," to her, but when I open my mouth, my broken teeth feel like they're being broken all over again. So instead of making her feel better, I wind up moaning like someone just kicked me. *"Dios mio,"* she says again, and the doctor says, "Hold on, Robert," and turns to walk her out.

After the dentist comes in and tells me what a mess I am, he whittles down the sharp, new edges of what are left of my four front teeth and he puts fillings in them. I lie there running my tongue over the crags. They're sharp now, like filed-down shark teeth. They'll make a convincing addition to my mask. I want to get up and take a look in the mirror, but when I try and stand up, my ribs feel like they're being split apart. I lay back down and give up.

Grams comes in again. I think about pretending I'm passed out, but I know it's better to get it over with for now. "Why?" she says. And I don't move or even try to say anything. I do look her in the eyes, though. She's been crying, but I can tell she's mad. "Why?" she asks me again. Even if I wanted to, I wouldn't be able to answer. My face is still numb and I've got stitches on the inside of my lips and a couple on my tongue. "You going crazy, boy?" She doesn't really want an answer. "You going crazy, boy." This time it's a statement. "Like your poor mama, going crazy, just going crazy."

She sits down on the chair next to the sink, her brown skin jumping out against the white antiseptic walls. "They gonna put you away, boy. They gonna put you away in the nuthouse before it's over. You try too hard to kill yourself when you got the devil already doing his best." She reaches across my body and pulls the sheet so that my right leg is exposed. "Look at that claw mark there," she says, stroking my shin where a rattlesnake bit me when I was just seven. "You think that was done by a snake?"

It's true. The doctors sliced me up good and the scar looks like some bear took a swipe at me. "That's the devil's mark, the dragon's mark. He wanted you then and he damn near got you." My grams never curses, but she's shaking now. "He tried to destroy you and just when he had you, God pulled you away. Hear that? He pulled you away and all the dragon got was a chunk of your little leg. That's there," she says stroking my scar, "to remind you that you've been saved. But it's also there to remind you that the dragon's always gonna be right behind. And now you trying to help him?" She shakes her head, angry, not crying.

They wheel me into a room for the night. I'm in the same hospital I was born in. Grams gets them to let her sleep in the next bed. I listen to her snore and I think about going crazy, about what it means, about my moms and when things finally snapped. Did she know when she was going crazy? Does anybody know? How do you tell? Is there a voice inside your head, like when you're drunk, and the part of you that never gets drunk is watching, and you can hear it come from inside somewhere and it's saying, "Damn, you are smashed," but it's helpless to do anything because your body is out of control? Does a crazy person just keep going till he can't hear that voice anymore, till it disappears somewhere behind him, swallowed up by the wind as he hauls ass toward the edge, the whole time thinking, *I know what the fuck I'm doing*, till he's flying and he realizes that he's jumped?

Moms took that leap after my Aunt Naomi came to town one last time to convince her that she needed to take care of business. She'd followed my old man around and she gave my moms the full details. It turned out that she'd gone and actually spoken to The Bitch, a young, stupid, mad-sprung woman, afraid that my pops would leave her soon to return to his wife and two kids. She cried for my aunt and my aunt actually *felt sorry for her*. I didn't. I wanted The Bitch dead. I used to pray for it because I figured with her out of the way, my pops would come home. But when Naomi gave us the lowdown, it made me see that it wasn't The Bitch who stole away my pops. It was my pops who had taken himself away.

A couple of days after my aunt told us where The Bitch lived, my moms got all dressed up. She put on her most businesslike suit and ordered me and Antony into the car. "Where are we going?" I asked her. She looked over at me, her eyes shining, and said, *"We're going to go see The Bitch."*

Maybe my moms just wanted to have a sitdown with her, tell her to back off because my old man had two kids. Maybe she just wanted to make her feel like a rotten slut, but by the time she got to the sleazy apartment, her face was red with fury. Her lips were working themselves up and down, and she kept mouthing words that I'd never heard her say. "Stay here," she said, and she got out of the car. She rang the button to 1F. No one answered, but she saw a curtain move. Moms started slapping at that buzzer like it was responsible for my pops leaving, by turns keeping her finger pressed so that the bell would continue ringing, and then buzzing patterns designed to unnerve The Bitch. I sat there, freaking out but not moving. It was like watching a crazy movie about a woman who's completely lost it, only the star was my mother and she was giving one helluva performance.

She came back and got in. She sat there crying, frustrated and ashamed. Then I think that she noticed that she was feeling ashamed and it pissed her off. She said, "It's that bitch who should be ashamed!" That's all she said. Then she got out and went around to the trunk. I looked back and said, "Mom?" but she didn't say anything. I could hear her rummaging around back there, throwing shit, *heavy shit*, all over the place like it was nothing. She found what she was looking for, and I watched her come back around with a tire iron in her hand.

I started to open the door, to try and stop her, but she gave me a look, a crazy look, and said, "Get your little ass back in the car. I'll be right back." She walked around the complex straight to apartment 1F. She knocked on the door loudly, banging on it with her tire iron like the fucking place was on fire.

No one answered.

She tapped on the windowpane in the front, peering through the thin curtains. "Open this door right now," she yelled. "I want to talk to you, you bitch!" Still, no one answered. But Moms knew she was there. She went around back, looking in the kitchen window. There was nobody inside. Then she spotted my old man's car parked in the back.

It was just sitting there, a shiny, new pumpkin-colored Mercury with a burnt-orange Landau roof. In the driver's seat was my pops's trademark comfy-seat cushion that keeps your ass from getting sweaty. From the rearview mirror hung a feather hatband that The Bitch had probably put there. That car was my pops all the way. He was forever washing it, telling me whenever I got to ride in it to make sure not to put my feet or hands on anything. *Godammit, I just washed this thing!* It was his love-mobile, his self-image, all the power and beauty that he wanted. My moms turned toward the green, beat-up Chevy Grams had given us. It sat there, dented, barely running. A manifest "fuck you" from our shitty lives. In it she could see me and Antony, who was crying, little-kid snot running out of his nose as he watched her go apeshit banging on windows and calling out her sworn enemy. She walked to the Merc and without a second thought lifted the tire iron up and brought it down on the car's vinyl roof. She did it again and again. I swear it looked like she was smiling and screaming at the same time. Then she smashed a window and knocked the side mirror off. Moms reached in and pulled out his comfy seat cushion. Then she came back to the green Dodge, where even Antony was quiet now. She didn't say shit. She put the cushion on the seat, sat down on it, and turned the car toward home. When we got there, she went into her bedroom and cried for two days.

I remember all that listening to Grams snore, and even though I'm high on painkillers, the whole thing makes me so sad I can't breathe from the fucking weight of it.

CHAPTER 8

I wake up in the hospital. Grams has gone to work already. I run my tongue over my vampire teeth and I decide. I'm going to strike first. I'm through waiting around.

They release me three days later. I have to wear a flack jacket thing that'll absorb punishment since my ribs are busted up. My teeth don't hurt now that they've plugged the holes up. My face looks like shit, though, like Frankenstein, all swollen and black and blue with stitches near my eyes and lips. I look like I'm coming apart at the seams and I can't hardly talk at all. I have to watch the way I walk. I got kicked hard in the back of my calf and when I go up stairs or even when I'm just walking, my leg goes limp with no warning. It's like a damn trick knee. With all that, I have a legit pass on school. But it doesn't matter. McNutt called and told Grams that I was out. So is Leo. Nacho isn't because he's not marked up, and Leo didn't say anything and neither am I.

My plan is simple. I'm going to call my old man and ask him if he'll let me go with him to L.A. They're recording there and I'm going to tell him that my moms wants me to show up and all I need is a ride. He won't check up on my story. He never talks to anybody over there. He wouldn't want to risk talking to Aunt Naomi.

When I get home, I count my money. All the dough I've made from the *molino,* from selling some of the Dexys we got from Nacho's old man, some odds and ends. I've done whatever it takes to get ready cash. I've got just over eleven hundred bucks. I've still got about thirty pills and I aim to get a job as soon as I get there. I can wait tables, bus dishes, whatever. I'm not going back to school anyway. I'll get a goddamn GED later. See, I'm going to lay the cash out for my moms, right in front of her, and I'm going to let her know that I'm not going to be any trouble. I've got that shit out of my system.

Both matters have to be handled delicately. Convincing my old man will be tough. He's probably ready for some wild times on the road and I'm likely to fuck that up for him. He's always trying to play the grown-up around me. So I have to catch him at the right time. Convincing my moms, that'll be harder because I've got to work on my other grandmother and my Aunt Naomi as well. It's a package deal, but I'm not going to let Antony forget all about me. It's been almost two years and little kids forget things quick. He cried like hell when I left. It seemed like everybody but him was glad to be getting rid of me. Well, maybe not glad, but relieved. But not Antony.

Diana comes to visit me, but Grams sends her away because I'm asleep. I'm taking Demerol so I can rest at night. I'm going to be leaving and it's better that I don't see her. I need to cut ties. She was cool, but I never felt straight with her.

After a couple of days, I get it together enough to dial up my old man. The phone rings about four times and I'm getting ready to leave a message when a woman's voice answers. I know it's not The Bitch's. That's been over a long time now. "Hullo," she says. I don't say anything for a second thinking that maybe I've got the wrong number. But I know I don't. "Hi," I say. "Yeah, hullo," she says again. She sounds kind of stupid and whorey, just like my pops likes them. "Hi," I say again like an idiot. "I'm trying to get hold of my father," I say.

"You must have the wrong number, kid," she says.

"I'm looking for Robert Lomos, Sr. This is his son Robert, Jr."

"Oh," she says. She says it like she still doesn't really believe it, but as if she's running over past conversations and events in her head really fast. "Hmmm," she says. She's remembered something. "Are you thin, black hair, cute?"

"Might be me," I say. It's getting aggravating. "But I'm sure that the guy who lives there is my father."

"Hmmm," she says again. She's really quick. "He told me you were his youngest brother. What a fucking liar. Is he married, too? Why do I always believe the fucking liars?"

"Is he there?" I ask again.

"No," she says. "He's gone. He's in El Paso and then he's heading for Los Angeles."

"He's not coming back through here before then?" Shit's falling apart.

"No. I don't know what the hell he's going to do, junior." She's feeling bad for herself. She hangs up. Just like that my plan is fucked up. But I'm not going to let it end there. I've got dough. I'm going to get there without my pops. He's never gotten me anywhere before, so why should he start now? The way I see it, after I think about it for a while, is that the journey will be all the more important this way. It'll have more meaning. My moms will understand then. She'll see that I took the hard way down, that I'm serious. That I can handle shit.

I decide I'm not going to wait one more second. It's nine in the morning. Grams is at work and won't be back until six or so. By then I can be halfway to El Paso. I'm not taking any fucking plane. Too much money. The bus will do. I'll stop in a couple of places.

I go to the bathroom and look in the mirror. My face is a real freak show. I've got to do something to make it less gruesome. With Grams's cuticle scissors I clip off the stitches that are still in my face. It doesn't hurt. Most of them have come out, anyway. They're the temporary kind that deteriorate right in your skin as your shit heals up. Some of them have already come loose and all I have to do is tug on them. After a while, my face is free of the thread. The scars don't look too bad. I'm all stubbly because I haven't shaved, but I figure it's best not to. If I'm going to be on the road on my own, anything I can do to make myself look tougher—scars, stubble, fucked-up teeth—the better. I make The Face, the new and improved face with authentic vampire teeth. It's enough to make *anyone* think twice before fucking with me. Cool, determined, untouchable. Crazy.

I go to my bedroom and pull out the duffel bag I use when I go on basketball trips. I'm going to travel light. I pack two pairs of jeans, six T-shirts, and six underwear. Three pairs of tube socks, my tennies, a belt, and I roll up a sweatshirt. I take the one that says *Sunnydale* as a laugh. I put on another pair of jeans, a T-shirt, and the brown leather jacket Grams gave me for Christmas. My heavy brown hiking boots are steel toed and I figure that they might come in handy. I put those on, too, but walking in them is not going to be easy with my trick calf. I put my pills and my Demerol in my tennies. Last, I go to Grams's closet and dig out my gramps's service revolver. After I load it, I wrap it up in a towel and pack it.

Now I gotta write Grams a note and that's the hardest part because she's the only thing I'm going to miss in this whole goddamned town.

CHAPTER 9

Dear Grams:

You were right about me going crazy. But you were wrong about me going crazy like Mom. She went crazy from heartbreak and worry. I went crazy from feeling pent-up, like the bubbles in a boiling pot that keep lifting the lid up, popping and fizzing, needing somewhere to go. But not wanting to disappear into thin air, to amount to nothing, I knew I had to act, to put all this energy to something. So I'm going to Los Angeles. My mom and Antony belong to me, don't they? I'm going to set things right. I'll send you a postcard from the road so that you know that I'm making progress and that I'm alright. I'll call you when I get there, and don't worry. I'll miss you.

Your grandson,
Robert

The bus terminal is on Houston Street, so I get to say good-bye to S.A. from downtown. There's a lot of people at the station, all of them looking as desperate and shoddy as me. About a zillion kids are running around and it seems like they're all screaming or jumping or crying, but it doesn't bother me because I'm in a bus station, a bus terminal. And this bus terminal is connected to the bus terminal in Los Angeles. There is a line, a direct line, between here and there, and I'm going to be riding that line, the bus punching forward, every mile bringing me closer. I am starting my journey today, *today*, after all those days of waiting and wasting.

After I buy my ticket I head over to the sign that says L.A. Most of the passengers are already on the bus. They are trying to thwart my upbeat mood, to make their gloom govern the ambiance. My fellow travelers look fucking morbid, like they are being deported to hell. I mean, I didn't expect a festival, but I didn't figure on riding with the damned. I don't get a choice of seats and the only three left are next to the winners of the Oldest, Scariest, and Fattest Passengers of the Day Contest: an old woman who's trying hard *not* to look at me with the one eye that works; Frank Zappa's identical, way more bizarre, more demented twin brother, and a fat guy with a crewcut who's sweating all the way through his black "Don't Mess With Texas" T-shirt and is wheezing like he's got a grapefruit stuffed in his nose. I can't hang with the fat guy. I need room, so I decide on Zappa. As soon as I sit down, I realize that I've made a mistake. This guy is definitely *un*clean.

He seems to be asleep until I sit down. "Yo man, good vibes, okay?" he says.

"Huh?" I'm not sure what he means.

"I'm dealing with only good vibes on this trip, right? I just want to keep the peace."

I guess he's not thrilled with my scarred-up face. "Yeah," I say, "I could use some good vibes." He seems satisfied with that. The woman across the aisle looks over and rolls her eyes to show me that either she thinks the guy is a flake or that he smells like a raccoon.

We get a move on, just ahead of nightfall. I lay back to get some sleep, but I'm excited. So I watch San Antonio disappear, each ten miles or so making it more final. A hundred miles outside the city, and I'm officially too far to turn back.

"Where you going?" Zappa asks me, his eyes still closed.

"L.A., but I'm stopping for the night when we get to El Paso."

"Don't do that," he says. "El Paso is the deep, dark asshole of the Southwest, man. You oughta avoid it if you can. I know, I was born at its bottom, and now I gotta go back, and let me tell you, I'm booking it as soon as I can get away."

"I have sore ribs. I figured it'd be better to sleep at a hotel than on this bus." He shakes his head.

"Not really. Only real reason to stop in El Paso is to buy drugs. That place is full of fuckers, dickhead Border Patrolers, and crooked, stupid cops, the worst in the nation. Treat Mexicans like shit there and the air is so polluted the lungs of old people and babies are known to spontaneously shrivel up and die."

"Why are you going there then?"

"I'm going for a funeral."

"Who?"

"My stepmother," he says offhandedly, a remark about the weather. "I'm just going for my old man, to be cool. I haven't been home in a long time and my sis called me. She was all broken up about it. I was already twelve when my dad married her. She never liked me, I was too wild." He looks around a little. "My buzz is wearing low. Wanna smoke up a little?" He puts a fist under my nose and opens it quickly and then closes it just as fast. Inside is a joint. "There's a toilet in the back. Everyone's asleep and we can blow the smoke out the window."

With hours to go before we hit El Paso, sitting next to Zappa is starting to look like a good choice. We walk to the bathroom and I glance around to make sure everyone is sleeping. I don't want to get kicked off the bus. There's no one except a Mexican couple sitting in the back. We go into the bathroom. Zappa is skinny and so am I, but we're still smashed in there. He lights the joint and I open the tiny window. We pass it around a few times, smoking it quick until things slow down, way down. Zappa smiles big, "Nice shit, right? Mellow buzz, too. Not harsh, no paranoia."

"Yeah," I say, growing more conscious that I'm balls to balls with a strange hippie. "How long have we been in here?" I ask. "Maybe we should go back before someone tries to come in." Just when I say that, there's a knock on the door. "There's someone out there," I say, "We better get out."

Zappa, who's ready to bug, nods. We open the door after he wraps the roach up and puts it in his jean pocket. There's an older man standing out there. He's not too happy when we walk out. "Probably thinks we're fagging off," Zappa says, looking at him with menace in his bloodshot eyes. But the old man knows we were toking up. The place reeks. We make our way back up the aisle to our seats, and it seems to me like everyone is awake now, watching us. Zappa is beyond caring. He's keeps meandering, oblivious to pubic opinion.

"Yeah, man," Zappa says, "why you going to L.A.?"

"Going to see my mom and little brother."

"That's cool. Who did that to your face? Your old man? Are you running away?"

"Nah," I say. "I'm just going to visit."

"Hey, I'd be the last to knock running away. You travel around long enough, there's not much difference. Not much difference at all. I left El Paso on a visit to my uncle's about twenty-five years ago and I ain't stopped yet. That old lady made it her mission to break me."

"How old were you?"

"Younger than you. I was fourteen. Didn't depend on anybody or anything. To me, my father was dead after that. He couldn't stand up to her. How's that for some bullshit? I couldn't respect that. I didn't go back to El Paso until about ten years later, and that was only because I wanted to meet my sister."

"Me and my moms were never on the outs like that," I say. "She just got sick. She needed some rest. I'm just going out to check on her, see if she needs some help."

"Cool," he says, settling back into his seat. "But there's lots of things worse than spending your time a free man. Drifting's been good to me. I've been all over the place, seen the best shit, cool shit, terrible shit, scary shit, groovy shit. All of that shit."

"That's a lot of shit."

"You said it."

"But still, don't you ever get tired of just drifting? Don't you ever just want to go home, sleep in your own bed, know that you don't have to go anywhere if you don't want?"

"Home is overrated, my man. When you've been on the road as long as me, you recognize that what's really important is that you can survive, that you can do with what's around. You learn to improvise, make do. That's when you know you're a free man. You ever read any Thoreau or Emerson?"

"No."

"Do yourself a favor. Pick up a copy, find out about self-reliance. It'll blow your mind. You'll see everything differently."

"Mexicans know all about that. We call improvisation *rasquachismo*."

"Rasq who?"

"It means making do. Improvising. But Mexicans don't like to wander. We do when we have to, like when my old man was a kid, his family had to travel up and down the Midwest picking crops. But they couldn't wait to get home."

"Yeah, well, a man doesn't get to know himself unless he ventures out, like you're doing. Drifting's the way."

"I'm tired of drifting. You don't have to be on the road to do it, either. You can do it right where you live." I stop for a minute and then decide just to keep on going. "I get this vision of myself like I'm a needle and I've got this red thread trailing behind me, and everywhere I've gone in my life, I've left this line, a threaded line, back and forth over this patch of white cloth, and if I look back to see if there's some sensible pattern, I find that there's nothing, just this messy crisscrossing web. It doesn't make sense. It doesn't mean anything. The way I'm thinking now is that this bus is the needle and it's punching across the land, and I'm going to look back when I get to Los Angeles and I'm going to see that I left a beeline in my wake. I've got direction. I'll be able to see that I knew where I was going and figured out, finally, that the shortest distance between two points is a direct line."

"Well," Zappa says, "they might say that the shortest distance between two points is a straight line, but what they don't tell you is that drawing a straight line is the hardest thing anyone can ask you to do."

"What's that mean?"

"Hell if I know. You're the one talking about lines and thread. I'm just going with it. But I'll stick with my drifting. Soon enough, you accumulate what you need. It builds up, but not so anyone can see it or touch it. It builds up in here," he says laying his hand on his chest. "That's when you figure out that you gotta live in here and not anywhere out there. No one tells me what to do. I'm my own man. Direct yourself or be directed by others. That's the choice."

That seems to be the end of the conversation. Zappa closes his eyes. Maybe I pissed him off, making like he's a lonely drifter with no home. Is that the only choice, though? Being your own man or having someone tell you what to do? Isn't there some other way? I'm on my way to something, a destination. I'm looking to stay put. I've made a fucking mess of everything up until now, but as I move up this line, I know something is going to happen to me. Something real, something realized. I can't put my finger on it yet, can't define it, that is. Maybe it'll be this thing where I'll look back at the pattern I've made and it'll all come together for me and I'll be able to say, "Ahhh! So that was it." But it's not gonna come down to me worrying about freedom. You can't build anything on a snow-drift. What's the use of accumulating a formless pile? I want to ask Zappa that. I want to ask my old man that. He's crisscrossed these highways, north to south, west to east, and I really want to know from him what it's gotten him.

I stare out at the dark miles, invisible, falling away exhausted, left behind. This isn't my first trip to California. I've been there twice. The first time was when my folks were still together. We drove in an old baby blue Impala station wagon, fixed and refixed, dented and gouged, heavy and clunky. We rolled out like the migrants of my grandfather's past looking for a crop to pick. We were just a Mexican family in a junky car, a typical sight on a Texas highway heading west. Moms and Pops and two skinny-assed kids, me and my cousin Juan. Only we weren't searching for a crop. At least one generation away from that life, we were looking for some-thing else, each of us with a different vision of what California meant. My parents were looking for a second chance, my moms desperate to make it work, my pops guilty and sullen. Me and Juan felt just like we were going to the moon, some heaven place beyond our imaginations.

We'd been getting ready for weeks, my old man delivering the station wagon to Mr. Lopez, the friendly church mechanic who'd trust my pops to pay him later for the work. My moms took me and Juan to something like a Pants, Inc. outlet, where we could find some generic blue jeans and look presentable to the California relatives. My pops wanted us to look nice, not like the poor family from the sticks who came to mooch, which is what we were. We couldn't afford the trip, but in one of those tragic deals, we couldn't afford not to take it. It was like some magic cure lay in the West and in the trip itself. They felt like I'm feeling now, that there was some redeeming power in moving, even temporarily, leaving their problems behind, as if the problems would just dissolve, or at least loosen their grip with every mile we made. Maybe that's why my pops drove like he was possessed with escaping. He wouldn't stop for anything. I stayed up while my moms and Juan slept in the back of the wagon.

I was afraid Pops would go to sleep while he was driving and kill us all. He knew that by getting there quick, he'd be able to get back all the faster. That way, he could feel that he'd tried hard and could then unload his guilty conscience, just drop it behind him like the miles, and just quit without being accused of having run out.

Pops didn't stop until the tank showed empty, and then only to fill up fast and get rolling again. That first day we didn't eat. Nothing. Me and Juan cried and my moms pleaded with him that we were hungry, but he kept insisting that we would stop "in a while." Finally, around eleven P.M. he stopped at some gas station where the only food he was able to find was a loaf of white bread, a package of American cheese, and about seven packages of Twinkies. My moms fixed us with cheese sandwiches. Plain, dry, and *good*. I swallowed it with some serious gulps and asked for another. Hunger makes everything taste right.

My pops was obsessed, though. He didn't stop, even when night swallowed everything up, even the horizon. He drove relentlessly, driving the six hundred miles to El Paso by midnight and swearing to me that he would have us to Tucson by the time the sun came up. It was exciting and scary at the same time looking at him from the corner of my eye while I fiddled with the AM radio to find some music, anything but the preachers and strange talk shows that make the road so depressing at night. "Are you keeping your father company?" my moms kept asking from the back. "Don't let him fall asleep."

We finally arrived, and L.A. was everything I'd imagined. Everything was good there. My parents acted like they were in love, and my days were nothing but fun because my cousins took care of me and Juan. In Texas there was nothing but heat, but here, cool, bright days. The place smelled like hope. My moms's mom, Abuela, even seemed happy to have us there. My parents told everyone that shit was cool now. They were going to make it. My tenth birthday was a blast. Abuela bought me a cake decorated with a football field. My cousin and his wife threw me a party and took me and Juan to Disneyland. I still remember this one picture. In it, my family is sitting together on some lame ride, the log one, I think, and we're getting ready for the rush about to come, but we feel happy, safe, because we're together.

At the end of two weeks, we drove back to Texas. We were still the poor, little Mexican family. We were returning from the search. Migrants looking for shit they'd never find. My pops drove back even more determined, even more desperate because his decision was too much to bear, and he needed the release that only action could give him. Not long after we got back, before I could even give Grams this dumb picture I'd taken of me with three parrots sitting on my arms at Disney, Pops had decided to split again.

When we get to El Paso, Zappa, the runaway, gets off. He gives me his hand and says, "Later." The bus empties enough so that I don't feel like getting off here after all. I want to move on. Straight line.

At about four in the morning, riding through the desert, a big city jumps up from out of nowhere. It's Tucson, the driver tells us. It doesn't look like it has any business being there, right in the middle of these desert flats. What could possibly have brought people here, and what made them decide to stop and build this city? Probably all the runaways living by themselves in the desert decided, Fuck it, I'm tired of being alone.

I get off the bus at the station. The driver reminds the passengers that the bus will leave in half an hour for Phoenix. I don't want to ride anymore, so I look for a place to stay. The sun is already coming up and I look around for a café or diner. There's an IHOP off the highway just a few blocks away and I head for it. I like IHOPs. The waitresses are always these older, motherly types. I get there and sit down. The place is empty but I'm not that hungry anymore, just really tired. My ribs hurt and my stomach is acting up and I didn't bring my goddamned ulcer medicine. The waitress, named Debbie, comes over and takes my order. She's sweet. "You look tired, hon," she says like she actually cares. "You been traveling?" She looks at my duffel bag. "Yeah," I say, "I'm heading for L.A."

"Well, hold on, you're almost there," and she smiles. It's nice to have someone smile at you when you feel lonesome. I order a glass of milk and some fruit. Debbie brings my milk and fruit plate and I feel a little like a puss eating melon balls and milk, but I force myself to down them quick. I leave a five on the table and split. Back on the road, I spot a motel and head for it. It's called the Scott's Inn and there are hardly any cars in the lot. The place needs a paint job bad, and half the lights in the sign are burned out so that it reads SC   INN. It's creepy even in the early-morning light, like any minute the walls might start wailing. The night clerk is this young black guy who's got really bad skin, pimply, maybe even boils. But at least he's not all scarred-up like me. He's checking out *Ghost Busters* on TV. He's cool. He asks me how I'm gonna pay, and when I say cash, he just says, "Fine, but you have to pay in advance." I'm down with that. I give him twenty bucks and he gives me a key.

The room is completely fucked. There's a big water stain on the carpet, the faucet leaks, and the door doesn't lock, but I'm so tired, I don't care. I turn on the TV and switch channels till I find *The Flintstones.* I have to sleep. But the more I try to sleep, the more I can't. Just knowing that I've got to *hurry* and fall asleep is making me even more nervous so I take a Demerol to calm me down.

I wake up around ten in the morning. The sun is beating down on my head. I get up and take a shower, which is a real hassle, an adventure in pain. I finish and dry up with my T-shirt because there's no towels in the dump. Fuck it. I'm not on vacation. I put the same jeans on and a clean shirt. I look at my face in the mirror. My lips aren't as swollen anymore, but the bruises look darker, especially around my left eye, where it's still swollen and the white of my eye is mottled with blood clots. I hope that clears up before too long. It's not very attractive.

Back at the station, I find out I missed the next bus to L.A. Now I have to wait until three P.M. I've got four hours. I don't want to wait in the station, but I'm too tired to walk anywhere. There's a newsstand and a couple of snack machines so I buy a package of Twinkies and a Coke for lunch, plus a couple of postcards. On one I write, "Grams, I made it to Tucson. Don't worry. I'm okay. I'm feeling much better, and you'll see, everything will work out." I sign it and put a stamp on it. The front of it has a picture of Tucson rising out of the desert, the sun coming from behind the tall buildings, ready to beat its light over everything. The other post-card's got a fat guy with his pants down just about to sit his bare ass on a cactus. The caption reads "Prickly Pair." I'll send it to Nacho. It's just the sort of stupid shit that will make him laugh.

Finally the bus gets there. It's full of Mexico-Mexicans on their way to L.A. to get jobs. I sit next to this older guy. He's got a big mustache and he's wearing a Dodgers cap. I nod at him because he seems cool.

"*Que te pasó a la cara?*" He wants to know what happened to my face.

"I fell," I say. "I'm alright."

"*Válgame,*" he says. That means "My goodness."

He's got a big bag of beef jerky and he offers me a piece, but I don't take it. I point to my front teeth. "Can't bite into anything that tough," I say. But he doesn't really understand me, although one look at my vampire teeth and he gets it.

"*Ta bueno,*" he says and rolls the bag up. The guy's old enough to be my pops. It makes me wonder what life might have been like if my pops hadn't been a musician. If he had just been a regular working guy like this man. Of course, this guy is on the road, too, but he doesn't look happy about it. It's too bad that I can't make conversation with him. I should've kept up my Spanish better. I can still understand it, but I can't conduct a serious discussion. Goddamn school ruins communication for us bilinguals.

I stare at him from out of the corner of my bloodshot eye. He looks like he's seen some shit in his life. His face is sunburned and dark from working all the time outdoors, and his hands are thick and hard looking. He's got lines around his eyes from having to squint. He's not like those bullshit stereotypical Mexicans you see in the movies, looking worried and scared and shit. Then again, he doesn't look like he wants any trouble, either. He just needs to make a living. I feel like shaking his damn hand and saying, *"Tenemos que hacer las cosas duras."* He'd understand that I'd seen the same thing in his face that I've always seen in my grams's face. "One has to do the hard things." Grams never gets tired of saying that.

I'm focused now. No more bullshit fantasies. I've got a job to do. I have a purpose. I'm into this positive visualization thing. Pastor Bud, who coached us basketball at Sunnydale, used to hand us that line all the time. "Just see yourself rebounding the ball," or "Just see yourself making that pass." Everyone would mock him later. Nacho would say things like, "See yourself banging that ass." Or, "See yourself *not* being such a fucking pussy." Or, "See yourself seeing yourself naked." But I tried it a few times. I don't know if it worked exactly, but it didn't hurt. I'd lay in bed, that old, creaky metal fan going while I was feeling lonely as shit, missing Moms and Antony, and decide that I was going to *visualize* what I wanted to happen, and not just the obvious images of me being with them, or of us being at some corny-assed picnic, but I'd picture the *process*. And here I am on this bus, so for what it's worth, I guess I'd have to say I'm a believer—at least as much as I'm a believer in anything.

In Phoenix, the Mexican worker gets out. I made the right decision staying in Tucson instead of Phoenix. It's too big a city, with huge highways and miles and miles of suburbs and malls and all that L.A.-style horseshit. I'm glad when we pull out. Nobody sits next to me. I like it that way. I can relax and just watch the desert.

Riding in a car has always relaxed me. After Pops was gone, my moms's first job ever was at Montgomery Wards. She'd work the night shift; at nine o'clock I'd put Antony's shoes on and we'd get in the Malibu Classic Grams gave us, and we'd go pick her up. Antony would stand right next to me as I drove. We'd get there and wait to see her come out of the employee's door. Sometimes we'd get there and go in a little early. We'd wander, nobody paying attention to us. Me and Antony, his little hand in mine, would kill time, usually at the candy stand. I'd buy us some fruit jellies. Antony's face'd be all delighted, his mouth aslobber as I handed him the sweets. They'd make the announcement that they were closing and we'd head for the car where we'd listen to AM radio. Two big windows, rolled down, Antony all the time standing next to me peering toward that employee door like baby Benjy in *Sound and the Fury*, at where Moms was gonna come out of. When she did, he'd howl. The car'd go on, me driving it to the sidewalk and she getting in and Antony jumping on her neck and Moms smiling, tired and sad because she'd been thinking all day. She'd cheer up a little, though, just when she sat in the car and we'd start talking. We'd head home, windows open, radio turned down because Moms didn't like it loud, and the wind blowing like mad all the while. I remember always feeling like that car could take right off the highway into the dark sky, like if we wanted, we didn't have to go home to that depressing dark house. Instead, if we really wanted, we might just fly off, and just keep flying, too.

CHAPTER 10

The bus rolls across the California state line, but it doesn't look like it's supposed to. I'd imagined that California would mean an immediate change, that as soon as I crossed the border, the grass would turn green, the ocean would be out there on the horizon blue as hell with surfers cutting across, and on the beach, hotties walking big, fancy dogs. But the desert just goes on and on until we climb over some small mountains and drop down into the twinkling L.A. basin. It's dark, and all the towns that list their names on the tops of highway signs seem to be wasting their time. It all looks like L.A. to me, all of it blending right into the same sea of lights and highways. I don't see any ocean, but the bus finally moves into the city that's been hanging on the horizon of lights for about an hour or more. We make our way into the bus station area. It's dirty and shady looking, not a lot of people walking around like in downtown San Antonio. Just a few homeless people and junkies. There's chain-link fencing everywhere, with aluminum warehouses that look abandoned but are still protected by rolling barbed wire. Gigantic trash Dumpsters, corroded and overflowing, line the alleyways.

The bus station is sleazy. Makes me homesick for the one in San Antonio. It smells like burning diesel fuel. There's a long line of people wanting to get out, and here I am, happy to be getting in. In front of the greasy snack bar, there's a cop, and he's keeping a lookout for poor homeless types who want to crash. He walks up to this one old guy, old enough to be his father, who's put his head down, and he says while tapping him with his fingers in this very official way, "This isn't a hotel." Not exactly a welcome wagon. I walk through the terminal and head out onto the sidewalk when it hits me that I don't know where I want to go or what I should do exactly. I can't call my moms. She doesn't even know I'm here yet, and I don't want to call out of the blue in the middle of the night. I don't know where my pops is staying, and even if I did, I wouldn't want to head there. I feel like calling Grams and letting her know I'm alright, but it's too late to wake her up.

I decide to take a cab to Mission Viejo, where my moms lives with Abuela. The ride there is long, much longer than I remember from the last time I was here. But I don't remember much about the last time. When Naomi came to S.A. to take Moms and Antony away, she told my grams that it would be "healthier" for me to come along, to see where they were going to be living so that I wouldn't feel like they'd dropped off the face of the earth. It didn't work.

The trip was miserable and long. We drove with my aunt at the wheel, a little U-Haul trailer swaying behind us the whole way, my moms out of control, crying a lot and then talking manic about how good it was going to be for her to get a rest and how I'd be able to come visit as soon as she got better. We played road games, but I wasn't into it. I sat in the back and didn't say much of anything. I was too down. I was mad, too. Mad at Naomi for bringing her big ass down there and taking Moms and Antony. I was mad at my moms for being weak, for not having the guts to say that I had to come live there, too. I was even mad at poor Antony because he was going to stay with Moms. When we finally got to Mission Viejo, I couldn't think of anything but that I had to go back to San Antonio. I never talked about it, hoping that maybe somehow they'd forget. But just a week later Naomi put me on a plane and that was that.

I pay the cabbie nearly sixty dollars. He made damn sure I had the money before we took off. After the bus drive with all those people all crammed in and hot, sitting alone in a car feels like a victory.

Mission Viejo is cool in a fake-assed way. It's full of malls and has this artificial lake right in the middle of it. There's huge stores, a gigantic Sizzler, and a movie gigaplex on every palm tree–lined street corner. It's early now, ready to dawn. I'm tired. I get the guy to drop me off at a Motel 6 just off the highway. I'm probably only a couple of miles from my moms's place. It's weird being so close but not being able to just knock on the door. I decide it's better to sleep here tonight, scope out the neighborhood, and think things through tomorrow. I've gotten phase one over with, and now I need to be creative if I want shit to go down right. In the motel room, which is nice for a Motel 6, I think about the reasons that I need to play up in my talk with my moms to convince her to let me stay: that Antony needs a father, that I'm going to work and help her out with the dough I've saved up, that I'll get my GED. But mostly that we need to be together and that I miss her and Antony.

I'm trying to keep it simple; I've changed and I'm here to prove it to her. Reasonable. Direct. Honest. How can I lose?

The next morning, I take a hot shower, shave, brush my vampire teeth, put deodorant on, and get in my best T-shirt and jeans. I head straight for the giant Sizzler I saw the night before. It's morning and there's no customers yet, just a few waiters and waitresses putting the salad bar up. There are two Mexican guys sitting at one of the tables. They both have mustaches, porn-style, and are wearing short-sleeved dress shirts, the type that make you look like a tent revival preacher. One's nametag reads JUAN AYALA/MANAGER. The other guy has a nametag that says SETH PONCE/ASST. MANAGER. Ayala and Ponce, a very good welterweight matchup, or a pair of knucklehead conquistadors who got lost before they found shit.

They stop talking when I get up to the table. Ayala looks up at me. He's got terminal fuckface. It's a lethal combination of stupidity, pissed off–edness, and arrogance that always equals asshole boss. "Yeah," he says like I just interrupted a meeting of the joint chiefs of staff.

"I'm just wondering if you need any help. Are there any openings?"

"How old are you?" he says, looking me over.

"Sixteen, but I'll be seventeen in a few months," I say way too quick. He laughs, looking over at Ponce like he can't believe the sight of me.

"You got experience?"

"I can bus tables. I've also worked in a *molino*."

"This isn't a *molino*. It's a restaurant, and we keep things tight. You want to work here, you gotta be quick, on time, and you gotta be available." He's trying to look intense, icy. Ponce is looking at me, too. The stares are supposed to be giving me a sense of just how *intense* they are, of just how tight a ship is kept, that they crunch balls like cough drops and eat nipples like potato chips.

"Yeah, I can work whenever you need me. I'm good."

"We'll see about that," he says, looking over at his silent partner. "Go get your shirt. You'll need to start tomorrow evening. I need a closer."

I get my Sizzler shirt from this sleepy looking white chick named Megan who's wiping down the front counter. "I'm the cashier," she says, handing me my brown polyester shirt. I guess I'm supposed to be impressed and I say, "Cool," and take my ass back to my room to plan my next move.

So right out of the box, I'm employed. Granted, a screwed job, but it's a start. Now I have to call Grams. I dial her number and after about two rings, she picks up.

"Hello?" She sounds tired.

"Hi, Grams," I say like I'm calling from down the street with nothing too important to say.

"Robert," she says, sounding excited. "Robert, boy, is that you? Where are you?"

"Grams," I say again and then stop, because I'm not sure what to say. "Grams, I'm in L.A."

"Oh Roberto, Roberto," she says, and the way she says it makes me sad, not only because I can hear how heartbroken she sounds, but also because there's something in her voice that tells me that most of all, she's sad for me.

"It's okay, Grams."

"It ain't okay, boy," she says. I know that it's true. "You're hurt, probably haven't had anything to eat. Where are you? Are you at your momma's?" It's a reasonable question, but one that if I answer will sound bad.

"I'm not quite there yet. I'm taking my time. I have money," I say, trying not to give in to the sad tone of the conversation. I want to sound confident, like I have a good plan. "I'm feeling good, Grams."

"How long you gonna stay?" she says.

"I don't know, Grams. I really can't say because a lot of that depends on how Moms and Antony are doing. They might need me."

"Boy," she says like she doesn't really want to say what she feels she needs to say, "I don't want you getting hurt on the inside like you've been hurt on the outside. Your bones'll heal, even your poor belly's going to heal up. I don't want you coming back here with your *corazón todo quebrado*." Funny to hear her talk about heartbreak. It shakes me up a little to hear Grams getting weepy.

"Grams, it ain't about that. I'm just here to make sure everything is alright." There isn't much more to say and she doesn't try. Before I hang up, I tell her to please not call my moms looking for me, at least not right away. "I need a few days to settle in. I have a plan. I'll give you a call so you won't worry."

First thing I do is to find my *abuela*'s house. Mission Viejo is complete suburbia. The streets are wide, with palm trees rising up every few dozen yards just to remind you that you're in goddamn California. It's sunnier than in Texas, only not nearly as hot. People look healthy, confident, like they don't have a goddamn care in the world. And cars? It's like a parade of shithead BMW-owners on every street.

I stop at the McDonald's just down a couple of blocks. I'm eating a cheeseburger when I spot Antony at the counter. He's with my Aunt Naomi. It catches me by surprise and I almost don't recognize him. I'm not ready for it at all. He looks twice as big as when I last saw him. His hair is darker, almost as black as mine, still curly, but long so that he's looking like a big boy now, not a baby like I still picture him. He's wearing white shorts and a light blue T-shirt that's got a Pokémon figure on it. They look baggy on him because he's skinny as me.

Naomi's got him by the hand. She pays for a Happy Meal and Antony and her go to the back where they can eat outside. She's gonna watch him play.

I can't feel my legs. It's a real shock, seeing him and almost not recognizing him. That means he wouldn't know me at all. Maybe Naomi, but not him. Or would he have? He *is* my brother. Is there something about that, a *sense*, a brotherly sense that made me notice him and would have made him remember me? I want to go watch him play, but I don't want Naomi to see me, so instead I dump my food and walk out. It's getting time for me to go to work. I walk back because I have a while and I can't help but think about Antony. It makes me mad, seeing him by accident. Shit like that shouldn't happen with your own brother. I mean that if someone should be living with you, or you with them, you should know where they are and they should know where you are, and there shouldn't be accidents.

After Moms and Pops split, Antony was my charge. My moms never had to ask me to take care of him; I just did. That kid was like my son since I'm twelve years older. I took him around a lot because even though Antony was a baby, he never acted like one. He never made a fuss or cried when I took him to the store. He wouldn't even ask for anything like other kids always do. What was most cool was that even though he was just a little kid, he saw me as his pops, but not some blurred vision. He saw me at my worst and at my best. The thing was that even when he saw me at my worst, fighting with Moms when she tried to get me to stay home instead of running off and getting high again, he still knew he could count on me. I always came home, always took care of him. That's important to a kid.

I walk to work, thinking about how goddamn big he's gotten. You know, he probably *would* have recognized me.

First thing I notice at the Sizzler is that everyone looks annoyed. Even the customers. There's a hundred people in line and dozens more milling around the salad bars. Everybody is poking their fingers in the bowls, scattering lettuce and egg crumbs to hell and back. Some of them are sucking down food right from the bar, and little kids are running around the ice cream machine throwing chocolate flakes and making a general shit sty for someone to clean. And for it being a salad bar, there are some hefty folks loading up on pudding and those little greasy meatballs. One guy, wearing one of those silly golf shirts that make wimpy dude's nips look even more chicklike, is sticking his mits right into the cucumber slices, like he's the only fucker alive in the restaurant.

Everyone is taking that all-you-can-eat deal seriously. People waiting for tables rubberneck at others who are done but still sitting around shooting the breeze. One guy says to his wife, "I'm going to shove my steak knife down that bastard's gullet if he doesn't hurry the hell up." Then I notice the busboys running around with brown plastic tubs and white towels wiping down booths like there's no tomorrow. I can see Ayala standing on the sidelines, trying to look imperious, convinced that he's more Caesar than salad.

I'm about to turn around and get the hell out, but just then he spots me and nods me over. He's got his arms crossed and he says, "Punch in and come back out with one of those tubs and a wet rag." I remember that I'm here to prove I'm a man, that I can work. Besides, I can always walk, so I go in the back area. There's a huge stainless-steel counter with a gigantic dishwasher and two sinks big enough to take a bath in. There's a stack of tubs with dirty dishes sitting on the floor and covering the counter, but because he is so short, I almost miss the dishwasher himself. He's an older black guy and he's working up a storm back there.

He doesn't even notice me. He's stacking the dirty dishes in a wire rack. When it's full, he pulls on this metal arm and the giant washing machine opens up and he pushes the rack inside it. Then he pulls on the arm again and the big door slides shut and the machine goes into action. It sounds like a miniature hurricane is taking place in there. After about two minutes, the machine stops. He pops it open, pulls out the clean dishes, and puts in a dirty batch. It looks cool except that the guy is sweating hardcore and moving so fast that it seems like he's afraid of being swallowed by the mountain of dirty tubs. Every five minutes, more tubs are brought in by sweating busboys, and they grab a clean one and head out.

Ponce, the assistant manager, gives me a blank timecard and I fill in my name. "Jus grab a tuv," he says, "an go to it, my fren." He sounds like Pacino in *Scarface*. I go back outside the double doors and Ayala is still out there. He looks over to see that it's me. "A few quick ground rules," he says sounding like a tough guy, but looking like the middle-aged guy going to fat that he is. "You got this job because this Dominican I hired a couple of weeks ago called in sick twice already. I don't go in for that shit. So you get to learn from somebody else's fuck-up. Next, my main rule is this, and it's simple. Don't mess with me. If you do, I'll make you wish you hadn't. You come in late or miss work, or knock off while you're here, I'll give you shit schedules and a very few hours to work. If it gets to be a habit, I just fire you. There's lots of wetbacks waiting for jobs around these parts. Get it?" He looks over at me and tugs on his pornstache. I try really hard not to smile. His tough-guy act is weak. My grams can be a hell of a lot scarier than that, but I nod. "Go to it," he says. "Got a lot of tables to clean. I hate to see dirty tables."

During a smoke break in the back, Jerry, this white busboy with manic blonde hair and a scruffy Fu Manchu, introduces me to Maurice, the black dishwasher. He's kind of short, with a lot of white hairs in his beard. He's sort of wall-eyed. Not too bad, but bad enough that you have to guess which eye to look into. He's older, probably more than forty.

"Hey man, we're at the bottom of this motherfucker. They've got hierarchy here. That means that there ain't no solidarity in the workforce. At other places, the employees stick together in hating management, see?" Maurice lights a joint. "Want a hit? It's the only way to work around this place. I need it to focus." I take a hit and pass it to Jerry, but he turns it down. "I gotta go back in," he says.

Maurice keeps on going. He talks fast and he makes what he says sound important, like he's on to something you're not. "See, at other jobs I've had, it don't matter what you do or what you make. If you're just expendable labor, you had something in common with everyone else around the place. But in the restaurant game, it's different. Goes like this, young man: manager, assistant manager, head waiter, waiters and waitresses, head cook, cooks, cockroaches, rats, bad meat, and finally busboys. There's no chance of mistaking that shit, either. That motherfucker Ayala and his little bitch Ponce, they mean that shit when they say they don't want to hear noise from you. The busboy's only reason is to whip around with a greasy brown tub and clean up after the guts as fast as your ass can take you." He takes another toke. "I better get my own black ass in there and start to washing. I'll give you some more info after work. You closing, right?" I nod. "Okay, then, I'll check you after." He walks inside and I hang back for a couple of minutes till I feel the buzz kick in and then I go inside and grab another tub.

The system is simple: As soon as the gut's ass is off the chair or squeezing between the table and booth, you must be there ready to clean off the scraps, wipe down the mess on the tabletop, rearrange the salt, pepper, sugar, and centerpiece so that the next gut can sit down. You carry around a white towel soaked with a solution of water and ammonia. The fumes get everywhere and give you a serious headache. Meanwhile Ayala is walking around in the back yelling his head off that you're not working fast enough.

"Sonuvabitch, there's a hundred guts in line tonight and you jerks can't keep those tables clean! If I walk out there and see so much as one dirty table and a line of guts waiting, I'm gonna fire the whole damned bunch of you useless fuckers."

But when you get in the groove, really get into a zone, and you're running around cleaning those tabletops, it's satisfying, almost a religious experience, setting things right, clearing away the shit to leave something behind that's clean, neat, everything in its place. The problem is, people are just waiting to sit down and fuck everything up all over again.

The guts, they're the worst angle of the job. Watching them eat is enough to turn you against humanity, make you wish you were a dolphin. It's nauseating. People waste tons of good shit. They're dirty, lazy, cheap, suspicious assholes. Any gut who comes into a Sizzler expects to be treated like a king. No matter what he may look like, what he's wearing, what line of work he might be in—minister, lawyer, bricklayer, prostitute, mailman, mechanic, house-wife, teacher—it doesn't matter. Guts leave one greasy mess behind and some of them even shoot you a look of contempt that says, "Hey, suck my gut slime, busboy."

My second day and I'm sitting there waiting for the Malibu Chicken, which I dig, and this waitress I haven't seen before brings it out to me. I notice her eyes first. They're light brown, and they're big and shaped like little leaves. She's got a pretty smile, shylike, with lips light pink, the bottom one real round the way I like. She puts the plate down and says, "Hi, I'm Marie. You're the new guy, right?" It's nice that she doesn't call me the new "kid" or the new "busboy." She's about thirty years old, a lot older than me, but she doesn't talk to me that way. "Well, I hope you like it around here.

Don't let Ayala get on your nerves. Just ignore him." And she walks away slow, knowing she's beautiful.

"That Marie is nice," I say to Jerry during a break that night.

"Yeah, she's cool. She's kind of fucked up, though."

"Yeah?"

"She's always being stressed by her old man. He's come in here a couple of times and got loud with her. Once he pulled her out of the restaurant after it'd closed and Ayala called the cops. He hasn't shown up around since, but you always hear her talking to the other waitresses, especially Flora, about what 'that asshole Joe' has done."

After we close, I notice her getting into a red Escort. There's a bearded man in there, way older, looking short. There's a little kid in the backseat who's psyched to see her mommy.

After work that night, I'm telling Maurice and Jerry how much I hate the customers. "Guts treat us busboys like we aren't even there. I don't know how the waitresses keep it together."

"Don't feel sorry for those bitches," says Maurice. We're sitting in the back of his old Ford pickup. Jerry nods. "Fuck no."

"They're pampered by Ayala. They're the upper class around here. They fucking call the shots. They shake that snatch for Ayala and Ponce and those two let 'em make up the schedules."

"Yeah," Jerry says. We're drinking a couple of beers that we got at the 7-Eleven. "They look down on us busboys. And let me tell you, don't let them fool you by trying to act nice to you. All they want is for you to do their shit for them."

"If you're going to make this gig pay," Maurice says, "you're going to have to steal some tips. Look, you do most of the work, and they sure as hell ain't going to give you a cut. And I'll tell you what, that's about the truest thing you'll hear about life. Remember it."

Maurice tells me that he's got a system down that's guaranteed to make us all some extra scratch, no risk. It's beautiful. We take tips and he backs us if we're caught. "Sooner or later, you'll get sick of working for peanuts and you'll start taking those tips, so you might as well never get caught. Number one, don't get greedy. This busboy last year, name of Jaime, used to go around to every table and sweep up everything, nickels, pennies, dimes, dollars. He wouldn't leave jack for the waitresses. Hell, even the dumbest-assed waitress gets suspicious if everyone in her station decides to stiff her. What you gotta do is set a daily limit, and no matter how tempting it gets, don't go beyond it. Don't be like those goddamn all-you-can-eat guts.

"For instance, when I started I set a reasonable limit—twenty dollars. Just enough to buy a six-pack of beer when I got out of work and some gas. Brother lives all the way up in Northridge. Now, if you know you got a big event coming up and you going to need cash, you can make an exception—*occasionally*. Rule three, don't get sticky fingers on really slow nights. Too much time for the servers to catch you in the act. The best nights are Friday and Saturday. And of course holidays. You can make a motherfucking killing on Mother's Day. You can get fifty, sixty dollars if you know how. Bitches won't know nothing. Rule four, never admit shit, even if you get caught red-handed. If they catch you with five dollars in your pocket, don't admit shit. Ever. If you get the technique right, you can cover your ass easy, although sometimes if a waitress bitches enough, Ayala'll come and have a talk with you. Just keep denying it, though. You got one of those innocent faces. I bet you could pull it off no problem. You down?"

I nod. "Fuck yeah. I can always use extra cash," I say.

"My man," he says, giving me his fist to tap. "The technique is simple. Your advantage is you get to the table first. Most waiters and waitresses won't pick up their tip right away. It looks bad, like they're only in it for the money. Those bitches gotta act like they're there because they *like* watching guts suck a plateful of fatty shit. Now right inside that nasty mess those motherfuckers leave behind on the table, you've got to spot the cash immediately. As you bend over to wipe off the booth or chair, give a quick, sneaky look to see if you're being watched. If all signs are clear, right in front of everybody put the tip in a "safe" place so you can clean the table. As you drop plates and utensils into the brown tub, accidentally brush a dollar or two along with the dishes. When you got this move down, you can progress to my patented move: tip-switching. That's the busboy's bonanza: When a gut leaves the waitress a five-buck or ten-buck tip, you pull a one lickety-split out of your pocket while pretending to clean something from under the booth. Then switch the one for the five or ten. It's lucrative, but it's risky business. See, there ain't nothing so eye-catching to the average waitress as a ten-dollar tip. If the gut drops it in front of them, their breathing speeds up, pussy gets moist. They'll hardly be able to concentrate. That's the warning sign not to pull the switch."

"Where do you come in?"

"If someone spots you, you just tell the waitress that you must've accidentally swept the money into the tub. Bring them back to check out your story. Act indignant. Say, 'Your money is in one of these tubs.' Then start looking and I'll shove a couple of bucks in a tub near me. Then I'll say to you and the waitress, 'If you're looking for money, there's a couple of bucks in this tub.' It'll work every time. We split the money fifty-fifty."

Ayala's got me opening the next morning. It's a Saturday and he's let me know I'll be on my own. "Get here ready to work, Robbie," he says fucking with my name. Maurice and Jerry sympathize. "That's screwed up," says Jerry. "I'd been here about two months before they sprung that one on me." Maurice drives me to the Motel 6. "Why you live here?" he asks.

"I'm just staying here temporarily," I say being too tired to explain it. Maurice doesn't take the hint. "Shit, I know it's temporary. No one lives in a Motel 6, man. But you oughta be able to find a place around here that's cheaper than thirty bucks a night. Hell, you'll go broke."

"I'm going to move in with my moms," I say. "She lives around here."

"Alright," he says, but I can tell he wants to keep asking questions. Luckily, he's tired and I get out of his truck. "Later," I say and go into my room and go to sleep after I wash the greasy funk out of my Sizzler shirt.

It sinks in right away that I'm going to hate opening the restaurant more than anything else I have to do around this place. Most busboys hate closing because it takes until midnight or longer. After the cooks and waitresses are done, the busboy is still there, cleaning all the pots and pans and mopping the kitchen and washroom floors. But opening means cleaning toilets and bathroom floors. Then you have to vacuum the entire dining room, fishing out whatever pieces of salad or gristle have fallen beneath the booths or chairs. A quick look at the baby chairs shows at least six or seven that are crusted over with Jell-O or some other nasty shit. Babies are little animals.

After cleaning baby-gut slop, I go back to the washroom and clean out all the pots and pans from the night before that were full of crusted gravy and other heart-clogging shit. And I get all of forty-five minutes to do the whole job. Ayala doesn't believe in giving extra hours. I run around the restaurant with the damned clunky vacuum, getting down on my hands and knees looking for that elusive chunk of meat that might start stinking up the place if it remains hidden. So I'm bustling to and fro, sweat's running down my face, and it being Saturday, the place begins to fill up fast.

Ayala comes into the washroom where I'm already washing

dishes. He looks at me hard. "Are you the one who opened this morning?"

I turn and look at him. "Yeah, what's wrong?"

"Well, for starters, it's hard for a gut to wipe his ass without any toilet paper." He gives me this sarcastic smile that makes me want to cram his big stupid head in the dishwasher. "If you can't do the job, you'll be out on your *culo* fast around here."

I think about my moms, who needs money, and instead of telling him to fuck off, I nod and say, "Yeah, I'll pick it up, boss."

CHAPTER 11

I've been here six days, and all I know about Mission Viejo is how to get to Sizzler and how and when to skulk around my moms's place. I'm going to make my move soon. I've got it planned like this: I'll get dressed up, go over on Sunday with some flowers, knock on the door, and pretend that this is all one big happy surprise.

One thing I've learned is that people play off of what you give them. If you fuck up and then act like you've fucked up, people get their stage directions from you and treat you like you fucked up. But I've gotten away with a lot of stuff just by acting like it was no big deal. Or if I was afraid, I just act like I'm not even close to scared, and most will back off just because they don't want to deal with somebody who isn't punked out. It's an act, but I figured out a long time ago that everyone else is acting, too. So why be a sucker and be the only one being real? That's the secret of The Face.

When Moms and Antony and me were still living together, I was driving home from the store. I was pulling into the driveway of our old house, the one Naomi put up for sale when she took Moms away, when this guy hits me. It wasn't really much of an accident. But it shook me up. I was fourteen, no license, no experience. You

114

get the picture. So as the guy gets out, instead of saying anything to him, since I'm right in front of my house, I go in to get my moms. Scared blind, I find my moms and I start blathering about "I just got in an accident. I don't know what to do." It's hysterical talk, like I'm losing it. My moms, who was already on the edge herself, comes storming out of the bathroom, and instead of taking control, wiping my forehead down, holding my hand—she looks me straight in the eye, her face in flames, and she says, "You stop acting this way right now! You act like a man. You hear me? *A man*. You go out there and you take care of this like a man!" The whole time she's grabbed me by the shoulders and shaken me as hard as I've ever been shaken. I remember feeling something fall down inside me: the absolute truth that I wasn't *allowed* to be a kid anymore. I wasn't going to have anybody to hide behind or to go asking to front for me. No pops, no moms.

So I walked into the bathroom for just a second, my moms watching me, not saying anything because she'd said it all. I looked in the mirror and I made The Face. Dead fucking serious. A wall between my fear and whatever motherfucker happened to be in my motherfucking way. I wheeled around and walked out, not fast, not slow, just calm. And as I did I thought to myself, I cannot be hurt. I am dangerous. I let those words come out my very eyes. Crazy, right? But that asshole took his cues from *me* that day. He didn't fuck with me, because I wasn't the same fourteen-year-old punk who ran into the house. He must've thought I went in and got my stone-cold twin brother to handle business.

In the same way, I'm going to roll into Moms's place with a big smile. Okay, not a big smile. One that'll hide my cracked teeth. They'll play along. When I get my moms alone, I'm going to tell her the plan, how I'm going to save her. She'll have to give me a chance. I'm going in there certain of that in my head if not in my chest. I am visualizing that right now. I am preparing to make The Face, to wait behind it for the good thing to become real.

I go to the mall. It won't hurt to bring a few presents. I hit the toy store first to get Antony some Pokémon cards. Kids love that shit, and he was wearing that T-shirt when I saw him at McDonald's. For my *abuela*, I buy a pair of slippers, and not those cheap-assed kind, either. These are nice and fluffy. The salesman told me that they'd make her feet feel "special." Shit was gay, but they *are* nice slippers. I get Naomi some perfume. For my moms, I pick her out a dress. Now this sounds risky, right? But I remember what she likes. When I was a little kid, she used to make me go dress shopping with her. I didn't mind really. It made her happy to have me around to ask me how she looked. I always said "good." I want to remind her of when she was happy. I pick out a nice blue one, kind of shapely, with folds in the skirt and brass buttons that I know she'll like.

I take a cab back to the Motel 6. It's familiar, the only really familiar thing in this town so far. That and the Sizzler.

The next day, I try and chill. I need to be rested and calm. I take a shower and start getting ready around one P.M. even though I don't want to get there till about five. I put my jeans, T-shirt, and windbreaker on the bed. I go into the bathroom and look at my face carefully. There's a few scabs left around my eye and mouth. I take a wet washrag and rub them away. Red patterns of circles appear where I've cleaned myself off, but it looks better than scabs. I study my face some more. I don't look nearly as bad as I did two weeks ago. I've got some scars, but I think they make me look older, more tough. If I don't smile, you probably wouldn't notice anything different about me at all. I comb my hair. I just got it cut and there isn't much to brush. I just had the guy run number-three shears across the whole thing. I think he's a punk, but Diana's always telling me I look like that guy from that runaway bus movie. What was it called? *Speed*. That wasn't so bad. Okay, I say to my reflection, and I take a deep breath and visualize.

I have the cabbie drop me off a few blocks from the house. I'm getting tense and I don't want to cause a commotion driving in to my *abuela*'s crib in a big fucking yellow cab. But now I have to carry everything and I look even more conspicuous because I had the department store wrap up all the shit I bought. In a way it's good that it's falling all over the place. It keeps me from thinking about ringing the doorbell till I actually come to the house. I can see my Aunt Naomi's car parked outside. I walk up to the door, but just before I ring, I get an anxiety attack. My stomach is killing me and my fucking knees are shaking, but my finger refuses to listen and it pushes the doorbell. It's not too late to get the hell out of here, but the door opens and standing right in front of me is my moms.

She looks at me for a second, like she recognizes me but can't make sense of what I'm doing there and so that makes me seem not real. I forget to bring up the flowers. Instead I'm standing there juggling all these shiny boxes and the flower bundle falls out of my hands onto the porch. I'm bending over to pick them up when I hear her say, *"M'ijo?"* And I freeze. She says it again, *"M'ijo, is that you?"* And before I can answer, she opens the screen door and hugs me, just like that. The presents all fall out of my arms, but she just keeps hugging me tight.

Screw it. I forget the boxes and I put my arms around her. She's thin still, my hands meeting up behind her back, plenty of room in the hug for maybe another person. I'd forgotten how it feels to have her arms around me. But not her smell. Her powder, gardenias. It comes at me like a wave I didn't feel in time, catching me up in memories I didn't know I had in me. Goddamn. I'm choked by it all, like her embrace is both something I want to stay in and something I have to get out of. I'm dizzy with it, feeling almost like I can just rest right here on this cold, hard doorstep because I'm nearly home.

We stand there, both feeling it, neither of us saying anything, and then I hear Naomi come in from behind my moms. "Teresa, are you alright?" Then she sees me. "Robert? Is that you? What?" and then she says, "Both of you come in here."

My *abuela* pokes her head through the doorway. She comes in heavy and slow, smiling like she's about to meet a friendly stranger. She sits down on a blue Barcalounger. I take a look around the place. It's big with pale green walls loaded with pictures of angels. There's little angel figurines, too. They're everywhere, like Naomi's trying to fool visitors into thinking they've gone to heaven. Above a small fireplace is a big-assed family portrait of my moms, Antony, Abuela, and Naomi. In it, everyone is smiling but Moms.

"Where's Antony?" I ask, but nobody answers. They all want to know what's up, where I came from, why my face and teeth look like they do, and mostly what the fuck I'm doing there. "Did you run away, is everything alright? Why didn't you call?" All that sort of shit. Finally, I see Antony. He's got a towel around him. He's just gotten out of the tub and his hair is dripping. "Momma," he says, and Naomi says, "I'll be right there, Antony, go back in the bathroom." It's strange because I half-expected, half-hoped, the kid would go crazy yelling "Robert" and come jumping into my arms. But instead he looks afraid, like he doesn't know who I am.

"He doesn't recognize me," I say to the three of them. "Of course he does," Naomi says. "Don't worry about that now. Tell us what's going on, Robert." My moms is sitting next to me and she's got her arm around my shoulders. She seems really glad. I tell them about saving up my money and deciding to take a visit up to see them. "Yeah, I just thought I'd come up and visit, you know, see how everybody is doing." I want Naomi and Abuela to get out. I want to talk to my moms alone, but they just keep sitting there. Finally Naomi gets up to take care of Antony, but my *abuela* doesn't go anywhere. So I give them their presents. My *abuela* is cool, but she's old as Moses. She's nothing like Grams, who's old, too, but still works and drives and talks up a storm. Abuela can hardly move around, and all she does is nod and smile a lot. She's not on top of things too well. But she seems to like the slippers. Moms puts them on for her and the old lady smiles and says, "Very pretty."

My moms opens her present. She pulls the dress out and holds it up. I can tell she likes it a lot. She hasn't changed in two years. She's maybe, if anything, a little thinner, but to tell the truth, she looks good compared to how she was looking. Her face doesn't look all pinched up with nerves and her eyes don't seem to be hiding so much pain. Her hair has grown back and it looks nice. I say, "Do you like it?" And she just says, "It's beautiful." She hugs me again and says, "Thank you," while she does it. I can't believe it really. It seems too easy.

Naomi brings Antony out of the bedroom where she's gotten him dressed. He looks over at me trying to hide even though he's completely in the open. His brown curly hair is damp and hanging nearly over his dark eyes. Naomi says to him, "Go give your big brother Robert a hug, Antony." And the kid smiles and comes over and gives me a hug. I say, "I brought you a present for your birthday." He looks at the small box and takes it. He takes a look around like he half expects someone to tell him he can't open it. "C'mon," I say, making a little rip, and he takes it from there. "Pokémon," he says, happy as hell as he tears off the wrap. "I got you something, too, Naomi."

"You shouldn't have, Robert. You really shouldn't have." She sounds funny, like she's not talking about the present.

Moms makes enchiladas, my favorite, and we sit around the dinner table eating and talking. Everyone seems cool with me being there. That's a good sign, but still, I've decided I'm not even going to mention staying even though the place is pretty big. The topic comes up when Naomi asks me where my stuff is. "I didn't bring much," I say.

"So where are you sleeping? Do you have friends here?"

"I've got a place," I say, but now my moms gets in it.

"M'ijo, you go get your stuff. You stay with us."

"Sure," Naomi says, "I'll take you as soon as we eat." Hey, I'm not going to fight it. If they want me around, then great.

Antony is the best. He's talking to me and asking me questions like where I live and where I've been and will I take him to McDonald's. I tell him San Antonio and he wants to know where that is. He's smart. He's five, almost six, and I haven't seen him since he was three. "I wanna go," he says when me and Naomi get ready to go get my bag. "You should stay here," Naomi tries to tell him, but the kid is already hanging on my leg and he's squirming around trying to get behind me so he won't have to look at her. "Can he go?" and I make sure to look at my moms when I ask. She nods her head. "Sure he can go. He wants to be with his big brother." Naomi doesn't like it much. I can tell she runs the show around here.

"Did you run off, Robert?" she asks after we get in the car. She's being direct now, the semitolerant act all done with. "You've gotten your other grandmother very worried I'm sure. You should have called. I'm afraid this is going to cause a lot of people a lot of problems and heartache."

I'm checking out Antony in the backseat, just watching him, but most of all keeping my eyes off of Naomi. "I told you guys that I'm only here for a visit. I didn't run away. I just decided to take off, see some things. Pops is in town, too. What's wrong with that?" But right away I know I shouldn't have brought up my father.

"Did he bring you here?" she asks like she's afraid he's back at the motel ready to jump out and surprise her with the high, hard one. "Is he staying at the motel with you?"

"No," I say. "I mean that if he can travel around, why can't I? I came on my own, to visit, to see Antony. I thought it'd be a good surprise."

"Well, *m'ijo,* it was a surprise. I don't want you to think you're not welcome, but I worry about your mother and your brother. You look like you're in trouble. Tell me, are you?" For a minute she sounds like she's actually worried about me.

"No," I say. "I'm alright."

"Well you look like you've been beat up . . . or fighting?" She's trying to figure out if I'm on the run from the cops or something.

"I fell down," I say, but I know Naomi is smarter than that and that she'll just call Grams and ask a lot of nosy-assed questions so I come clean. "Okay, I got in a fight. But I had to. You know how things are in the neighborhood. Sometimes you have to fight, but I didn't come here because of that. I came here to see Moms and Antony."

"What?" he says from the back, thinking I called him.

"Nothing, kid," I say from the front and I turn and smile at him. He smiles back. He's very friendly.

"He's a sweet boy," Naomi says. "I can tell he likes you, that he's remembering you. It's only natural. A little brother always wants to be like his big brother." She sounds like she's trying to get to something. She turns into the parking lot.

"What do you mean, Naomi?" I say. "I'm not here to cause trouble. I'm here to visit because I missed Moms and Antony."

"I know, I know," she says, trying to be empathetic and innocent at the same time. "I just want to know what you're going to do while you're here. I want you to be aware of how delicate the situation is, *m'ijo*. You're right. You aren't a child anymore. You're a man, or very nearly one. You couldn't have made it this far if you weren't, only it worries me that you've come in *this way*. That your grandmother is probably worried sick, that you've been fighting, that you're not in school. Where did you get the money you have? There are a lot of questions. They're questions your poor mother won't ask you because she's so happy to see you, but I have to ask them because since your mother took sick, I've had to look out for her and for your brother. Your mom probably looks very good to you, but she's not all that well yet. She's getting better with the medication, yes. But I wouldn't want her to get worse just when things are finally getting good." She's looking at me now. She's trying to be very serious, very penetrating. It's supposed to be a moment of truth, but I figure, fuck her. I've got a plan and I'm going to see it through. The wrinkle is that I thought I was going to have to convince my moms, and it turns out that it's Naomi who's got to be convinced.

"It's like this," I say, trying to sound like I'm confiding in her, like I'm trying to be *real*, "I know I've done some stupid stuff that didn't help out Moms. But I've got my act together now." To this, she smiles, but I know that smile. It's the smile McNutt gives when she thinks someone is trying to snow her. "See," I go on, "I do want to stay. At least for a while. But you don't have to worry about me messing up anymore. I've got a job." She wrinkles her fat little brow at this one. "I work at Sizzler. I've got money that I saved up, too. I had jobs in S.A. and I want to give the money to Moms to help out. I'm getting my GED, too. I'm not going to wind up a *burro*." When I say that, I think about Grams and I feel my heart sink a little because I miss her. But I go on. "I'm here to prove that I've got it together and that I can be a help to Moms, and to you and Abuela. See, I know that Antony needs me. He needs a father figure. Not like the one he's got, but a real one. I'm here to do something about that." I'm talking too fast now, but I'm worried that she's going to interrupt and tell me that it's better if I don't come home with them. I'm past being able to stay in this goddamn motel now. I want to go home, even if this bitch is there. "I'm going to be good for Moms, for everyone. All I need is a chance, see?"

She sits there, her arms on the steering wheel, and she reaches down and turns the motor off. "Go get your stuff, Robert," she says like she's just made a big mistake. I don't wait for her to finish the thought. I jump out of the car and head for my room. Before I close the door, I hear Antony say, "I wanna go with Robert," and I feel so fucking happy that my heart is beating like crazy.

I don't have to work until the weekend, so I can kick around the house for a couple of days. I unpack, making sure to wrap my gramps's service revolver in an old T-shirt and sticking it way underneath the mattress. I wrap my dope up, too. I don't want to make any mistakes.

Putting my things away makes me feel like I'm actually home. I walk around the place like it's mine, like I'm this regular guy in a regular family. I start thinking how I'm going to take my moms and Antony to the beach or Magic Mountain. Family shit. Something touristy, buy them dinner and maybe even get one of those dorky hats for my brother. Why shouldn't I? All the time playing the tough guy down in S.A., making sure to not break down or do the uncool thing in front of Nacho or Enrique or Grams, playing it hard. Fuck that. Naomi is wrong. I'm here now, and I'm going to do everything right. I can't wait to mail Grams and my friends goofy pictures of me and the family barbecuing at the beach, smiling in the sunshine, and having a great time.

Just then, Naomi comes out of her bedroom. Seeing her face

brings me back to earth. She gives me a toothy smile and says something fakey like, "Make yourself at home." She's leaving for work. She's a registrar at the community college. Basically, she gets to tell kids what they should do with their lives. It's a good gig for her. She's the type that's always got the answer even before she hears the goddamn question. She leaves and me and Moms finally get to spend some time together alone. I get a big glass of orange juice and I make some Pop-Tarts. Moms has got a cup of coffee. She's drinking it lukewarm with mad sugar the way she likes it. The thing is that I can tell she's nervous. Her hands are shaking a little, but mostly when she's not holding the cup, so finally she reaches for it and just keeps it in her hands.

"Maybe you shouldn't be drinking coffee," I tell her. She's taking a big gulp of it. She swallows hard and smiles.

"It makes me feel calm. That's funny, isn't it?" I don't say anything. I eat my Pop-Tart and drink my juice. I look around the room because suddenly I don't know how to start the conversation.

"You're mad at me," she says finally, but she says it to the wall. It stops me cold because I am, but I don't want to say that.

"Nah, Mom. I told you, I'm just here to visit. I'm here to help you out."

"Oh," she says, but she doesn't sound convinced. "How's your stomach?"

"Good," I lie. "Better."

"And your trip?"

"Buses, you know." Moms nods her head like she knows all about buses.

"I always hated the drive here from Texas," she says. "I hated the desert and all that flat road. It doesn't go anywhere. Just more of the same thing as far as the eye can see. I told your father that when we came here the first time together. He hadn't been to California and he didn't believe me. I wanted him to go north before we turned west, to drive through the mountains of New Mexico. He didn't want to. He kept insisting it would take too long." Moms has her cup in both hands now, holding it out in front of her chest, almost like she's forgotten about it. "That seems like so long ago. Almost another life, a dream of another life. Do you remember?"

"I remember," I say. "I even thought about it on my bus ride."

"You did?"

"Yeah, of course."

"Nothing I could do," she says after a couple of seconds.

"About what?"

"Everything."

"Oh," I say.

"You don't believe me."

"Doesn't matter. That's the past. I'm here because I want to talk about the future."

"That would be nice," she says, "to talk about the future. I think too much about the past. My father used to say, 'You don't belong to the past, the past belongs to you.' But Papi was wrong."

I want to cut through the bullshit and flat out ask her if she ever thinks about me. I want to ask her if she loves me. "What about the past, Mom? What would you change?"

"Oh, *m'ijo*," she says, "that's something that would take me days to tell," and she takes a sip of her coffee like she's out of words and that's the only thing she can think to do with her mouth.

"How's Antony doing?" I say. "I mean in school and whatever."

"Not too good." Moms sighs. "The teacher calls him the Tasmanian Devil. He doesn't like to listen. She told your Aunt Naomi that he doesn't respect authority."

"Jesus," I say, "the kid's only in first grade and he's already being pegged as a troublemaker?" It occurs to me that my own school record doesn't give me much room to criticize. "Mom," I say, "why did the teacher tell *Naomi*? Why didn't she tell *you*?"

"Your aunt handles a lot of these things for me, *m'ijo*. I'm not good at things like that anymore." I can see that I'm putting her on the defensive, so I try another tack.

"I can dig how Antony feels, though. Maybe that's one of the things I can help out with. Schools can be awful for kids. Maybe I can do something, maybe talk school up a little."

"You think you could do that?" she asks. She seems genuinely hopeful.

"Sure. That's what I'm trying to tell you. I can do things like that and a lot more, Mom. I've got a job, too. I'm getting my stuff together. I've grown up."

She looks at me, smiling like I remember her smiling at me a million years ago. "You're a man now." I can't tell if she's asking or stating.

"Yeah," I say just to be sure. "You're gonna see, I promise."

I volunteer to pick up Antony from school the next day. It's a nice walk. The sun is out, but it doesn't feel hot. I breathe in the air like I'm in some fucking movie, like I just can't get *enough* of the fresh California breeze. But I want to feel that way, really, truly *feel* it. I want some cleansing process to take over, like a smoker's tar-stained lungs cleaning themselves up after years of a two-pack-a-day habit. I saw that in a film they showed at school, that lungs are capable of returning to almost new if only you quit. I use that image for my visualization on my walk. I'm trying to let the California air clean up all the shit I've got going on in my head.

The school is only a few blocks away and I get there a little early. Already there are parents waiting for their kids. You can't let your kid walk home alone anymore. You gotta watch them from the minute they get out, and even that isn't safe, not with all the nuts shooting them up in the schools. They're probably safer never leaving the house.

The kids start to come out from the different doors, each one connected to a different grade. I watch the first grade, and after about twenty kids come running out, I see Antony. He's talking to a buddy.

I walk toward him and his friend. When I get close enough, I yell out his name. He says real loud, pointing me out to his buddy, "I'll see you later. That's my brother." After he runs up to me he says, "That's Curtis."

"Is he your friend?"

"Nah," Antony says, "he just sits next to me in class. We play kickball. He picks me if he's the captain, and if I'm the captain, I pick him." It's impressive to me, because the kid is sort of cool. I look at the paper he's carrying. He's gotten an "F" in spelling and there's a note from the teacher at the bottom saying that my moms needs to sign it and have Antony return it.

"Not doing too good, huh?" I hand the paper back to him. "What's the matter? You don't like school?"

He's walking next to me now as we leave the schoolyard. "School sucks," he says.

"But you gotta do good in school," I say. "You want to be a *burro*?" I say it the way Grams does, sounding like it's a terrible thing to be. "I have to tell you, they're saying some things about you, some nasty stuff."

"Who? Who's saying stuff about me?" He's concerned enough that he stops walking.

"People."

"What did they say?"

"That you can't cut the mustard, that's all."

"What?"

"Don't you know what that means? Cut the mustard. That's an old one."

"What's that mean?"

"Well, it means that you stink at school. That you're not . . ." I pause like it kills me to say all this to him. "Well, Antony, I guess it means that you're not overly smart. That you're dumb!"

"I'm not dumb," he says.

"I know you're not dumb. I never said it. I'm just telling you that I've heard it thrown around as a theory."

"I'm not dumb."

"Can you read?"

"I don't like reading," he says.

"But I heard you can't do it," I say right back.

"Yes I can!" he says loudly.

"Well, prove it. What's that sign say?" I point at a paint store.

He stops in the middle of the sidewalk and squints at it, like if he just stares hard enough, the words will reveal themselves. "Pant Store," he finally says. Then he adds, "I think."

"That's close," I say, trying to give him some credit.

"Oh," he says, looking a little embarrassed. "I stink at reading."

"You just need to practice." I tell him about this book I had when I was his age and how it turned me on to reading. "Imagine that you find this horseshoe and if you put it on the ground and think really hard, it gets big, as big as a door, and you can walk through it and every time you do, you walk into a new planet, or country. See, reading is like a magic door. Whenever you pick up a book, you walk through that door and you can go anywhere you want. You can even become somebody else, even become an animal or a superhero." It sounds corny to me now, but it makes Antony think.

"You can?"

"Yeah," I say. "I bet you could be reading just as good as anybody if you tried. What if I make you a deal? What if you kick ass in school, even though it sucks, and on Fridays I'll spring you early and we'll go to a movie."

Antony looks up at me like I'm bullshitting. "Really?" he says.

"I wouldn't lie to you about something like that. All you have to do is be good in class, listen, and do your homework. I want you to learn to read."

I respect the kid for not jumping at the idea as soon as I say it. If I'd gotten an offer like that when I was his age, I would have blown my wad immediately. But he thinks about it for a few seconds and then ups the ante. "What if I do so good that you can't believe it? Can we get pizza, too?"

"Well, it would have to be very friggin' good, little man. You'd have to be able to read PAINT STORE like it was nothing. You'd have to bring home a book from the library and be able to read it to me out loud. That's a big deal. You think you could do that?"

He doesn't say anything, but by the big smile on his face I can tell that he sure as hell is going to give it his best shot. This big-brother stuff is going to work out. "But look, Antony"—and I stop so I can look right into his eyes—"this is just between you and me. It's a secret. It's a game we're going to run on our own. No one gets to know, not Moms, not the teacher, and especially not Aunt Naomi."

CHAPTER 12

Marie is my favorite waitress, hands down. Not just because she has a beautiful face and a slamming body, but because she doesn't kiss gut-ass like the others do, then come back to the kitchen and bitch and complain about them. Out of respect, I don't rip off her tips. Those others, that's a different proposition. Every time Flora brings her fat Filipino ass back to the kitchen and starts screaming that she needs help "right away" loud so that Ayala or Ponce can hear, I smile because I know I'm taking her shit to the cleaners whenever I get the chance. Delores, too, although she's not as obnoxious as Flora. But she's malevolent in her own way, always talking down to us when some fucking gut complains about no salt or that there's a grease streak on the table. "You gotta keep things clean," she'll say, shaking her droopy little face so that her chin waggles like a chicken's. She's skinny and smells sour. I take her shit, too. Fuck 'em both. But Marie. She's different. She gives me something to look forward to, something besides the home situation to think about.

One night I'm standing at the edge of the kitchen door during a momentary lull, waiting for some table to free up so that I can clean it. I'm the only busboy working because Tuesdays are dead-dog slow. Marie comes up and stands next to me, just taking a breather like. She leans up against the wall. I can smell her hair because she's standing close. It smells like coconut. It's straight, thick, reddish brown. It looks soft, like if you ran your hand through it, it'd make you feel like keeping it in there all night. "What are you thinking about?" she asks, a big sexy smile playing across her face. I can't tell her that I'm thinking about running my fingers through her pretty hair so I say the first stupid thing that runs through my mind.

"I was wondering how high the center beam of the roof is." I gesture up at the ceiling. Stupid, I know.

"Why are you wondering that?" she says, looking up at where I pointed.

"Oh, I play basketball and it just came into my head what an incredible leap it would be to be able to take a running start and just jump so high that I could touch it, maybe jump out of this whole building."

She gives me a mercy laugh and bumps her hip against me. "I bet your legs are strong, aren't they?" She gives me another smile and goes back to work. I look at her walk away. Even through that clunky uniform, I can see that she's got the full package, and I'm thinking that there's some chemistry thing going on between the two of us.

That night Marie trades with Flora so that she can close with me. I'm back there cleaning up, and Marie comes in and stands against the wall.

"You need any help?"

"I can handle it," I say, sweating my ass off.

"Mind if I wait back here with you?" She's just watching me.

"Nope."

"Robert," she calls out to me after a couple of minutes. "Do you have any dreams?"

"What do you mean?" I ask. "Dreams as in I want to be a lawyer or the first *chuco* president, or do you mean dreams like I'm naked, flying through the air on a big fudge Popsicle?"

"Well, neither exactly." She laughs a little. "I mean things that you wish would happen. Things you want to happen." She's acting kind of shy now, very coy, a little-girl-like smile, her eyes looking at me and once they catch my sight, turning downward. "You know what I mean, a fantasy; do you ever have fantasies?"

"Sure."

"Can I tell you mine?"

"Sure."

"I'm kind of embarrassed; lean over and I'll tell you." I lean close to her and she brings her lips to my ear. "I want to make love to someone who's never made love before. You're a virgin, aren't you?" She leans over a little closer and kisses me below my ear. "You're salty," she says, licking her lips slightly. "I've got an idea. Why don't you let me help you finish cleaning up, and then I'll give you a ride home and I can tell you more about it." I work faster than I've ever worked before, putting the dishes away, using all the shortcuts I've learned over the last couple of weeks. When we finish, we go out to her car.

We're in the Escort. There's a doll in the backseat, a Barbie whose hair has been cut off. It reminds me of her kid, the little girl who was in the car before.

"Hey," I ask, turning back around, "you want to smoke a j?"

"Sure," she says.

The whole time I'm rolling it, though, I keep thinking about that little girl and how Marie is a mother and what the little girl would think of me if she knew what I was about to do to her mommy.

I light up and pass it to her. "You're not worried about being seen?" I ask her. She hits it quick and passes the joint back, but doesn't say anything. She's holding her breath. She exhales.

"Seen by who? God? I know you don't mean my husband. He's banging somebody in a hotel somewhere." I wonder about the kid, but I don't ask.

Instead of a motel, this crazy woman drives up on a house. "Where are we?" I ask her. She puts her hand behind my head, and pulls me toward her. She kisses me, not very long, but soft, like she means it. Her lips are warm and full. She leaves her bottom lip tucked between mine and I open my mouth and softly suck on it for just a second before it slides out.

"My house," she says.

"What?"

"My house. I want to do it in my bed." She's kissing my neck, but I'm pretty fucking freaked out now. "That's the other part of my fantasy." She kisses me again. "You've really never had sex?" she asks like it's no big deal that she wants to screw in her husband's bed.

"What about your kid? What if your husband comes home? I'm not trying to get shot."

"My kid's with my mom, and *he* never comes home anymore. He's got himself a *bitch* in the Valley." As soon as she says it, I get this horrible picture that I'm kissing my moms. That I'm about to jump in the sack with my moms.

I shake my head. "I'm not down with this."

"C'mon, let's do it. I can show you." She seems more desperate than sexy, like she has to do this or something bad is going to happen to her. "I'll turn on the shower for us and I'll show you how to do everything," she says. She unbuttons her dress and opens it clear down. Underneath she's wearing white panties and a bra. Her shoes are off, too. She's not wearing stockings. Her skin is white and her stomach is just slightly round. I reach out for it and she lets me put my hand there. It's warm and I can feel it pulse with a heartbeat that's getting quicker. "You look excited," she says. "Like you really want to touch me. Do you?"

"Yeah," I say, but I can't move.

"Put your hand down my panties," she says in the same whispery voice, moving my hand down from her stomach. "Do you feel how wet I am?" I nod. "Are you going to fuck me like I tell you?" I nod again. Before I know it, she's sitting on top of me. She keeps on saying "C'mon, c'mon, c'mon," and the more she says it, the less I feel like I can keep it up. As much as I try to concentrate on her face as she grinds and slides up and down, I can't get it out of my head about the kid and her being a mom. And underneath it all is this fucking picture of my moms alone all those nights at home not being able to do anything about anything. It's all I can do to keep from losing my woodrow.

After about four minutes, Marie moves over to the driver's seat and puts herself back together. She doesn't say anything and the car is filled with this thick, musky silence. I button up and keep my mouth shut, but the whole time I'm trying to think of something to say. Maybe she's trying to find something to say, too, but finally settles for starting the car.

We're both quiet on the way to my moms's house. I'm thinking how in a way I'm almost lucky that my moms got sick, that she broke down and was depressed, because at least that way, I didn't have to deal with her doing shit like this. At least I always knew where she was.

Marie drops me off a couple of blocks away. I give her a half-assed kiss and slip out without saying anything. The first thing I want to do is take a hot shower like maybe I can wash my thoughts away.

As I creep toward the stairs, I pass my moms's room. I hear her say, "Robert, is that you?" I poke my head through her door. She's lying in bed, a dim nightlight casting a small, sad yellow glow on her face. I get this weird, stoner déjà vu thing, only it's like I'm in my pops's head, feeling like he must've when he crept in late after fucking in a car or motel and having to face Moms with the smell of another bitch on him.

"*M'ijo*, come in here." I walk into her room. It's pretty empty, just a bed, a small sitting chair, and a bureau that I remember from our old house. She's got a few pictures on it, mostly of Antony, but I notice she's got one of me there, too. It's this dorky school picture taken when I was in fifth grade. I'm wearing a goddamn safety-patrol belt and this stupid grin that says I don't know shit and never will. It's the picture of a kid in need of a good beating. "Sit down for a few minutes," she says. I sit on the chair.

"I smell bad. I should go take a shower," I say.

"No matter. Let's talk a little."

"Okay."

"Do you like your job?"

"It's okay."

"Do you have a girlfriend?"

"Not really."

"No?" she smiles.

"Don't you ever get lonely, Mom?" I say suddenly, maybe too suddenly, but I keep going now that I've opened that door. "I mean, I'm glad you've rested up, but don't you, you know, want to leave sometimes?"

"Where would I go?" she asks like maybe we're going to finally *talk*.

"Anywhere," I say sharp and hard, like maybe I can pull her through. But she shuts me down, turning her face toward the little nightlight.

"I'm already here, *mijo*," she says, kind of sad but also sort of determined. "I'm okay and your aunt takes good care of me. I know you don't like her, but nothing that's happened is her fault. She's done the best she can for me. I'm grateful."

"I don't see it. She runs your life, that's all it is. It's like you're hibernating. Why should you be grateful for that?"

"Does it seem that way to you?" she asks. She seems hurt by what I've said but I want to be real with her while I have the chance.

I nod my head. "Yeah, it does."

"Don't you remember how bad things had gotten?" she asks.

"You're asking *me* that," I say. "Me? I was there every minute, every night. Do *you* remember?"

My moms sits up looking at the wall just on the other side of my left shoulder. "I was sitting at the house, our house in San Antonio just after your father had left for the third or fourth time," she says, "and I was praying, but I had gotten so tired of everything that I didn't even know what I was praying for or to, and I remember I started to cry and I looked up at that dresser mirror behind you," she says, looking at the bureau against the wall, "and I saw myself, what I'd become, my hair falling out in patches, my eye twitching, my face so old and drawn that I looked like I was fifty and not thirty-three. I felt like I didn't have the strength to get out of bed or even the first idea of where I'd go if I did get out of bed. That's when your Aunt Naomi came, and she helped me to do the things I needed to do to keep from giving up. From dying."

"But why did that have to mean getting rid of me?" I ask her.

But she doesn't have an answer. We sit there for a while longer not saying anything really. Moms settles back down into bed and she gestures for me to give her my hand. She takes it and says, "I think about you all the time." That's something I guess, but only if I don't think about it too long.

I pick up Antony from school on Friday like I promised him. He's held up his end of the deal. For two weeks he's taken care of business: no notes, no F's on homework assignments, no phone calls. He's taken to bringing his schoolwork to me. A couple of days ago, he came in excited because he'd gotten a couple of check-pluses on his addition worksheets. The kid's turning into a little egghead.

I go into the school office and tell them that I'm there to pick up Antony Lomos. I forged a note this morning saying that he could get out of school early. It's about lunchtime and I figure we'll go to Pizza Hut, then a kid's movie. The lady at the attendance desk calls for him on the intercom. I imagine Antony getting up from his desk kind of proud, like he's just been chosen for something special. I remember how it used to be in elementary school when you had to leave early and they called your name out. You'd get your stuff ready to go and all your classmates would be looking at you with envy pointed like a shiv because you were going somewhere and they had to stay in purgatory for a few more hours.

Antony comes into the office with his backpack and I sign out for him. I can't believe it's so easy. Outside, Antony is all smiles. We hang out at the theater arcade before the flick. I was thinking I'd show him a thing or two but he's better than me at video games. He's really digging it, though, beating his big brother, and it seems like we haven't been apart at all. These last couple of years haven't happened. He's making fun of me when I blow it, and then giving me advice about how to play this kickboxing thing. "Hit the A button twice before you move the joystick up and then hit the B button three times really fast." I catch the hang of it and Antony seems happy that he's taught me something. Goddamn, it makes me feel good to know I can pull this big-brother stuff off, that I'm showing my little bro a good time.

The trouble is, kids don't keep secrets, especially when it's a secret about them and it's something they're dying to tell other kids about. I hadn't taken Antony out of school but three times before his teacher, who I guess was already getting suspicious—they hate for kids to get out of school early—overheard him rubbing it in to his buddies at recess that his big brother, Robert, was taking him to a movie every Friday. All hell broke loose then because the teacher couldn't wait to tell the principal what she'd heard. They went over the sign-out book and the notes and it didn't take long for them to see that Antony was being "kidnapped" by me on Fridays. They called my moms while I was at work and by the time I got home, Naomi was in the picture.

"Do you know that you could be arrested for pulling this little stunt?" she asks me like I've taken Antony to a titty bar. "Do you?" She wants an answer. Meanwhile my moms isn't even in the room. "I'm trying to save your mother more pain, and I'm certainly trying to keep you from influencing that poor baby in the wrong way. God knows that we have enough trouble without him turning out like—" and she stops because she's just about to say "you."

I figure I have to defend myself because, like most adults, Naomi has completely missed the point. She doesn't understand shit. "I'm trying to help," I say, but before I can go on, she's all over that.

"Help? How? By turning your five-year-old brother into a tru-ant? By forging your mother's name? By teaching that baby that deception is the way to get what you want? Your father—" and she stops again because she's just about to say that my pops has already fucked me up by teaching me how to lie and that she doesn't want it to seep into Antony. I'm just like my pops, she wants to say. I sti-fle what I want to say—fuck you—and instead stick to doing what I can to help Antony. "I knew that if I gave T something he wanted, something he could look forward to, he'd do better in school. He's been doing better, too. Just look at his work."

"Who is 'T'? Is that some sort of gangster name you're giving him?"

"Just a nickname," I say knowing I've lost.

"Well, don't think for a minute that this short-term bribery is a good solution. It's not. What's he going to do when you're not around anymore?" She keeps going but I stop listening because she's said it. *Not around anymore.* I know it now, that she isn't going to let me stay. She's been looking for a way to make me go back since I knocked on the door, and here is a way for her to kick me out.

She calls in my moms, who acts all mousy and just nods her head when Naomi looks at her for approval of what she's saying. Then they bring in Antony and tell him that what I've done is wrong and that he needs to understand what a lie is and why it is bad, and how I am a liar. Naomi pulls him on her lap and speaks to him like he's an idiot, using a fakey soothing voice. I feel bad for him because he can't really understand what's going on. I don't want him to think it's his fault. But the kid's scared. He can barely look at me and when he does, I can't tell if he's buying all of Naomi's shit. I should do something but I don't know what.

After a while it's over and everyone rolls out of the room and I sit there alone for a while not saying anything. I do my best not to think about it, but what else is there to think about? After a while, I get up, take a shower, and head for the Sizzler.

I'm blowing smoke with Maurice during a break and I wind up telling him most of the story, I guess because he seems interested and because he's older, almost as old as my pops.

"I was just trying to get Antony to read, keep him from being 'anomic.' "

"What's that? Weak blood?"

"No. My Aunt Naomi says it means he's 'consciously and purposefully maladjusted.'"

"Shit," Maurice says, "she ought to know better than that. It's life that makes you be anomic to survive."

"Yeah, but I wanted to help him. Show my moms I got it together. That I'm useful. Not a fuck-up."

"I don't know," Maurice says, "sounds like you think maybe you can control shit, like maybe life's a story, like you writing a script. You too young still. Take it from me, best you can do is put a spin on shit. It only took me till I turned forty to learn that."

"What do you mean 'spin'?"

"Spin, motherfucker, *spin*. You know, like those goddamn politicians do to everything."

"Like lie to yourself or act a part?"

"No," he says, getting frustrated. "It's not lying or acting. It's framing the shit right, that is, to your benefit, to where you can live with yourself and with your circumstances. You gotta believe it, get it?"

"What, like a comedy or tragedy?"

"Just like a motherfucking comedy or tragedy. Or romance, if you like that shit. But whichever way you frame it, you get some choice, and that's better than no choice."

"What about other people," I say after a minute. "What if they're set on framing their lives like a tragedy and you know that it won't work out with your story? What do you do then?"

"Shit, that's why I can't stay with a bitch. You gotta cut some people loose if they won't let you frame your story or if their story don't flow with yours. Sooner or later, one of you will wake the other one up, make them hip to the fact that what they're seeing as their lives ain't nothing but a mirage. That ain't cool, man. Above all, you gotta sell yourself on your own story. You gotta believe it so that it will be true. I don't need anyone trying to change my perspective. I believe in the old saying, 'Don't truth me and I won't truth you.' I'm trying to spin my shit like Shangri-la and people keep trying to wake me up in Compton. I'll kick a bitch to the curb for that."

I'm working in the back, elbow deep in muck, ankle high in grease water because the drain in the kitchen is clogged like an all-you-can-eater's heart, when Ayala pokes in his head and tells me my old man is in the restaurant and wants to talk to me. "Make it snappy," he says, "and clear out that fucking clog before you come out." I prefer sticking my hand into the slimy drain to having to go talk to my pops, but after I clear out the gunk, I walk out into the dining room. He's sitting in the farthest booth drinking a big glass of iced tea. He's wearing a black T-shirt, his shades and keys sitting in front of him like he's a busy movie star, the king of the joint daring someone to come up and talk to him. When he sees me, he gives me a fucked-up little smile while he shakes his head.

"How'd you know I was here?" I say, beating him to the punch.

"Your grandmother phoned me after your aunt phoned her. Naomi's got her worried. Something about you getting yourself and your little brother into trouble already."

I stand there trying to make a hard face, but I can't find it right now and instead I probably come off like a fucking kid. It's been a hard day.

"Sit down," he says.

"I can't. Boss won't like it."

"Yeah," my pops says, "he seems like a real asshole. I was getting ready to fill him in on what's what. No one tells me when and where I can talk to my son."

Toe to toe, my pops wins the heavyweight asshole division by unanimous decision. Ayala's only shot would be a lucky knockout blow. I almost smile.

"I'm here to tell you you've got to go home, Robert," he says like it's a closed case.

"What?"

"I know you heard me. You've got a lot of people worried. Your grandmother, your mother, me. It's been decided."

"By who?"

"By me, Robert."

"That's not enough," I say.

"Yes it is. I'm your father."

"Look, Pops, you've gotta give me a chance here," I say, my fucking voice starting to shake. "I'm here to make things right, to make amends. Like a man."

"Make what right? You can't make things right. You're a kid."

"I don't want Naomi to win," I say. Mentioning my aunt has the effect I want on my pops. He keeps his mouth shut now, waiting for more. "I can't go out this way. I can't let Naomi win, because if she does, then I lose everything that I want. Antony loses me and Moms loses herself. Naomi is as bad for Moms as her other problems. Moms was never this weak. Never. Even when shit got at its worst. She used to cry and she'd get depressed, but when she needed to, she found the energy, the strength to go to work and make decisions. Now she's lost that. She doesn't seem depressed, but she doesn't seem happy, either." I sit down. "She just seems lost in some deafening buzz where nothing seems to reach her. Everyone likes that buzz for a while, but who wants to live there? I need to reach her and bring her back, her and Antony. I'm not going to let Naomi stop me."

My pops seems surprised, like he's seeing something he's never

142

seen before. My adrenaline jumps because I've reached him. Fuck it if he's the reason my moms is so messed up, if he's the worst thing that ever happened to her. I've got him buying my spin and that's what's important.

"I don't know, Robert. I'll think about things and let you know what I decide." With that, he picks up and gets ready to leave, but before he does, he tosses a twenty on the table. My tip, I guess.

Shit has changed. It's been subtle and silent, but I've felt it just like you feel roaches lurking in a dark kitchen before you hit the lights. All week, no one's talked to me except Antony, who likes to come into my room when I'm home and ask me to listen to him read. He's getting good. I shoot him a buck every time he finishes a book. He's got a little stash going good now.

A few days after my pops blindsides me at Sizzler, I come home with my latest pay in my pocket. I walk into my bedroom and count out my dough. I've been adding to it since I got here. I've got close to two thousand bucks. I decide I've got to talk to my moms now. I have to make a move. Let her know about my plans once and for all. I need to draw out the scenario, give it my best shot. Give her what she hasn't had in a long time, a real choice. I tell Moms that I just got paid and that I'm going to get us some dinner. Some pizza. She's all smiles and I ask Antony if he wants to come. He does. The two of us jam into the car and head off to California Pizza Kitchen because I don't want greasy pizza. I want to make like it's a celebration.

We get home with the pizza, but my moms is catatonic. She's so quiet, it's spooky. Antony can sense it; he walks over to her and she sits there holding him. "What's wrong?" I ask her and then I look across the room to see my father sitting in a chair. The backstabbing motherfucker is wearing a beige cotton jacket and jeans and a pair of California-asshole sunglasses. He's been here only a couple of months and he's already looking West Coast. He's sitting next to Naomi frostylike, the way you might with somebody you hate at a party—with a half-smile while your eyes say fuck you till you die.

I stand there watching them for a second feeling more and more like a punk. I haven't changed from work and I'm still wearing my goddamn Sizzler shirt. They don't seem to know how to start but before anyone can open their mouth, I turn around and head up the stairs fast as shit.

I hear my pops call my name, but I keep going. I close the bedroom door and lock it. No one follows me up, but I can hear Naomi talking all sorts of shit, sounding like a goddamn shrink, like she's trying to be protective and patient. Oh-so-fucking rational. I grab my money from underneath my mattress. I almost pull the gun out by mistake. Both are wrapped up in old T-shirts. I walk back down and stand in front of my moms. I know I have to say everything now, in front of them all. It's my last chance and so I do my best to block everyone else out.

"Mom," I say and she looks up. She seems to not recognize me. I keep going, "I know that this looks bad, but I want to show you something." I hold out the stash. My hands are shaking like crazy and I can barely contain myself. I hold out the money, trying to play it cool. It's mostly twenties and it looks impressive. "I can get us out now. We can leave. We can fix all this shit." She looks at it without expression. "I've been saving up," I say. "I'm thinking that we can use this money to get our own apartment, you, me, and Antony. It'd be better that way." She smiles at me sweet, like I remember her doing when I was just a kid.

"Don't worry, *m'ijo*," she says. "Don't worry." And she makes a motion with her hand for me to sit next to her on the couch. I sit down, still holding the dough. She puts her arm around me, keeping the other one around Antony. She strokes my head like she used to when she was trying to help me go to sleep.

"You worry so much, *m'ijo*," she says. But she sounds dreamy. "You've always worried so much. That's what used to hurt me so much about you. You were always trying to be so grown up, always with your brow wrinkled, being a big boy even when you were a little one. I've been bad for you," she says more to herself than to me. "I've been so, so bad for you. Not strong, not strong at all. That's why I had to leave you."

"Mom, you didn't leave me. You just needed to get away. I understand, but now I'm here and we can make it. You're stronger than you think."

She traces the scars around my eye with her finger. "You always wore your pain on your body, all the pain that was in your soul, your spirit," she says. "You used to worry me so much when you were a baby. Always falling and cutting yourself. And now with your poor stomach. Always your body telling me what you couldn't. Every time your skin got covered with that rash, I knew what you weren't telling me. I thought it was better to leave you with your grandma than to have you keep trying to tell me how bad I was for you."

"Mom," I say, trying to snap her out of it, "We don't have to stay here. We can leave. We can be together. It's all coming together." But even as I say it, I know it isn't true.

"I can't go anywhere," she says, "I'm no good even to little Antony. Anywhere I go, it would be the same, so I should stay here. Don't you see?"

She hasn't said "we" once. "What about me?" I ask knowing the answer.

Naomi opens her big mouth. "I know how hard this is for you to understand, Robert. But we've come to a decision. It's not easy. Maybe later, when you've had some time to grow up a bit more."

I don't even look Naomi's way. I have to get through to my moms fast, or it's over. "We can leave. Look," and I fan about five hundred bucks on the coffee table.

"Where did you get that money, Roberto?" Naomi doesn't bother to think that I've saved it from my checks. "Drugs?" she says. "Drugs? Is that where? I had a look in your room. I know what you're doing. I know about the pills, about the marijuana. Do you think I'm blind, that I can't smell, that I would tolerate that sort of thing in my house? You are corrupting your little brother and hurting everyone around you."

"Shut up, bitch," I say and she jumps off the couch like she's thinking about getting in my face.

"Stop it," my moms yells out, "you stop it. All of you." And then she gets up and practically runs to her room. Naomi follows after her shooting me an I'm-not-through look.

I look at my pops. He looks almost embarrassed. He's trying to distract Antony with some electric piece of shit he brought him.

"Why'd you come here?" I tell him, picking up the cash from the coffee table. "I thought you were going to give me a chance."

"I never said anything like that. And now Naomi tells me about drugs." I just sit there looking at him because even with all I know, I can't believe what a rat he is.

My moms is a mess. She doesn't want to come out of her room. I can hear Naomi knocking on the door saying, "Teresa, come out. Big Robert came here to talk to you. It's important that we resolve this thing right now. Come on out." Moms doesn't make a peep.

"She won't come out," Naomi says, stalking in. "She's very weak and this whole thing has been unsettling for her." She looks at me when she says "this whole thing."

"Well, I hope I'm not making things worse," Pops says, looking up from Antony. "I just want to help. Also, I've missed my Antony. I want to be a part of his life if Teresa would only let me." The two of them are talking there like conquering generals. "You've got your grandmother very worried, son," he says at me, trying to look like a fucking TV dad. "You know that?" He wants me to answer him. He doesn't want to be shown up in front of Naomi. I nod because I don't know what else to do. I'm in a kind of shock.

"Can I talk to her?" he says to Naomi. "It's important that she be in on this conversation. I don't want to come in here like some jerk. I'm here to help her out, really." My pops is trying to sound sincere now. Naomi buys it, but she doesn't want to give up control in her own house. "No, Robert. Let me try again. I know how she gets. She's not likely to come out if she feels threatened. This whole thing has just been too much." The bitch looks at me again when she says "whole thing."

She walks to my moms's bedroom door like a zookeeper at the cage of a stubborn animal. "Teresa, come out. We need to talk about some important things." She waits outside the door for a few seconds without saying anything. Finally, Moms says something, but it's mumbled. "What?" Naomi yells out. She's steaming. "What was that, Teresa? You have to speak up!" There's nothing for a few more seconds. Then I hear my moms say more loudly. "Please leave me alone. Please. Do what you want, but just leave me alone."

"That's not going to be good enough, Teresa. You're going to have to come out here sooner or later."

I don't like sitting here watching them fuck with my moms like this. "Just leave her alone," I say finally. My pops turns toward me and shakes his head, but I keep on. "Naomi," I say loudly, "just step away from the goddamned door already. Leave her alone. If she doesn't want to come out, she doesn't have to!" My pops is pissed not because I'm being too loud or rude, but because I'm throwing him crazy in front of Naomi. He tries to reach for me, but I move off the couch quick and stand up, walking toward Naomi. "Why don't you just back the fuck off my mom!" Naomi steps back.

"You get back to the living room. I know what your mom needs better than you, I think." She's trying to front like she's in control, but I can tell that she's pissed and even a little scared. I've managed to surprise her. My pops comes into the hallway.

"Robert, go sit down now. Leave this to us."

"So what? So you can finish the job on her?" He gets this look in his eye that for a second reveals what's really there, like his skin can't contain it and from out of his sockets comes something you don't want to know.

"Shut up now," he says. "The trouble with you is you don't know when you're beat. Look around. It's over, Roberto. You're not wanted here. It's time. Go get your things." Naomi is turned toward me now, the two of them standing side by side, a living wall of don't-give-a-shit.

I know they won't ever let me in, won't ever let us be. "I'm not going anywhere," I say. "If you fucks would let us, we could make it." My pops reaches out quick and slaps me hard. "You watch your mouth, *malcriado*." I can hear my moms crying and Antony is crying now, too. He hangs back in the living room poking his small head through the doorway. I smile, my vampire teeth in full view. "You better back the fuck off me." My pops makes a grab for me, but I slip it and jump up a couple of stairs so that I'm standing above them. "You can't do shit to me, motherfuckers. Neither of you." I hit the rest of the stairs but just before I reach the top, he grabs my foot and trips me up. I fall hard on my knees, and he's holding tight onto my left foot like he wants to drag me down to where he is. I'm trying to kick loose and I catch him on the side of his face. *"Cabrón,"* he yells, but the shock makes him let go and I get to my room. He's there a second later and starts working the knob.

"You're going home!"

"Fuck you," I yell back, and I grab my duffel bag and go to throw my clothes in when I hear him start kicking at the door.

"You're nobody to tell me where home is," I say. "You wait," he yells while Naomi gets there. I can hear one of them fucking with the lock. Before I can finish grabbing my shit, they're in and my pops comes up fast taking a wild swing that catches me on the back of my head because I've turned toward the open window to crawl out on the roof. I spin around on him, dropping my bag, but he's quick for an old man and he catches me across the eye with the back of his hand, almost like a karate chop that sends heavy thunder rolling through my head. But he doesn't knock me down. "You can't hurt me," I say and I mean it for the first time. "Stop it!" Naomi yells, scared now because it's gone further than even she wants, but my old man is on a tear and he slaps me again, hard, and goddammit, I know I'm about to cry. But I swallow hard and smile, fucked up like, and I say, "You can't hurt me." There's blood running down my eye. I feel it trickling, mixing with the blood in my mouth. "Can't hurt me," I say again, and this time I am crying. And then crazy shit, like I'm watching it. And I lick my bloody lip, the weird iron taste making it like the words are liquid pain, like the blood's been squeezed out from my insides and I want them to see some more of it right there on the fucking walls, on the goddamn shag carpet. I move backward toward my bed. I put my hand under the mattress and pull out the gun. "I could blow my fucking brains out right here for you," and I point the motherfucker at my head. "Would you like that, bitch?" Both of them stand there looking like they've forgotten how to breathe. "Hate you motherfuckers," I say and I spit a bloody mess right on the floor. "Hate you god-damned motherfuckers!" And for a second I feel like I'm gonna squeeze it off, just end the shit.

"Robert." It's Antony, looking in the room, crying same as me. "Robert," he says one more time before Naomi grabs him quick and disappears out into the hall.

My father still hasn't moved, hasn't said shit, and I think, Fuck him, and I move back quick finding the window with my ass. I climb out keeping my eye on him, his face as scared as I've ever seen it. Outside, I try to keep my balance on the mad-sloped roof made all the worse because I'm dizzy. I have to jump or I'll fall. I drop the gun and then take a quick look down to make sure I'm not going to land on a rake or some other crazy shit and I leap, landing on my feet for just a second, before I roll onto my back. I get up fast and grab the gun, but the TV cop effect's ruined when I nearly split my head kicking a full bottle of beer some scumbag left in the middle of the street.

I get running and from behind me I can hear my pops finally yelling my name. A stranger's voice that doesn't mean shit.

CHAPTER 13

Jerry's brother races Mustangs. Not the horses, but the cars. He actually belongs to a club that races them. I find this out when I get to Jerry's apartment. There's a party going on, and Jerry apologizes for not inviting me. "Dude, I'm glad you're here. I would've told you about this thing, but it's really my bro's doing. These fuckers get together every couple of weeks and race their cars and then party together. Shit's gonna get wild, man. You gonna hang?" He notices my puffy eye and lip and my grass-stained Sizzler shirt. "Hey, what happened to your face?" he asks. "Did you and Ayala finally mix it up?"

"I need a place to crash. Got home problems, man."

Jerry's cool. He doesn't need to hear the whole story. "You can stay here, but don't plan on getting too much sleep. Not tonight." Jerry gets called in to the kitchen and I head off for the bedroom. His room smells like he's cooking old socks and ass soup. It's depressing that I've got to sleep here.

I roll a joint and smoke it next to Jerry's window. I'm all worked up even though I'm so goddamn low. I need to calm down, keep my heart from exploding right there. I feel the gun in the waistband of my pants and I think about how close I was to blowing my head off back there. The gun's cold and ready and I get this urge to head right back and put that fucker in my mouth and pull the trigger in front of them all. My moms would feel like shit.

It'd serve her ass right, and I can't think about anything else but how much I wish I could hate her, could just walk back to that house and do it, just blow my fucking brains out right in front of her, and just before, shout, "I'm doing this because of you, you weak, crazy bitch!" But right away I start to repent for it. I ask God to forgive me and I realize that I don't deserve to get what I want, that my moms doesn't deserve such a demented fuck-up son. And I start to panic, wondering what they did to her after I ran out like that. What she must've done when she heard me and my pops fighting. Did he tell her? Did she hear me? And what about Antony? What did he see? What a fucking mess, and I keep saying that to myself in my head, What a fucking mess, what a fucking mess, what a fucking mess. I want to take it all back, but I know I can't. And I see it in my mind's eye, my insides, all blackened, rotted. My spirit, its outline shaped just like me, but made of ashes, burned and coal black. I am a piece of shit. "What a fucking mess," I moan from so far deep inside me that I can taste the words sliding out of my mouth, vile and heavy and true.

I hear my voice and it hits me. I'm stoned. I'm tripping. I gotta catch hold of myself. I tighten my fists and I slam them against my thighs hard, then harder, then harder still, until my legs are aching and the physical pain tears me away from my thoughts for just a second, long enough for me to take a long peep at myself in Jerry's dresser mirror. I reach back and pull the gun out, put it to my head, and watch my reflection for a second. "Fuck you," I say finally, flipping myself off. I smile big and suave and give myself the thumbs-up sign. I say it: "I am untouchable, goddamn it! I am untouchable. I am untouchable." With that I shove the gun back in my waistband. I walk into the bathroom and stick my head under the faucet, soaking my hair, using Jerry's soap bar to wash off the goddamn grease. I take off the Sizzler shirt, wash my armpits. I look in the mirror, and The Face is there, in the middle of all this craziness. It's there. It isn't gone. It hasn't failed me. I can go out. I have to.

The strange people I saw when I first entered now look a lot stranger, almost like aliens. They are *not* cool and collected. They are freakish, off-the-hook defectives yammering away in a dingy two-bedroom apartment with old, stinky, cigarette-burned carpet and a beer-stained couch. Only the TV is new, a thirty-six-inch model Jerry and his brother probably bought hot. I make my way to the kitchen and to my surprise it's clean, the only room in the joint that doesn't inspire nausea. I guess it's because Jerry's a busboy.

The keg's tapped and I go back out to the living room. I move around listening to conversations, not wanting to join in till I find something that won't wig me out. I don't want to hear other people's horror stories, but I'm damned sure that these freaks aren't going to help. There's about forty people bobbing and weaving in threes and fours, smoking cigs and holding cups that look like they're filled with piss. I walk around listening to them laugh at shit that only a heartless asshole could find amusing. The women look ugly, overly made-up, like demonic clowns wearing skanky halter tops and faded Levi's. The dudes look mean and suspicious, a roomful of flat-out junkies talking stupid shit about motors and mag tires and horsepower. It hits me that I don't know a goddamn person in this city. This apartment has become the center of all loneliness. I am a stranger amongst the strange.

I make my way over to Jerry, who's sitting on his urine-y couch with his girlfriend, Gina, and her cousin Gloria. Gloria's been drinking all night and she's right away interested in finding out why I'm sporting a shiner. I'm not even close to wanting to explain it. "You get in a fight?" she says. I say no, but she doesn't get the message. "You a boxer? What happened? Does it hurt?" I try to ignore her, but the mystery is killing her and it seems to turn her on. She starts hinting about how ready she is. "I'm feeling *gooood*," she says, trying to wink, but she's so drunk that the wink looks more like a wince, making her almost-pretty face look psychotic, a crazy woman who eats tubes of red, red lipstick. It's scary.

Then from nowhere this goth-looking figure appears. He's wearing a pair of black shorts and an unbuttoned black wool overcoat with no shirt underneath. It's gotta be ninety degrees outside, but the guy isn't even sweating. His skin is white with a rash of ugly pimples and scabs running across his forehead. The dude's so skinny that I can see his spine ridging from below his belly. His face, emaciated, is dominated by black-lined eyes under which he's painted bloodred teardrops. I knew a few goths back home and they were a freaky bunch. But this guy is so hardcore, it hurts to look at him. He seems nervous, one shout away from a meltdown.

It doesn't seem like anyone knows this cat at all. He seems just to have wandered in, but soon he's telling us how blood is the only real bond with chicks that counts. "We cut each other all the time." He's got a bored-like affected tone. It makes him sound sedate and fruity, almost English. "I drink her blood and she drinks mine. You should see it." He pulls the sleeve of his overcoat up and reveals his puny white forearm. Every half inch or so lies a razor-blade–thin red scar. "She'll take our blade and slice me and I do the same to her. It's better than fucking."

I go try to find a beer. I can't listen to that sort of shit right now. It's too much. I focus on drinking. The vampire follows me, though. He wants a beer, too. "I thought you just drank blood," I say. He smiles at me. "I drink all sorts of things."

From outside I hear a loud motor revving. The Mustang racers are heading out to look at Jerry's brother's car. "We gotta check out my bro's car, dude," Jerry says, poking his head into the kitchen.

He's obviously loaded, but people seem genuinely excited to see the car. Jerry explains that his brother has taken the air-condition out of his Mustang to make it even faster. "It's hotter than two rats fucking a wall socket," he tells me as we walk out to the street, "but that bitch moves!"

His brother's car *is* pretty cool. It's a '67 Mustang, bright red, tricked mags, black ragtop, and a kinghell engine that sounds like it's ready to fuck a herd of elephants. I realize right then and there that what I want, what I *need*, is a car. Something that'll move me the hell out of here. "You think your bro or any of his friends can get me a line on a car? Nothing fancy, just something to get me around," I say.

Jerry nods. "Fuck yeah. You came to the right place for that."

I go back into the apartment wanting to get away from the noise, and I find the vampire there alone. He's sitting on the couch, his black wool overcoat splayed out, his knobby, pale chest acting as a resting place for his beer. He has razor scars running across his stomach, too.

"You into that devil shit," I ask him, but in a friendly way. "You one of those goths that go around killing their parents?"

"No, oh no," he says. "Those people are giving us real vampires a bad name. They've listened to too much Slip Knot. Now everyone thinks that just by blowing a boy and cutting their wrists, that they're vampires. It doesn't work that way."

"Just how does it work? What do you have to do, watch *The Hunger* and drink blood?"

"Let's not get into it if you think it's a joke." He doesn't say it angry, just like he's getting bored being asked dumb questions.

"I don't think it's a joke," I say. I flash him the smile. "See?" He nods his head understanding that I'm part of the brood.

"So what's there to do around here tonight?"

"What do you have in mind?" he asks.

"Anything, nothing, whatever. I just want to be occupied."

"Well, that gives us a lot of leeway," he says. "How long have you been here?"

"Long enough, but I've been spending most of my time in Mission Viejo."

"Don't spend too much time in Orange County," he says. "Spend time in L.A. It's worlds better."

"To me," I tell him, "this whole fucking mess is L.A. The whole goddamn place."

"We need to take you on a tour," he says. "My bar's in Hollywood. Coven 13." He looks me over, "But you're not dressed, Sizzler boy."

"This shirt's got more blood on it than you or your girl could drink in a week," I say.

"Oh, *I* believe you, but that won't get you into 13. We could go to a rave my girlfriend knows about. It'll get going at about one, out near Laguna, dance till the sun comes up with real children of the night."

"You got a car?" I ask him.

"No."

"You and me must be the only two assholes here without wheels. Do you fly when you need to go somewhere?"

"That's funny," he says, making bored. "Why don't you ask that girl that you were talking to if she wants to drive us. She seemed *interested*."

It's only about midnight, but I ask Gloria of the red, red lipstick if she's interested in heading out, maybe drive a little bit. She's cool with it. "You'll have to drive. I'm fucking drunk," she says, giving me a kiss. She's gone, boozy breath sour and not all that attractive, but at least she's willing to roll out. "Let's go, *papi*," she says.

———

She gives me the keys to her (big surprise) Mustang. It's not a show car, but it runs. The vampire directs us to his girlfriend's place. She lives near Newport in a nice house, big palm trees, open, roomy avenues, with a fancy, rich mall featuring all the mind-numbing, asshole department stores. She comes out, a pretty used-to-be-blonde, now jet-black-brunette. She's wearing black, her addict-eyes dark holes. Her name is Blair. "Like in the Witch Project?" I say. She takes it like I'm being an asshole.

"My real name is Blair," she says, giving the vampire a big kiss. She calls him Stevie. So much for good vampire names like Cassandra or Victor or Raul or Lestat. Even Lomos is a better vampire name than that.

The car is almost out of gas and we have to stop on the way. After I pump, I go in to buy some cigarettes. As I walk back to the car, this kid, probably a couple of years younger than me, maybe fourteen or so, comes out of nowhere and he says, "Hey man, hey. Can you help me? I just need directions. That's it. No shit, no joke. Hook me up with some directions." He looks scared, sad, empty, a runaway probably.

"I'm not from here," I say as if it's a mystery to anyone. "I'm just as lost as you." He's lanky, with black hair like me. He's got a scab on his forehead. He says again, "Man, help me out. Help me get home." I look at him trying to figure him. "Help me out, man," but this time he's out and out pleading even though he's trying to smile. "How about a ride? Where you going?"

"Laguna," I say.

"Man, I just want out of here." I feel bad for the guy, but Gloria starts honking the horn. "Let's get the fuck out of here," she yells, laughing.

"I'm lost, too," I say and I throw him a couple of bills, whatever I have in my front pocket. He looks at the money, but doesn't jump at it. I get in the car and drive looking at him in the rearview. He stands watching the car move off and I think I see him bend to the money before I have to turn onto the highway.

Gloria is hitting some hash the vampires gave her and I take a couple of hits, turning off where the vamp Stevie directs me. I got no sense of where we're going or how long it takes to get there. These people could be driving me to some demented witch meeting, some coven ritual where they're going to cut me open, take out my burned heart, and whip each other with my intestines in a no-holds-barred satanic fuck frenzy.

That's just what I'm thinking as the traffic drops off to the odd pair of headlights moving in the opposite direction. After a while, though, we seem to be heading toward the beach. Just before we get there, we turn into a warehouse-looking building. There are hundreds of cars in the parking lot and I can see a line of people waiting to get inside the doors, smoke rising above them, music pounding. I try to calm myself down a little. "This is going to be good," Stevie whispers a little too closely in my ear. We get out of the car, but Gloria is already pulling that sick shit, talking about being dizzy and tired and she just wants to lie down for a minute. "Just leave me here," she moans. I got the keys, so fuck her; I say "cool" and we leave her there.

We make our way to the front. It's all kids, hundreds of them waiting in line, talking, smoking, laughing, rubbing each other, a real love fest. "Everyone's rolling," Stevie says right in my ear again. "I'm gonna score a couple of hits for us. This won't be good unless you get some E. Are you going to try it?" I nod although I don't need any more distortion. Already I'm seeing goblins and ghosts under and behind every car. "Twenty bucks, you gotta give me twenty bucks for yours." I hand him a twenty. We get up to the front quickly, but long before that I can hear the bass and computer bleeps pouring through the walls, already making me ever so slightly rock my head back and forth even though I don't want to. The hash was good, good enough to almost drown out my anxiety. The sounds make it seem like I am getting ready to enter a really soothing but haunted pinball machine.

We get in and the place is alive. The place is one big light show with a beat, strong and primitive, flowing, pulling everybody in their own direction. It's pac-man gone wild, with limitless silver quarters dropping from heaven, the game gone public—louder and brighter than ever. Motherfuckers are high, hand-jiving, looking like brain-dead hippies just rocking to the beat and that beep, beep, beep, beep, beep. The vampire Stevie sneaks up behind me. He leans toward me and says something but I can't hear a word, then he slips a pill in my hand, blue, small, a cure for what's ailing me. He yells something else in my ear that I don't hear, something about letting go. I pull a stray Dexadrine from my pocket and stick both pills in my mouth and swallow without water. I'm here, I figure, and I might as well go with it.

Just as the beat breaks loose, I look up to see Gloria come running through the crowd like either the greatest thing that ever happened to a human has just happened to her or like she's just woken up to find some horrifying, green-eyed demon slurping at her tits. Somehow, seeing her, seeing how confused she looks and how stupidly she runs, gives me the assurance that my mask is still good. I give her the grin, a grinding vampire grin, a friendly warning that I might bite her fucking head off if she gets too crazy. She keeps pulling, though, and we start dancing, rubbing each other, but not like we're horny, just like she's this incredible soft living warm thing that moves with me that's moving with everything else, and I close my eyes and move with her, with myself. I move against the wall, alive with vibration and thunder, as if there's a hundred trapped miners behind it screaming and kicking to get the fuck out before the air ends. Then suddenly it's so loud in there that I can't even hear my own sadness. All of us, deaf to what we don't want to hear, dancing like we're being pursued by some invisible terror, like we can get away from it if we just keep running in placé. And I know it's too late, because it will catch me, I know it will, with a bang, *and I don't give a fuck*. Gloria's trying to whisper something in my ear, but all I can sense in this deafening wave is her puky breath. I don't move a facial muscle, I just stare. She won't get to me, no one will. Not anymore. I'm cool, detached, aloof. No one can hurt me now. I'm putting everyone on alert because I'm fucking dangerous.

Hours of bam-dance-distortion and more dance. Thirsty and sweat-drenched, shrunken but still aware, the E fades and I feel my nerves returning to tautness. I can make it out of this crowd now. I need water. I need another Dexy. I say, "Let's go" to Gloria. We start to walk out. No water in sight, so I pop the pill dry. I'm ready to get the fuck out of here, out of California. I'm not digging this shit one bit. We hit the door, the vampires Stevie and Blair behind trying to get my attention, but my attention will not be got in here. Not anymore. I *will* walk out of this motherfucker before my skull implodes, and as we make the door, the cool ocean air hits me square in the face like a cold shower the morning after. I feel the up coming on already. I stop to face them. "What?" I say, the first voice I've heard since we came in, my own, sounding small in my numb ears. "We're gonna stay," he says, "but you got some of our stuff in your car."

"Oh," I say, glad that I don't have to lose my shit with these people. There's a crowd outside, no longer waiting, just grouped out there, talking, smoking, laughing. I need to stand there for a couple of minutes, get my senses adjusted, wash out the echoes of the hours' sounds with something close to silence. I pull a cigarette out to buy me some time. I need clarity. Which way to walk? Where did I leave that jacked-up car? If that Gloria moved that mother-fucker . . . Then I hear somebody from behind me say real loud, "Hey, Sizzler, you steal my wallet?"

I turn around and I look over at him and he's looking at me, in my direction, a white boy wearing a baseball cap backward, with three or four other white boys. His nose is pierced and he's wearing a wife-beater, his hair bleached, trying his best to look like that ass-hole Eminem. Some kid, maybe a couple of years older than me, probably from the valley. I make eye contact and I can tell he and his crew are here to bomb on someone, and they've picked me. I check my mask. It's on straight. Tight. Ready. "Hey, Sizzler, I'm talking to you," he says.

Gloria and my vampires sense the trouble and they try and pull me toward the parking lot, thinking that it can be avoided. But I know better.

"You must be tripping talking like that," I say, but I say it with an out. All he has to do is take it, walk away, just turn around. But I know he won't.

Because he's ready. He thinks *he* is cool, detached, dangerous. "You motherfuckers are always stealing." He says this to his friends more than to me. One of them says, "Fuck up that spic, O." O's on it. He starts walking up on me, his boys right behind, and I know it's on. "We oughta call the border patrol on all you wetbacks, espe-cially you, you spic-assed, cockroach-loving, motherfucking bus-boy." But before he can say anything else, I flat out hit him with everything I got as he walks right into the punch. I put all my weight into it and follow through like a homerun hitter swinging pure and swift and *hard*. I know at the instant I make contact that his nose is gone, obliterated, fucked like frozen mashed potatoes. He's got a lump where his shit used to hang and as he falls down he says, "Jesus," and before I can put my steel toes to him, his boys jump in catching me from all different directions, going wild with their fists, hitting my face and chest and back, till I go down and they start kicking. All the vampires watch, clutching their toys, their goddamn Big Bird stuffed animals and their Teletubbie backpacks, just a playground brawl set to a pulsating beat. "Motherfucking spic, goddamn Mexican," his boys yell. They want to crush my teeth, to pound my ears flat, to break my last rib. No one jumps in to help me till a bouncer or two comes tearing out of the club, yelling what we already know. "The cops are on their way, you assholes."

They pull back and Stevie helps me up while I look at Eminem who's still covering up like he's being kicked. His face is laying flat on the concrete and his blood, black in the dark, is pooling and now he's putting his hand in it, trying to roll over, maybe push himself up. His boys pull him to his feet and disappear fast into the parking lot.

"You alright?" Stevie keeps asking me. I don't answer, feeling this sick exhilaration because I've left blood on that concrete, relieved that for a while I can concentrate on my physical pain, that for a minute I can locate its source exactly. I can touch it and see it, not like this other shit weighing my heart down, boiling my stomach, felt everywhere and nowhere. "At least *I'll* know I was in California," I say walking away toward the car where the girls are already waiting. They're nervous, saying, "Hurry up, hurry up," but I don't because I don't give a fuck. I remain cool, detached, aloof. No one can hurt me now. My mask is on straight, tight, ready.

"That was crazy," Gloria says when we pull away. "That was really crazy. Man, that was *insane*."

"Shut up," I say, the adrenaline pouring out in a cold sweat. "Or at least learn another goddamn word."

"Fuck that asshole," the vampire says. "Fuck those racist fucks. Why do they have to do that shit?"

Finally everyone shuts up, and I drop, just like that. My energy, the juice, is gone. My heart's beating like hell, though. I need to relax. I feel like my chest is gonna explode, like I'm going to puke out all the acid that's been building up in my stomach all night long. And then I do. Stevie pulls over just in time for me to throw up all over the 5. "Are you alright?" someone is asking me. I wave them off. I just need everyone, everything to be fucking quiet. But of course the cars keep rolling by, a few even honk at me and scream drunken curses.

"Come on in if you're finished," Stevie the vampire says from the driver's seat. "You don't want a cop pulling up with the drugs we've got. They'll take all of us to jail." He's got a very good point. I wipe my mouth off and swing my legs back into the car. "Do you want some water?" Gloria has a bottle in her shopping-bag-sized purse. Usually those things drive me crazy, the whole bottled water obsession that all these fucking Californians have. Polluted ocean draining into everyone's consciousness. But I take it, grateful to wash out the blood in my mouth. I got to get out of this town, but I know that it isn't just this crazy fucking madhouse. The madhouse is in me, and I can't run fast enough to get away from me. I've tried. I've tried hard. The vampire hands me the pipe. "Take a good, long pull. That's what you need. Chill out."

I suck some smoke in, and feel it rush through my teeth and over my tongue. I try to become that smoke, to get into the rush fast. My window is open and the wind blows over my face, same as the smoke, drying the sweat and blood on my forehead and my eyes that have teared up from the labor of vomiting. I need to calm down, I keep telling myself. I think about where I'm at and who I'm with and what I'm doing and anyway I look at it, it just seems completely surreal, completely empty. I feel like jumping from the car right then and there, out into the crazy SoCal night, just get away from the chaos I've invited inside the car, inside my life by coming out here and thinking that I could make my life sane in this insane shit town. This fucking place is as bad as I am, worse, and you can't shake your demons in hell.

Gloria's place is way up near Hollywood, but the drive gives me a chance to clear my head a little. The sun is coming up and I can see my face in the rearview mirror. My face isn't so bad. My lips took a couple of shots, but mostly my back and legs got the brunt of it. By the time we get to the apartment, I'm just hoping to get a little rest. The place is nice, soft and girly, with wicker shit everywhere, and pictures of flowers. But Gloria's room is different. It's got books and a poster of the Farmworkers Union eagle. I'm tired, but she wants to fuck. Violence turns her on.

"You like that one?" she says, pointing to another poster, this one a nude by some famous painter. "Give you any ideas?" We start to kiss and I've got her half-naked when she reaches under her bed and busts out a Polaroid camera. She wants me to take shots of her giving me head, playing with her own pussy, spreading her legs. She wants the shit down on film, for posterity, for whatever. "I keep the pictures in this box," she says, pulling an old, purple school box from under her bed. "You want to look at them?" she says, spreading a handful on the bed next to where I sit. I look down at dozens of pictures of her with other guys and some even with girls. I can't handle this trip. I couldn't get it up right now if she were to break off into a lap dance. I say, "I'm going to sleep," and before she can even start to complain, I walk out to her living room and lie down on the couch. "Punk-ass," she says, coming out of her bedroom a few minutes later. She's naked. Behind her she's dragging an old Scooby beach towel. She goes into the bathroom and turns on the shower without closing the door.

I shut my eyes, but I can't fall asleep so I turn on her TV. The morning news is on. Some little girl got hit by a car last night and instead of stopping and checking on her, the fucker rolled over her trapped body so he could make his big getaway. They got her moms on the screen, crying, her eyes looking for someone to tell her that all this is just a horrible dream. I shut the set off and limp out before Gloria can drag herself out of the bathroom.

I stand on the pavement, my Sizzler shirt torn to shit, my face puffed, my legs weak and bruised, and watch the people driving out to the highways to get to work. I only got one place to go and even though I know what's gone down, that I'm not welcome, that sick part of me that hangs on to hope when even God would give up, wants to see the thing through to the very end. So I find a payphone. It's early enough that Naomi answers. "Hello," I say after almost hanging up.

"Robert," she says like she's smelling baby shit. Long pause, then, "you've got a lot of people worried. You need to come here. We need to talk." That's all I need to hear. "I'll be around tonight," I say. Of course, I have no intention of talking to that bitch tonight or any other night. I'm going to wait for her to get out and then try one last time to get through to my moms.

I can't get a cab looking like I do, so I get on a bus. People on their way to work do everything they can not to look at me. I swallow another Dexy to keep from falling asleep and concentrate on not throwing up.

By the time I get to the house, I'm shaking all over the place, like I have Parkinson's or something. My gramps died of that, and I don't remember much because I was so young, but I do remember that his hands were in constant motion, always shaking in time to some deep, unutterable fury, like he was directing some mad symphony in his head. My hands are shaking, too. My stomach doesn't feel any too good either. Between the acid swishing around in there and my jittery hands, I half-turn around and fuck the whole thing off. Just leave. I know this isn't going to get me anywhere. But I push on ahead. I gotta see this thing through all the way so when it all explodes, I'll know I did everything, said everything.

I'm aware that I haven't prepared: no speeches, no laundry list of my best features, no top ten reasons Moms should forgive me for being such a fuck-up. Nothing. All I got is a nervous stomach, jittery hands, and useless, raggedy vampire teeth.

Instead of knocking at the door, I go around to the back and peer in through the windows. Antony is at school and Naomi is definitely gone. I can see my grandmother napping her old age away, but Moms is nowhere to be seen. I climb up to the second story, to where my room had been. It's not easy. I use the tree, dragging my sore body up a little at a time. The pain is coming in steady and sharp now, my chest, back, and legs begging me to be still, to lie the fuck down.

I go in through the bedroom window that I left unlocked, and real quiet, take off the scraps of my Sizzler shirt. I put on a clean T, rinse my face, cupping big gulps of water because I'm so thirsty I can't stand it. Then I creep downstairs to my moms's bedroom door. It's half-closed. I stick my neck out and take a look. Moms is lying down, her eyelids pressed together, but I can tell she's not asleep because her forehead's knitted.

"Mom," I say, my voice shaking all over the place in almost a whisper. "Mom," I say again. This time she responds but she doesn't open her eyes.

"M'ijo," she says. "Roberto. Come here, *m'ijito."* Hearing her say "my son" makes me feel so good for a second that I forget the razor blades in my stomach and the blood on my shoes. I walk over to her and before I can even say a word I slide down on my knees right in

front of her. I can't even talk. All my energy is gone and all I can manage is to fucking start crying. A perfect beginning. "Stop. Stop." I order myself in my head. I can't, though. I can't maintain my shit. I just kneel there weeping, only no real sound is coming out of my mouth because I'm still hoping I can control it, keep it from her, hide how lost I feel, how lost I am because I don't want her to know that I'm such a goddamn mess, that I need my mommy, a mommy, any mommy. This isn't part of my plan. Goddamn it, I came here to show her that I was past that. That I was gonna take care of her and Antony, and how can a goddamn baby do that? But before I can get it together, she puts her arms on me and draws me to her.

Finally, she says, "I'm sorry, *m'ijo,* I'm so sorry." I tell her she's got nothing to be sorry about. Nothing. "You haven't done anything to me," I say, but the words come out small and choked up. "Can't we just be together?" I ask.

"I'm not strong enough," she says, "I can't get away from my sadness. I've tried everything to swim away from it, but it's not something I can swim away from. It's the ocean itself. I thought for a while that I could just float on the top of it, just keep kicking my legs and my arms and that I'd get past it. It's too broad, too deep. I can't find the bottom. It's in me now. I've swallowed so much of it that it's in my blood and I can't wash the smell of all this sadness away." Her eyes are open all the way and she's looking dead at me.

Her pain washes over me and I want to look away because I recognize myself in there. I look closer and I see my father, too. I see in that reflection that my father and I are the same thing, are the same *package* for her. We're the Siamese twins of pain and memory. I can see him staring back at me through her anguish and I realize that it will always be like this for her. I'm not going to change that. She says "I'm sorry" again. I hug her tight, tighter than I've ever hugged her or anybody before. I want to tell her that I love her and that it's okay, but I can't move my tongue in my thick fucking throat. Instead, I just give her a kiss on the cheek. My lips linger there, and I soak in the feel of her skin for just a few seconds thinking, like a punk, like a sucker, that I better remember that—the feel of my mother's face. In that instant I know that my mask is for shit, because I'm still nothing but a kid, no bigger, no better, no harder than my little Antony.

I stand up and I look at my moms, and I know. I know it's time to leave for real. I limp out of the room like I'm just going to the bathroom or something, but once outside the doorway, I walk up to what was my bedroom, grab my bag, and crawl out the window like a straight-out thief who's found an empty house where he was sure he'd find riches.

Jerry has a line on a car for me. He has me meet him at the Sizzler during his break. Jerry notices how much worse I look than I did last night. "Jesus, what happened to you? Last night it was a puffy eye, now you look like you got jumped into a gang."

"Nothing," I say, but it makes me realize that my moms didn't notice. "Where are the wheels?"

The car isn't fancy or even very attractive. It's an old '85 Mustang, but it's black and the inside is in good shape. "It's a decent car. It'll get you where you're going," Jerry says.

"I'll take it," I say, surprising myself. We exchange money and keys. As I'm leaving I see Ayala. He starts talking shit about why didn't I show up this morning. "Fuck you, shit brains," I say, and I dump my rolled-up Sizzler shirt into the deep fryer as he watches, his big, stupid mouth open.

I can't leave without saying good-bye to Antony. Could try to use another fake note, but with my face the way it looks, they'd never buy it. Could just make my way into the school, kidnap him. Could unload the gun, leave just one bullet. I'm not looking to pull a Columbine. Just get my little brother, maybe take him to Mexico. Why not? My moms won't do him any good, and leaving him for Naomi is worse than stealing him away, right?

I roll up to the school. I'm sweating like crazy, wondering what I'm going to do. I got no plan, got no real idea what it is I'm doing here. A good-bye? A kidnapping? Offing myself? I got one bullet in the gun, a regular Deputy fucking Fife. I sort of laugh at the idea of it. But it's not funny. I check the piece, making sure the round is next up. I get out of the car, reach behind, and slide the gun in my waistband again. I walk toward the big glass-and-aluminum double doors. In the reflection I see myself for just a second, skinny, fucked up, bruised, face all puffy. My breathing is quick, like I've run a mile, but I walk in steady. The office door is to my right, with the old bird who runs the desk sitting there drinking her god-damned coffee, just a normal day. I have choices, I gotta think, what am I here for? Antony, but what? I walk right past the office door, just like the breeze, no fuss, no muss, and I head for the hall-way to the first-grade classrooms.

Just take him because he's mine. Take him to Mexico. Just get in the car, run off, live free and clear. I peer into the classroom, hid-den most of the way by a column in the hall. Antony is sitting in his desk, his hair slicked back, combed neat. His face is clean, white, smooth. He's writing something down, maybe working on a math problem. Whatever it is, he's concentrating, his face scrunched up a little because whatever he's doing, he's finding it hard. It makes me smile, makes me want to cry, makes me wish I was little like him, maybe that I was him.

But I'm not. I need to think so I head for the bathroom. I go inside one of the stalls and sit on the toilet, the gun poking my back. I'm not him. He's not me. I don't want him to be me. It's then that I know I'm not going to do shit. Not to myself, not to Antony.

But maybe if I chill in there for a little bit, I can catch him, at least say good-bye. I wait a little while. But he doesn't come in. I hear two other kids, but they're older, already talking about fuck this and fuck that. After they leave, I figure my little bro doesn't need to see me like this, anyway, big fuck-up that I am. But with a marker some kid left behind, I write on the wall in big black letters, "I love you Antony, Your Big Bro Robert."

I sneak out, nobody knowing I was even there. Maybe I wasn't. I get back in the car, take the gun, toss the bullet in the backseat. Fuck this shit. Daytime is burning and I can only think of one thing now. Getting the hell out of California and getting back to San Antonio.

I drive like my ass is on fire until I get to I-10. It's going to take me straight through to S.A. A 1,200-mile shot, back the way I came. Here I am, a needle, pulling red thread again, but this time I don't want to look back. It's a mess again, no pattern, nothing that would make any sense. From the time I got off the bus at the L.A. terminal, I've left a confused trail, a path not even Sherlock Holmes could follow. If I could see the pattern, I'd see that it's a thick coil, its center my moms's house, such a confused mess of a coil that it's no wonder I got tripped up in it.

By the morning, I'm almost in New Mexico. Somewhere between here and there, I bury the gun right in the fucking desert. My gramps's service revolver finally laid to rest.

I haven't slept in two days and I park at a rest stop and nod off. After a few hours of sleep, I'm back on the road. I have this running conversation in my head with my moms. In it I ask her what I wanted her to answer for me. "How am I going to know who I am; who you are?" And nothing comes to me except her stories, the ones she would tell me way back after Pops had first left. Thinking about them, they pick me up a little.

I would keep her half-cheerful by asking her questions like "What were you like as a teenager?" She'd get to remembering her youth and her old boyfriends and how she liked to make them jealous. How they chased after her, because my moms was a knockout with her dark brown curly hair and her big green eyes and dimples. She would tell me, "Your grandfather was very strict." She liked remembering him because he took care of her like a father should. When he died, he left her alone just like my old man.

He was a preacher. He didn't take money from his congregation because it was the Depression. So Moms's family had to live in a tent for a long time and drink water from the river, water that was polluted and killed her baby brother. "Your grandfather had to sell vegetables to keep us in food." I never got to meet him really, because he died when I was only three. But my moms would tell me his stories and how he was strict, but had a soft spot for her. "He would let me get away with a lot more than the boys. He never yelled at me, and if Momma got mad, he'd say, 'Esposa, leave my Teresa be.'" I liked hearing my moms telling me those things. It took us out of that dark room to another place, like a movie in my mind, where my moms was the star of one of those fifties romantic comedies she liked so much.

I stop only to get gas or at the occasional McDonald's. I've got about a quarter ounce of weed left, and that's enough to get me home. There's a cassette tape someone left behind, *Who's Next*. I listen to it for almost the entire drive until I see the city lights and I catch FM 99.5 on the radio. It hits me that I'm back in San Antonio, that I'm going to see Grams, that I'm alive, and for a minute I feel almost good.

CHAPTER 14

I drive into San Antonio coasting through downtown till I hit Culebra, where I turn off to get to Grams's house. I've missed knowing where I'm at. L.A. is this crazy-assed maze of highways and zones, but I get San Antonio. I know *its* divisions, its fractured body and spirit. It's split into five areas, and growing up here, you know which one is which, and you figure out quick which one you belong to.

As I creep down Culebra, I pass the westside landmarks I've memorized without memorizing. There's Las Palmas shopping center, the only real spot for shopping on the westside of town. Grams buys all her groceries at the HEB, and when I was a kid and it was time to go back to school, she took me to get my dorky-assed clothes at Joske's department store. They let you put shit on layaway, at least until they went out of business. Las Palmas had it all: a Niesner's pharmacy, where you could buy anything from a cockatoo to a cheap, awful cup of coffee at its lunch counter; a Western Auto where Mexicans went to get parts to keep their clunkers moving; there were dime stores and cloth stores and piddly, bizarre boutiques. You could get anything from a turtle to a nice dress for your daughter's *quinceañera* at Las Palmas. The place has changed in the last few years, but it still feels Mexican even though lots of the stores have gone out of business or moved to the north side to the big white mall. Las Palmas isn't fancy with Muzak pumped in from invisible speakers. It's still got masonry work that makes it look like some Spanish colonial outpost. The stores are all arranged in a long line with HEB providing one of the ends of the bracket-shaped strip.

All along the wide passageways of white concrete stand tall palm trees transplanted from Florida or California. Each store has its own canopy, brightly striped or colored in a sharp, solid green, blue, red, or yellow. In the middle of the market there used to be this small carnival where Grams would let me ride the carousel and the small Ferris wheel when I was Antony's age. If I was good, Grams would buy me a *raspa* at the stand where an old guy would scoop the ice into a cone-shaped paper cup and pour whatever flavor syrup you wanted. I dug coconut. Still do. Out in the parking lot, on the outskirts of the market, stands the old public library. It's round, with high ceilings, and Grams would take me there on Saturdays and let me get two books. Across the street taking up about ten blocks of space lies San Fernando Cemetery, where Grams told me that only Catholics could be buried. There are always hundreds of flower displays lying on the graves. There's tons of flower shops specializing in arrangements for the dead. Loud, funky bouquets set in bundles in green-and-red foil-covered pots are ready for the next religious holiday.

Even in the earliest part of the morning, the westside is alive, cars and trucks speeding down General McMullen, the main road, toward Commerce Street, which leads directly to downtown. The westside is split by Commerce and McMullen, and again, farther down on Commerce, by Zarzamora. There are a dozen Catholic churches, the most beautiful on Zarzamora, Church of the Little Flowers. It's got this high belltower that you can see from miles away.

St. Mary's University sits on the northern edge of the westside; Grams says that this is where I should go to college. When she wants to get on me, she says, "You better watch out or you'll never end up at St. Mary's, unless you plan on mowing the lawn." At its eastern edge lie the railroad tracks and the *matanza* near Alizondo Courts where that skinny-assed Renaldo lives. There's a produce market close to the tracks where Grams always goes so that she can buy twenty-pound sacks of oranges and grapefruit. Grams's brothers all worked at the fruit market during the Depression, making a dollar a day stacking boxes, cleaning, and unloading trucks. I pass the Mariposa Projects. Grams's house is only two blocks from the courts. When I was a kid, she didn't let me go anywhere past her street in that direction except for Calderon's store. As I creep closer, I decide to make a stop at the Cinderella Bakery that stands between the Mariposa and Durango Projects. It's worth driving there to get the best *pan dulce* in the whole city. I figure I'll bring some as part of my homecoming. I always get a couple of *maranitos* for Grams. She digs the pig-shaped molasses sweet bread, but they're out of them, so I buy her a yam-filled *regalito*.

As I edge home, I cruise past the *molinos* and the rent-to-own joints that charge four or five times the price of whatever piece-of-shit furniture or appliance they happen to be "renting." There are bingo parlors where old people sit for hours peering down at their cards trying like hell to win the five-hundred-dollar prize. That's enough dough to hold off disaster in lots of westside houses for at least another month. There are too many fast-food places to count, selling cheap, fatty hamburgers, tacos, pizzas, and fried chicken. One thing, though: it doesn't take a fortune to get fed on this side of town.

I drive past Dr. Flores's office, around since I can remember. Westside doctors don't take insurance. Cash Only. For thirteen bucks you can get a shot of penicillin. There's always dozens of people waiting outside. Sick, feverish kids crying and coughing, waiting for their turn to get a shot and a prescription for cough medicine that their parents can't afford. Cheap-clothing stores are always busy around this neighborhood, places where you can buy a blouse for five bucks and a bad-fitting polyester dress for eight. What I like about this place, and what I'm realizing as I make my way home to Grams, is that even though it changes, it doesn't feel different. It's still there, still where I can get to it.

The house is dark except for a glimmer of light coming from the kitchen window. Grams is up getting ready for work.

"I thought that was you," she says when I come walking through the kitchen door. She acts like it isn't any big deal, no crying or big hugs, no hurt feelings. None that she lets on, anyway. She's behaving like it's school I'm coming home from, not California. It makes me grateful to her because after the shit I've seen and felt these past weeks, I need her to be herself, her strong, nonemotional self. No-nonsense Grams. "You hungry?" she says, ignoring the way I look. I hold out the bag of sweet bread. She takes it and I sit down. She turns back to the stove and takes the boiling water. She grabs the handle with her bare hands. I don't know how she does it without getting burned. Me, I'm a wimp when it comes to heat. She pours some of the water into a cup and drops a couple of heaping tea-spoons of instant coffee and stirs slowly. No sugar, no milk. She drinks it still boiling hot, not bothering even to blow on it.

"I brought you a *regalito*," I say, pointing at the bag.

She keeps looking at me, though, until I feel like I gotta say something. "Aren't you mad at me?" She reaches out and touches my face for a second.

"I got no reason to be mad at a boy just because he wants to see his momma."

"I'm back if you'll let me," I say.

She looks me in the eye and says, "Boy, this your home. You oughta know that."

"You were right," I say because I can't think of anything else. "Things didn't work out too well there."

"Sometimes people can't help themselves," she says. "Your poor momma, she's one of them. You pray for her." She takes another drink of her coffee.

I want to apologize because I feel bad looking across the table at her. She looks smaller than when I last saw her, older, not the same. I hate to think about what my running has done to her, but I haven't had much time to do that. People always think that when they leave somewhere that things will be the same when they get back, but when they do, they start to notice that things have changed. Maybe not a lot, but enough so that the surfaces of things look different. That's how my grams's face looks. More worn, thinner. I never recognized it before, but my grams is not just older, she's old. "You been okay?" I ask.

"Been fine. You don't need to worry about me." She's not trying to guilt me. Grams gets up to go get dressed for work and just before she turns to go to the bedroom, she comes around and gives me a hug. "Nice to have you home, boy." That's it. She goes off and twenty minutes later I'm alone because Grams has gone off to clean houses. My room is the same as the night I left, and I put my shit away.

After, I go out and sit in the living room. There's nothing to do. I think about calling up Juan or Nacho, even devil-boy Enrique, but they're all in school. I'm a dropout and anyway, I don't feel like answering a lot of stupid questions about how everything turned out. Instead, I watch the tube. *The Price Is Right* with old-assed Bob Barker still giving free shit away. That never changes.

Grams has been getting up two or three times a night. I'm a very light sleeper and I can hear her moaning quietly and then getting up and taking that Doan's back pills bottle off the counter, opening it, and drinking a couple down. It happens at two and four and just before six, when she usually gets up. When I ask her about it, she gives me a quick answer that means I should mind my own business. "My back hurts, boy. Your back'll hurt too when you get as old as me, and with the type of *burro* work you're going to have to do, you'll be taking them Doan's pills, too."

"Maybe you should take it easier. I'm going to be working now and you don't have to do as many houses. You should go to the doctor."

"Doctor?" she says like I just suggested that she should go to a witch. "What's he going to do? Send me to the hospital? That's what kills old folks, going to the hospital. Now go worry about yourself. I don't need it. I got work to do." And with that, she pulls herself out of her chair and makes for the bedroom. She does it painfully, with too much effort, and it makes me feel worried, but with Grams, there's not too much I can do.

I call this kid from Sunnydale whose uncle owns a construction joint. He told me he could hook me up with a job. I gotta get work and summer's always good for construction. The guy who owns the company is used to hiring illegals and desperate-types, so hiring me isn't really much of a stretch. He pays me six dollars an hour, which is about a buck more than he pays the illegals. The place is called P.J. Enterprises, but from what I can see, the only enterprising going on is the employees finding all sorts of new ways of not doing shit.

P.J. tells me how he's trusting me to work on his top project. His "crack team" is supposed to be putting up suspended ceilings in an elementary school that needs to open by the end of summer.

They're on a break when I show up. Four guys sitting on stacks of precut tiles like stunned iguanas sunning on desert rocks. I introduce myself and get a few waves and a come'ere gesture from Brace, the foreman. "You're the new gopher, um?" he says as he sits leaning against a stack of throwaways. "You'll do fine here if you remember one thing. You's just shit labor." The others nod lazily. That seems to be the orientation.

Our crew is one of the last ones in because the building has to be up already before we put up the ceiling. We also put in insulation, either laying rolls of itchy fiberglass or spraying glop above the ceilings. Brace told me not to ask what's in the shit. "I don't know, so don't come to me if you start shitting blood."

We hang the wire from the underside of the roof. After that's done, we put up the fiberglass panels. The work is hot and itchy because the air-conditioning doesn't work yet. It's a bitch. Outside the temperature is in the hundreds. The only way to keep from going crazy from the thousands of fiberglass slivers inside of your collar and underwear band is to move around as little as possible and that means not working. But that isn't a problem for Brace or his crack team. We take a ton of breaks, long ones, too. Brace says, "Fuck P.J., he's kicking back at the office."

The guys on the team look sketchy, pretty much solid losers. There's Phil, a Willie Nelson–looking druggie with wrinkled, leathery skin and a stringy mustache and beard. Brace says Phil was once so fucked-up he took a walk out the back of a van while it hauled ass down the highway at sixty miles an hour. Bob is an unhappy-looking white kid a couple of years older than me, with blond hair and a really thin, scraggly goatee that reminds me of Shaggy from

Scooby-Doo, only he doesn't look as bright as either Shaggy or Scooby. He's married, lives in a mobile home park, and doesn't talk much. Rollie, a fat, hairy guy, seems nice enough, but he stinks like he hasn't stepped in a shower since he was in high school.

I get home that day tired and itchier than I've ever been before, but at least the crew is going to be okay. We didn't do much, but even that got me tired. I'm not cut out for the heat. People always give me a hard time about that. "You're a Mexican from South Texas and you can't take the heat," they'll say. Even Grams says it, but there's nothing I can do about it. I'm just no good in the sun.

I go straight to the shower and stand under a cold blast of water until the itching stops. After, I grab a Coke and walk out to the porch. Ruthie and Tina are playing outside. I haven't seen them since I've been back and it makes me glad that they're out there. "Hi," I say. They run up to the fence. Ruthie looks excited, but Tina just smiles and waves a little. I get up and walk over to them. "Where you been?" Ruthie wants to know. She's always the gutsy one. "You haven't been around."

"I know," I say. "I went on a trip. Went to see my mom."

"Where's your mommy live?" asks Tina.

"In California," I say, expecting that they don't know where it is.

"Did you go to Disneyland?" asks Tina.

"Yeah, Mickey Mouse," adds Ruthie.

"Nah, I'm too old for that."

"Your mommy didn't take you there?" asks Tina.

"I wouldn't have wanted to go," I say, remembering my stupid plan to go there with Antony and Moms.

"That's dumb," says Ruthie. "Everyone wants to see Mickey Mouse. Bet your mommy doesn't have money. That's why we don't get to go!"

"Shhhh!" says Tina. "Don't talk so loud. He's gonna hear you."

She's talking about their alky father. "Yeah, well, I probably wouldn't have gone even if my mommy would've had the money," I say. "You two been good?"

Tina nods and Ruthie shakes her head. "It's you that ain't good," says Ruthie. "You ran away from home. I heard your gramma telling my momma."

"Well, he's back now, Ruthie, so shut up." Tina turns back toward me. "Don't listen to Ruthie. She talks too much. We're glad you're back from your trip." Ruthie smiles at me, "Yeah, you got any money for ice cream?" I dig out a couple of dollar bills and put them in her small hand, which she's shoved through the chain-link fence. She takes both dollars and runs around to the other side of the house. "She's going to look for the ice cream man," Tina explains. "I better go over there, too, or she'll forget to buy me some. Bye." And she gives a little wave as she starts off after her sister.

I go back to the house and order Grams and me a pizza because I know she'll be tired when she gets home. Grams comes in a couple of minutes after it gets there, but she doesn't want any. "I'm too tired to eat," she says, and she goes straight to her bedroom and lies down. It worries me some, so after a while I go to her room with a plate and a glass of Pepsi, her favorite. "Brought you something to eat," I say, coming in. She's laying on her side and she's got a heating pad on her back. "How can you have that thing on when it's so hot, Grams?" I try and put the plate down next to the bed. "No, you," she says. She sounds like she's in pain. "I'm not hungry. You bring me some of my Doan's pills. Maybe I'll feel better in a while." I go to the bathroom and get a couple of the tablets and come back in. She drinks them, the whole time keeping her eyes closed like it might hurt her more to open them. "Grams, you oughta go to the doctor," I say because I can't think of anything else.

"You go on now," she says. "I got better things to do with my money. I need some rest, that's all. What a life I got working like a *burro* for them white folks. Work, that's all it is," she says, half-complaining to make herself sound tough, but all the while I can hear the pain in her voice.

"How long has your back been hurting?" I ask even though I know she won't like it.

"You, Roberto, you quit bothering me now. You go worry about your belly and stop worrying about my back."

Bob talks a lot, but only about how much he hates being married and how his kid gets on his nerves, and how his favorite song is "Freebird" and how he's going to leave that "bitch" one of these days. His favorite insult is to tell anyone complaining that "you bitch more'n my old lady." But near the end of the week, he loosens up when P.J. hires these two girls to help us out for the rest of the month. They're young and not too bad looking. Bob's falling in love with the one named Nancy. I think she's the other girl's lover, but they're trying not to let on, so Nancy flirts with him. Bob's coming to work a few minutes early so he can set up his scaffold. He'll load it with enough ceiling panels to last for two or three hours. Then he puts his boom box on the scaffold. He plays his Lynrd Skynrd's greatest-hits tape and as soon as the girls come in, he asks Nancy to be his scaffold partner. He likes to explain the meaning of each of the lyrics and their personal significance for him. "See, that's how I see myself," we hear him say when "Freebird" plays. "I'm just waiting to leave, to head on down the road. It's in me, you know. I got a taste for adventure. That sounds stupid, right?"

"No," Nancy says. "It sounds like you should."

"Yeah, well, I'm going to."

Rollie says, "I got your free bird," and he gives him the finger. We all laugh except for Bob and Nancy.

Bob's bringing double sandwiches to work, sometimes an extra banana, and he shares the food with Nancy. Her friend—we call her the "manster" because she looks masculine around the eyes and jaw—doesn't like it. She's taken to asking Bob about his wife and kid whenever she can work it into the conversation.

"But how can you leave if you've got a wife and kid? That sounds shitty to me." Bob stops talking whenever the manster comes around. But the love affair isn't meant to be. Brace tells the girls that P.J. isn't going to keep them around after all. They have only a couple of more days on the job. On their last day, Bob's fidgety and short-tempered. Nancy acts nervous, too. At lunchtime she goes to her car and comes back with a black T-shirt that she gives to Bob. It has "Freebird" spelled out in silver letters across the chest. Bob blinks hard and rolls it up, sticking it in his back pocket. For a minute, he looks ready to cry, but instead he just says thank-you. The girls want to stay on, but P.J. says he can't afford it. "They's just shit labor," Brace says to Bob in explaining why the answer has come back negative.

The guys ride Bob hard the next day, asking him where his "Freebird" T-shirt is, and why he hasn't brought his boom box to work that day, and could one of them be his new scaffold partner, and does he have an extra sandwich, and would he please stack up their ceiling panels. I feel sorry for the guy, though, but all I can say is, "Man, don't listen to them, that shirt's pretty cool." Finally, at the end of the first two weeks, I'm psyched because it's payday. I got plans for the dough. Big plans. But the day is torture. The way it works is that P.J. calls in all his employees from the different work sites and he tells them to take a seat around his desk. His office is a mobile home he's put up on an empty lot he owns on the south side. There's all sorts of supplies stacked outside with a six-foot fence surrounding the place. Inside's a tired-looking dog he calls King, who doesn't seem interested in barking unless he's hungry. I guess it doesn't matter because I don't know why anyone would want to steal a stack of precut ceiling tiles. You can't use them unless you have the wiring up, and P.J. keeps that locked up at his house.

P.J. likes to sit on his hot young secretary's desk while she sits behind him talking to her boyfriend on the phone. She doesn't do a damn thing that I can see except talk and drink Diet Cokes. Brace and the guys say that P.J.'s banging her, but nobody really believes it. I think that P.J. likes her around because he imagines that everyone thinks he's banging her, and that's something.

For over an hour after we get there, he just sits and stares at us as other guys come drifting in from the sites. He nods, but he doesn't talk. His aim is to make everyone feel uncomfortable, to see who looks guilty. When everyone's there, and not a minute before, he begins to ask questions. He does this shit till eight, but no one has the nerve to complain, much less ask for his check.

"How's the Piedmont project going?" he asks one of the guys from the northeast side. The guy nods his head and says it's going on schedule. P.J. goes down the row, asking everyone how their project is progressing. Of course, no one admits that things are dangerously behind, or that the floor people or painters are threatening to report the crew because we aren't getting the job done. It's more of a ceremony than a fact-finding meeting. I figure that it's P.J.'s way of buying time before he has to part with the green. After everyone has shown their determination to "keep up the good work," P.J. signals his hot secretary to pull the checks out from the check drawer. As he sits on his desk, his secretary hands him one envelope at a time, and P.J. grasps it, gives it a little snap, reads out the name, and gives the lucky winner a personalized message as he goes up to get the check.

"Rollie, buy some soap. You smell like a yak fucking a rotten cantaloupe."

Next check.

"Brace, don't drink it all. I don't give a good goddamn about your Vietnam nightmares. You better get that job site humming come Monday or you'll have a whole lot more to worry about than agent orange."

Next check.

"Bob, get your pretty wife something before she gets wise and leaves you. Good thing them carpetmunchers are gone. Wife mighta gone over to the other side."

Next check.

"Robert, might wanta spend more than a few of them dollars on a dentist. Those teeth are spooking my dog. You look like a god-damn wolfboy."

Next check.

"Phil, please boy." He takes a deep breath, like he's really con-cerned. "Stay off of the pot. I don't want you taking a midnight stroll off a moving truck." And so on. Each check-wanter grins and nods their thanks so they can get their dough. After, our crew drives to the Sigmor up the road and buys a case of beer. The topic stays on what a bastard P.J. is and how one of these days, "by God, I'm going to pop him in the mouth, take my check, and walk out that fucking door for the last time."

I don't stay long. I'm starting a new routine, a payday routine. Every other Friday I'm going to bring home some groceries, order a pizza, and give Grams most of my cash. I bring home stuff I know she likes: a big jar of Folgers, Pepsi, chocolate ice cream, and some nice steak for *carne asada*. I've decided that one way or another, I'm going to make Grams go to the doctor and that one way or another, I'm going to make her quit her houses, or at least most of them.

Grams is happy with the groceries, but she won't take all my cash. "You save some of that, boy. You planning on being a *burro* like me?" she asks, being more serious than usual about being a *burro.* She sighs. "You young now, but not always. Not always," she says, emphasizing the word "always" in a way that scares me a little. "I just want you to slow down," I say, "because you've been feeling tired lately."

"I slow down now, I'll never be able to speed up, boy. Now you go get yourself a shower and stop nagging me," she says in a way that I know the conversation is over.

After I get out of the shower, Grams tells me she's going to call it a night. I'm bored so I call up Enrique and Juan. Enrique tells me he's got a "cutie" he wants me to meet. "She's got a friend, man, and you can tell us about California. It's good to have you back. You had us worried." I figure a night out won't hurt, so I drive my Mustang to his house on the northeast side. For once, I feel kind of proud to be there. Not even Enrique, with his fancy house and his rich parents, has a car. He checks it out and tells me how cool it is, but he can't help himself and he tells me how his pops, my uncle, has promised him a new truck if he pulls his grades out of the shit-house. "I'm gonna do it, too," he says as he messes with my stereo so that it sounds right to him. Juan gets there a little later. He's cooler than Enrique and after a hug he makes out like my car is a Ferrari. "This is awesome," he says. The three of us take off together for a girl's house. Enrique swears that she's in love with him and that she's going to hook us up. Me and Juan give each other a look because we've heard this shit before.

Enrique always, *always*, blows it with girls. They usually dig him at first, but he inevitably does something to chase them off after only a couple of weeks. We get to the girl's house. Her name is Karen, and Enrique's been talking her up the whole ride, and to our amazement, she's all he claimed. She's got that fresh look, young and pretty with straight, long chestnut hair. Enrique's had one date with her. He took her to a dollar movie and tonight he's decided to surprise her with a gift he's picked up at some five-and-dime: a cheap, visibly fake gold bracelet that's already turning green.

"I'm gonna give Karen this present," he told us just before we got out of the car. When he held up the bracelet, thin and so cheap looking that I turned red from embarrassment when *I* saw it, I was straight up with him. "You're gonna give that shit to that girl?" He gave me an angry look. "What do you mean 'shit'?" He snatched the chain from my hand. "This bracelet cost almost twelve bucks." He gave it a closer look, turning it over in his hand as we walked up to the door. "Do you think it looks fake?" He seemed a little concerned. "I don't want her to know it's fake. Won't get any snatch that way." Juan laughed. "That thing looks like it'll give her a fucking infection."

Karen introduces me to her cousin Beatrice. She's cute but dumb. Usually I wouldn't mind this combination. It's worked for me before, but tonight I'm more in the mood to talk, and this girl can't carry a conversation at all. At least one that I'd give a damn about. She just wants to talk shit about how hot Karen *thinks* she is. She's boring the hell out of me and about the only thing I can do is stare at her belly button, which is pierced. I have to admit, it does look hella good. But it's not enough to keep me interested. Juan is talking to their friend from school, this Mexican girl who's sitting on the sofa. She catches my eye right away, not only because I think she's beautiful, but because she has this sad smile that's got something deep to it. It's kind. She's gotta be that if she's listening to Juan tell one of his dorky-assed stories. After a few minutes of listening to Beatrice go on about herself, I give Juan a shout so that we can combine our group. Enrique is off somewhere with Karen. I can tell that the girl with Juan is happy to get some other people into the action.

"This is Amelia," Juan says. He likes her, but I can't help it, I gotta horn in on her. Her eyes are big and dark brown. They tell me that she's smart. Her smile makes me feel like I need to deserve it. We all start to talk about whatever, and I work it so that I'm talking to her. I tell her about just getting back from California and she tells me that she's never been there, but that she's always wanted to go. When she leaves for the bathroom, I notice that she's got a little limp. Beatrice leans over and says in my ear, "One of her legs is almost an inch shorter than the other and she has to wear a special shoe. It gives her terrible backaches." She says it pretending to be sad for her, but really she's being a bitch because she can tell that I'm into Amelia. Juan can tell too, so when we're in the kitchen getting a beer, he tells me that if I want, we can switch girls. I'm all for it.

I find out that she lives with her mom and stepdad, an ex-cop who now works security for the nearby high school. She doesn't say it directly, but I can tell she doesn't care for the guy too much. "You guys want to go downtown?" Enrique says, coming out of the bedroom with Karen. She's wearing the fake bracelet and Enrique is obviously happy because he tricked her. We head off for the Tower of Americas that overlooks San Antonio. We park near the Alamo so that we can take the riverwalk to the tower. I look over at Amelia worrying that she might not be able to make it. "Are you going to be alright if we walk?" I ask. She's embarrassed but she doesn't show it too much. "I'll be fine. Walking doesn't bother me." We take off along the banks of the river. It's dark and not too many people are out tonight because it's getting late. Before I know it, and without thinking about it, I take her hand. It's warm and soft, small in mine, and it feels so good that I get a crazy idea to kneel down right there and then and ask her if she'll marry me. I feel like I'm drunk with her and I'm so got that I can't even look at her. Instead, I concentrate on her hand and the feeling of her round, warm fingers in between mine. I feel so happy all of a sudden that

I start joking with everybody, Enrique, Juan, Karen, even that bitch Beatrice.

Up at the tower, I let the whole thing get to me. When I feel happy, I get a little stupid, so as soon as we've left everyone on the other side of the observation deck, I ask her if she'll marry me. I straight out propose, "Please marry me. I'm serious. I want to support you, come home to you, the whole thing. The house, the kids, a goddamned dog." I do it like a joke, like I'm only kidding, but I'm only half-kidding. Amelia looks down at me, smiling that sad-like smile and she says, "Don't play. Some girls would take you seriously, a beautiful proposal like that."

"Oh, you should take me seriously," I say. "I'm always straight up when I propose."

"I see," she says, "you do this a lot?"

"Every time I come up with a pretty girl to the tower it happens. I can't help it."

"What's so special about the tower," she says, playing along now, but still holding my hand so that it makes me feel almost fucking giddy.

"It's where my secret lair is located. I'm a vampire. You'll never see me during the day, only at night."

"Do vampires get married?"

"Not usually. They collect a bunch of women. You know, keep a harem. But every hundred years or so, they find one that they really fall in love with because they remind them of the one really special wife, the wife they had before they became a vampire, and that woman, they make their wife. Their vampire wife."

"Doesn't sound so great for the woman."

"It's actually a good deal. You get to fly, turn into a bat, smoke without giving a shit about your health. You can read minds."

"Flying, that would be nice, I guess." She's looking through the suicide bars on the observation deck. "From up here you can almost imagine what it would be like to fly."

I shut up for a second and look through the bars, the both of us still holding hands. It's beautiful from up there, the city with its lights and tiny, crawling cars, with no disturbing sounds getting this high up. "Yeah, flying is a perk. If you sign up with me, we can do it tonight."

"How do I know that you're on the up and up, a real vampire? Give me a demonstration."

"No problem," I say. "I'll just climb up to the top of these bars and take a swan dive off the top, a perfect arching fall, and just when you think you've made a terrible mistake, daring a lunatic to take a flying leap, I'll surprise the hell out of you and pull up just before I splatter on the concrete. I'll come soaring up about ten feet in front of you, right to that spot in front of these bars." I point directly to the space in front of her. "Then I'll do a graceful figure eight, a couple of spiraling loops, and for the grand finale, I'll come down like a freight train to this very spot with a goddamn pigeon in my mouth. Strictly a gift for my beloved." She's laughing.

"That would convince me," she says.

"Or," I say, "I could just kiss you."

"You could do that," she says. "You could do that." And I lean my face into hers, softly kissing her and knowing at that moment, that I am got good.

I work on Saturday this week and next because we're trying to finish the job by the deadline. It's a drag, but Rollie brings *yesca* and we all light up during lunch. It's like a communal meal. We hop in Brace's beat-up Chrysler, drive to the nearest Stop & Rob, and buy the vacuum-sealed sandwiches they keep in the refrigerator, along with two or three candy bars, a sixty-four-ounce drink, and a big grab bag of chips. No beer. Beer might be spotted by some snooping contractor who'll be sure to let P.J. know that his workers are getting drunk on the job. The weed is a different story. It can be smoked in the car as we drive around the block. "It's for medicinal purposes," Brace says, inhaling, "to keep you from thinking about the heat and the itch in your pants."

It's cool because we don't do a damned thing after that except talk. Amazing what people will tell you about themselves when they're high. Rollie's daughter is selling LSD at her high school, but Rollie doesn't care because she doesn't have to ask him for money. "One time, I laid one of her friends at a party her mama let her throw. Whoowee, that was the sweetest-tasting pussy I ever ate!" He laughs, remembering the night.

"Didn't it bother you that you were screwing your daughter's friend?" I ask. The guys look at me like I'm crazy.

"Hell, no," Rollie says, "my old lady don't give it up anymore hardly. She's fatter than a friar. I can hardly get it up myself, and here some young baby girl wants to throw some of her sweet little poontang over to me?"

"What if your wife would have caught you?"

"You ask a lot of silly-assed questions, Robert. First of all," he says, trying to look tough in his cheap aviator sunglasses, "I run the show around my place. I know it looks funny me letting my little girl sell LSD and shit like that, but I only let it get so far, see? And my old lady, she knows not to talk shit to me."

"Fuck off," Bob says, "I seen your old lady. She's bigger and stronger than you are. I saw her bringing you to get your check that one time. She was the one driving and she made you turn over that check as soon as you got in."

Rollie's on the spot now. "She's the only one with a check-cashing card."

"You ain't never had fifteen-year-old poontang," Brace says finally. "I know you haven't. When I was in Nam, you could fuck any sweet little whore for five dollars. Hell yes," he says, remembering it a little too clearly. "Some got hooked on heroin, some got hooked on killing zipperheads, but I got hooked on sweet young 'tang thang."

"How long were you in Vietnam?" I ask him.

"Two years."

"What was the scariest thing you ever had to do?"

"They had this thing called elephant grass, and when you jumped off a helicopter, you couldn't ever judge how high that grass was. It looked regular from up above it, but when you jumped, sometimes it was five or six feet deep. Enough to break your fucking legs. I hated jumping off that helicopter more than anything I had to do out there, and that includes standing watch."

"I hates jumping out of the back of moving vans," Phil says and everyone laughs.

"Why'd you do it?"

"I was high, man. I was sitting in there, tripping, and I just decided, I want to go outside and I did, just walked out the back door while the fucker was doing sixty miles an hour. I broke every fucking bone in my body." He isn't laughing anymore, but that makes it seem funnier for some reason and the guys laugh even harder. "Yeah, laugh, motherfuckers. Go ahead and laugh, but I'd be willing to bet that every one of you assholes is jumped out of a moving van or into elephant grass without taking the time to figure out what the fuck it was you were jumping into. You sure as hell wouldn't be here if you had."

"Look before you fucking leap," Brace says. We're supposed to be pondering that bit of wisdom when Bob breaks in. "Hey man, don't bullshit us, how much longer we got on the job?"

"Hell, I don't know," he says. "We're just shit labor here. I wouldn't count on all of us being around past the end of this job, though." Brace turns toward me. "That ought to be good for you, Robert. You can get back to school. Shouldn't you be in school, anyway?"

"School don't pay my bills," I say, trying to be tough like the others, but it doesn't come out right.

"You oughta be in school," he says again. "You're wasting your time here with us, that's for goddamned sure."

"Leave him alone," Phil says. "School never did shit for me or anybody I know except make them an asshole."

"Nah," Brace says, "that kid's making a helluva bad decision if he's trading school for shit labor. Shit labor just fucks you up. Ain't you smarter than that?" He looks at me expecting an answer, but I don't have one. "You look smarter than that. I hope to hell you're smarter than that." We spend the rest of the day waiting for five o'clock.

When I get home, Grams is so sick from her back that she can barely move. I don't even ask this time. I call the hospital. They send the EMS. Grams can hardly speak except to moan once in a while when the technicians roll her onto a gurney. They tell me that she's going to the Baptist hospital and they take off. I find my pops's home phone and call, leaving him a message with his girlfriend. All I can think is, Motherfucker, motherfucker, motherfucker. What now?

CHAPTER 15

Pops doesn't call back. I guess he's still kicking it in California, getting laid, having a helluva time. It better be a hell of a time. He's not around when the doctor comes out and gives me a fishy look, looking to see if there's an "adult" to talk to.

"I'm her only relative," I say, getting pissed off with this white dude who doesn't give much of a shit in the first place. Grams doesn't have insurance and these fucking sharks don't care about anyone if they aren't getting paid. "It says here that she has a son. A forty-two-year-old son." He says it like I was going to try and slip one past him. Why I'd want to take responsibility for all of this is a mystery. "He's not around. I'm her grandson. I take care of her." He gives me the once-over taking in my shark teeth and old scars. After a second though, he lays down a kinder, gentler routine. "Well, Mr. Lomos. Your grandmother is in a lot of pain. We gave her something for that. She told us that it was her back, but after some preliminary tests, including X rays, we don't think that it's a back problem. How long has she been complaining about pain?"

My stomach is going off like a fire alarm, warning me with a flood of acid that something has gone really wrong here. "A long time," I say. "More than two years. When she didn't go to work the other day, I knew that she was really hurting. I tried to get her to come in, but she wouldn't."

The doctor nods his head sympathetically. "Wouldn't really have mattered. What's your name, son?"

"Robert," I say.

"Robert. It wouldn't have mattered. If it's what it looks like on the X rays, she would have needed to come in months ago. There's nothing conclusive for me to tell you right now. Best thing is for you to—"

"Look, Doctor, I'm not going anywhere right now. I want to know what you think it is. Is it her appendix? Did it burst? Has she got a hernia? What is it?" Deep down inside I know what it is, but I want to give this sucker a chance to prove my stomach wrong, that it's just a chickenshit worry-wart. "Tell me, Doctor."

The guy hems and haws for a couple of more minutes, but finally he gives it to me. "It looks like she has a growth in her liver. It looks like cancer. But," he rushes in, "there's a chance that the tumor is benign."

"What's that mean?" I ask, trying to keep myself steady. "That mean that she isn't going to die?"

This guy isn't in the hope business. "Look, we can't tell anything until we get in there. We're going to have to operate and we won't know how serious it is until we do a biopsy of the tissue."

"Is my grams going to die?" I sound frantic, like a kid.

"Son, go home and get some sleep. We're going to operate tomorrow afternoon and we won't know for a few days."

I'm about to tell him that I'm not his fucking son, that I'm nobody's fucking son, when it registers like a thunderstorm that my grams is going to die. She's going to die. My grams, the only person I got that gives a good goddamn about me, is going to die. I stop listening as my stomach fills with bile and without bothering to say excuse me, I head for a bathroom. Just as I hit the stall, it comes pouring out and I puke all over the shiny, white porcelain, little red threads and clearish acid that I can't flush away quickly enough. I hit that fucking toilet handle four or five times, trying to clean up my mess, erase it. I sit there and moan, feeling like I just got a face full of mace, my eyes tearing up from the strain of throwing up.

She's always talked about her death. I guess all old people do. You can't get old without starting to think about dying. I'm only gonna be seventeen and I think about it all the time. But Grams, she's been talking about it since I can remember. Always warning me about what relatives do when people die. She used to tell me, "When I die, you make sure to come over and get everything you want before I'm even in the ground. The first thing people do when somebody dies is come over and steal everything from them. *Especially* relatives. They're the worst. So you come here and you get it all or there won't be nothing when you finally get the courage to come over." It used to bug me at first, but then I got used to it. Whenever we drove past San Fernando Cemetery, she'd point it out. "You see all those flowers? That's respect. That's how the living show the dead that they remember them. You going to leave your gramma's grave empty and all alone?" I always told her that I'd visit, but I never thought I'd actually have to do it.

She's so strong, but all that death talk is where she's always kept her vulnerability. That was just supposed to be a mental trick, though, a way of putting all the bullshit she's had to deal with in a coffin in the ground somewhere, which she can visit when things get tough. She wasn't supposed to go ahead and die! She's always seemed unkillable, undie-able to me, secure in her own immortality almost. How do you kill a tank? Not that she's big. She's actually compact, though she gives off this aura of being armored. But those little fucking cancer cells found a way in where other things, other things like me and my pops and my moms and having to work like a goddamned mule, never did.

"I don't want no silly, fancy funeral. We're not rich people. I want a cheap wooden one. When the time comes, they're going to bury me with your grandfather over there in the military *campo*. There won't be no need to be spending money. That'd be a sin. All I want is a simple burial. A few songs, and to make sure that you ain't going to forget to come visit me." What a sucker I am for not seeing that God would pull the last rug I had to stand on right out from under me and leave me flat on my ass.

When I get home, I can't manage to go to sleep. I'm supposed to go to work, and I figure that Grams would get mad if I don't go, so I take a Demerol to knock out. I clock in for a couple of hours the next morning, till I figure that Grams will be up. I make it over to the hospital by ten A.M. Grams is awake, sort of. They've given her all kinds of pain medication and she's barely coherent. "I'm going to give you your dollar," she keeps saying. She thinks that I'm still a little kid and that she needs to give me my allowance.

"It's going to be alright," is the only thing I can think to say. It's a weak thing to come out with. I feel like I should be praying for her, something more serious, but I can't think of how to do it, even. I don't think God's listening anyway, not by a longshot. I run it around in my head to call my uncle, but I don't want him coming around here right now. I don't want any relatives here. I know once they come, everything will turn out in the worst possible way. I want them to stay the fuck away. I don't want them wringing their hands here, trying to comfort me by giving me phony hugs and pats on the back. Grams belongs to me, not to them, and

Grams doesn't care much for them anyway. They never really come around unless they need something. I stay with her till a couple of nurses come to take her away. "I'm going to be right here," I say to her, but Grams is freaking out a little. She's drugged up, and she doesn't really know what's going on.

"We need a next of kin," another nurse is saying to me; meanwhile I'm trying to keep Grams from scampering off the goddamn gurney. I don't want either of those nurses to touch her. "It's going to be alright, Grams," I say even though my stomach is telling me that it isn't going to be alright, ever. "Don't worry, Mr. Lomos. Let them take her away. We're going to get her all better." She's talking to me like I'm four years old. "Look, lady," I say, "let's cut this. What are they going to do to her?"

The nurse keeps up the sympathetic act. "The doctor is going to cut out the tumor and then we're going to run tests on it. But right now, I need you to sign some forms and to answer a few questions." I do what she wants and finally go to the waiting room with a lot of other people who look just as miserable and hopeless as I feel. I'm so fucking nervous that I keep getting up feeling like I gotta throw up. Maybe like I *owe* it to Grams to throw up, feel sick, to feel a shitload of pain. I didn't bring my ulcer medicine. Funny, I'm usually stocked like a walking hospital, but today, no pills.

Next to me there's this older couple, maybe in their fifties, and the man is hugging his wife and she keeps blowing her nose. The guy, a poor-looking Mexican who probably does day labor because his hands are thick and calloused, keeps telling her, "God won't let him die. You'll see." It's more than I can take right now, so I head off. I go outside and have a cigarette.

I never realized how fucked up it is to be stuck in a hospital like this. I've been in plenty of them, what from the snake bite and my ulcer and all the other crazy shit that's happened to me. But I've always been the patient, never the person having to wait and worry.

Mental torture, mental pain, that's the real hurt. I can see that now. Physical pain you can locate, and people usually treat you nice because they feel sorry for you and they're getting paid to look after you. But mental pain? Who can locate that? What cure is there for that? What about when no one gives a shit? Where do you go where someone'll understand and be able to actually help you? The best someone can do is say, "Well, Mr. Lomos, we've got it narrowed down to your heart." Well, thanks a whole helluva lot for that one, Doctor. I knew it was my heart all along, but why does it hurt everywhere and why can't I get a moment's goddamned rest?

Everyone I know is suffering something awful, some deep pulsating pain that has completely fucked up their ability to navigate through life. My moms is a wreck; me, I'm a lost son of a bitch; poor Antony, he'll probably wind up the same way as me. Now Grams? This is too much now. I want to tell God that I give up.

Then I want to find the fucker who runs the show down here, burst into his office, grab him by his fucking power tie and tell him, Look, you *win*. I give up with this whole thing, this whole *endeavor*. Okay? I'm serious here, pal. I give up. I'm gonna be good, I'm gonna follow the rules, be kind, whatever laundry list of things I need to do. I'm just gonna be here, chilling, not bothering anyone, not asking anyone for shit. So if I don't make any noise, can you just go on to someone else? I realize I'm being melodramatic, but I don't give a fuck because it seems like that's the only answer sometimes. Only I know I can't do that, the not-give-a-fuck thing. I've tried. So I throw my half-smoked cigarette against the hospital wall like it's some grand act of defiance, and I go back to the waiting room with all the other tortured.

When I get in there, the older couple has gone. I'm afraid to ask where they went because it's probably some really bad news. I'm glad I missed out on that scene. After a while—just over an hour because I've watched back-to-back episodes of that lame-assed

Leave It to Beaver—the doctor comes in. I'm so drained all of a sudden that I can't stand up. I can tell just by his face that it's all bad news.

"Robert Lomos?" he says. I'm the only guy in the room. "Your grandmother came through the operation fairly well. We took out the tumor and we've sent it for a biopsy, but I have to be honest with you. It looks malignant."

Malignant. That word. I've never thought about it much, if ever. But now, it's the ugliest word I've ever heard. It means death and being alone and saying good-bye to my grams. I can't do it. I *can't.* I *can't.* I *can't.* The phrase keeps floating through my head, bumping into *malignant*, and I know, my stomach knows, that somehow *I can't* is not going to be enough. I'm going to *have to.*

The doctor goes on, but I'm hardly listening. Something about waiting but it looking bad. "Can I see her?" I ask. He hesitates a second. "You can, but you might want to wait till tomorrow. She's just coming out of the anesthesia, and she's going to be discombobulated and nauseous."

"I don't care. I want to see her." He nods and tells a nurse that it's alright. She walks me to a room, my grams's hospital room. There's a nurse in there with her. Grams is moaning and gurgling like she has to vomit. "It's okay, Grams," I say, but it doesn't do any good. She can't really hear what I'm saying. So I just sit there and stroke her hair, trying to do what I can to calm her down.

I sit there for a long time. She keeps falling asleep and then waking up startled, like she's heard some loud noise. But as the night goes on, she seems to get better at recognizing that I'm there. After midnight sometime, she says "Robert," and goes to grab my hand not realizing that they've tied her down so that she won't pull out the IV. I hold her hand. It's strange what you do and what you don't do and when you realize what you haven't done in a long time. Holding my grams's hand is something I haven't done since I was a little kid. It's been so long that I'd forgotten what her hand even feels like. It seems so thin and delicate, like the skin of an onion, so that I'm afraid that I'll tear her hand if I press too hard. I feel sad because I never even missed it, that is, holding her hand. Being alive, it seems to me, is about walking around forgetting everything, forgetting even that you're alive. Forgetting that holding the hand of someone you really love, is something you should be conscious about when you do it. Obviously you can't go around holding everybody's hand all the time, but when you do, you should really think about it. Recognize it, you know?

I don't want to go off on one of those "love your life" things like some fucking New Ager might, nodding with a silly, distant, *empathetic* grin. I'm talking about fucking losing things around you left and right and not even knowing how important they are, like you're some kind of kid with too many toys and you don't give a shit when one breaks or gets lost because you think you have so many of them. I'm talking about being a spoiled brat. It makes me want to hate myself, and it makes me so goddamned confused because my plans haven't amounted to shit and I've been all over the place thinking that I'd get what I needed. Only I've been going in circles around what I already had, trying to find what I'd lost. "Is it my fault?" my stomach nudges me. "Haven't I tried to tell you?" Grams moans again and I come back to her. For a second I'm mad at her for making me come back, for making me feel so bad, for making me focus all my energy and thoughts on her, and for making me feel guilty that my mind strayed off of her and on to myself.

Then I get this idea. If Grams dies, the disaster will be complete and her dying will be my way of showing the world how fucked up it is for doing so many things to me. It'll be my way of shouting at everyone that I hate them and this goddamned life. In a sick way, it has me almost *wishing* for her death the same way a kid hopes he'll die after he gets belted so that his mom will get hers. Only I don't know who'd get theirs if Grams dies. Only me, really.

Grams drops back to sleep and I go on sitting there in the dark trying to sleep but not being able to because I'm so angry with everything.

I don't tell any of the guys at work what's going on. I don't want to talk about it with them and I don't want them giving me any of their sympathy. I stay quiet most of the day. But they don't notice. They've got their own problems, and it's so hot that nobody's much in the mood to flap their gums anyway. I get off, go home, and try my pops's house again. This time I'm a lot more hardcore with his girlfriend. "You tell him that his mom is in the hospital and that she might be dying and that if he gives a damn, he better get down here." I hang up before the bitch can even get a word off. I try to eat, but my stomach won't let me. While I'm taking a nap, the phone rings. I wake up and the house is dark and I'm confused for a minute because I don't feel like it should be nighttime already. But the phone keeps on ringing and I stumble to pick it up expecting that it's going to be my pops. "Hullo," I say like I'm drowning.

"Robert?" a girl's voice says. It's Amelia.

"Yeah, it's me," I say, trying to wake myself up, but it's hard because I'm so groggy. I feel like I just got kicked in the head.

"It's Amelia, from the other night?" She thinks I don't remember.

"Hi," I say. "Yeah. Of course."

"Should I try you some other time? You sound like you were sleeping."

"Yeah, I mean no. I needed to get up. I have to go to the hospital." And there it is. I've already started confessing my problems to other people. I was going to keep my mouth shut, but hearing Amelia's voice makes me feel like telling her even though I don't really know her.

"The hospital? Are you sick?"

"Yeah," I say, "but it's not for me. My grams is there. She's the one who's sick."

"Oh no. Really sick?"

"Yeah."

"Are you okay?" she asks. She says it so sweetly that it makes me feel worse. Sympathy will do that to you. It gives you an in to your own pain. I don't want that.

"Sure," I say. "I'm okay. I just gotta go over there and you know, keep her company."

"Do you want company?" I didn't expect that one. She makes me feel how alone I am and she makes me realize how much I really *do* want company.

"No," I say. "I'm fine. I just gotta go do this thing." She's trying to be *nice*, but goddammit, I don't want that. I can't start accepting that kind of sympathy. I gotta get to a mirror, make The Face, defend myself from all the scab-poking that motherfuckers are going to unleash. All for their own satisfaction, bastards, so that they can then disappear into their own lives as soon as they can do it without looking like— She interrupts my thought.

"Okay," she says. She actually sounds disappointed. For a second, despite myself, it makes me feel a little better.

"Thanks," I say. "Listen, I'll give you a call. Maybe we can hook up somewhere later?"

"Sure," she says. "Only, I can't be out late. My stepfather . . ." and *she* trails off.

"No problem," I say. "But I have to go right now. I'll call you early." We hang up. Just before I head out the door, the phone rings. This time it is my pops.

"Robert," he says. He actually sounds scared. "Robert," he says again when I don't answer right away. I'm not trying to be mysterious or a bastard, I just can't talk because if I do, I'm afraid I'm gonna go off like a little scared kid, and I'm not going to let myself do that. It'd be too easy right now and I'm not giving him the satisfaction of playing Daddy for me.

"Yeah," I say quick and strong. "Yeah, it's me. Grams is in the hospital. I think you better get here as soon as you can. The doctors keep telling me it's bad."

"What's wrong? You're not giving me any real information. What's happened?" He sounds nervous. I've never heard him like this before. He's the one that sounds like a kid, but in a way, he *is* the kid, because Grams is his mom.

"She's got cancer. They say it's probably malignant." That word again. My pops doesn't say anything for a minute until finally I hear him say, "Oh God," just two words leaving his mouth like a last breath.

"Are you still in California?" I ask him. He doesn't answer my question. Instead, he gathers himself together. He's not going to be punked out by his punk kid. "I'll be there tomorrow. Delia will bring me to the hospital." Delia's his girlfriend. "Which hospital is it?"

"The Baptist," I say. He hangs up without even asking how I'm doing, but I don't let it bother me. Much.

"Can I please speak with Amelia?" Her pops has answered the phone. I didn't intend to call but I couldn't get my mind off that girl and her limp and how she was able to make me feel better. In the middle of all of this shit, I keep remembering her fingers and how they felt in my hand. Her pops is going to be a prick though. "No you can't," he says. It's a strange thing to say right off the bat. I mean, he doesn't know me. I've never really been out with his daughter. He doesn't really have a reason to dislike me yet. Although I could understand if in the future he decides I'm just a little, nowhere *chuco*. But now? That I don't get. It takes me a second to come up with a response because he's not saying anything and he's not hanging up. He's just waiting, listening, probably *thrilled* by my discomfort. Then I remember, the bastard used to be a fucking cop. Finally I say, "Is she there?"

"Yes," he says, leaving it at that. Again, there's silence, ex-cop silence. Heavy, almost menacing.

"Can I speak with her for just a second?"

"No, you can't." And then the bastard hangs up on me. Now I'm puzzled and pissed. I'm waiting around for my pops to come barging in to play Daddy dearest and now this other prick has just made me feel like a snot-nosed punk, a snaggle-toothed waste case. As I'm steaming about the balls on that guy, the phone rings. It's Amelia and she's crying. "That asshole," she says. "Come get me, please. I'll meet you around the corner."

"I'll be there in ten minutes," I say, and as soon as I put the phone down, I'm out the door. I drive to her house. It's a nice house in a "good" neighborhood. That means the guy keeps the yard looking neat and shit, and that it isn't on the westside.

Amelia is waiting where she said she'd be. It's dark and she comes bounding out of the shadow waving her arms so that I'll see her. She doesn't run too well and she's out of breath having come only about thirty feet or so.

"I'm sorry about my stepdad," she says a little breathless. "He's an asshole."

"I can relate."

"How's your grandmother?" she asks right away. "Is she okay?"

"Not really. I think she's going to die." It's the first time I've admitted that out loud. I've been thinking that for the last two days, but I haven't said it. Mostly because I've had no one to say it to.

"I'm sorry," she says.

"You got nothing to be sorry about," I say. "You didn't give her cancer."

"Cancer?"

"Yeah, malignant." She doesn't say anything. She reaches for my hand instead. "You want to go to my house?" I ask her. "No one's there." I regret saying that as soon as I've said it because it sounds like I want to take advantage of Grams being in the hospital so as to fuck her. She doesn't take it that way, though. "Sure," she says instead. When we get there, I take her inside. She sits down in the living room and I get her something to drink. "All I have is orange juice," I say. But she doesn't mind.

I sit down across from her. She's on the couch and I'm on Grams's chair. The place is real quiet. I'm used to having the TV on for noise. I get up and turn on the big metal fan. It makes me feel like Grams is home. "Is that your grandmother?" Amelia asks. She's pointing at a picture of Grams when she was young. It's a big black-and-white portrait, her straight, then-black hair pulled back and tied loosely behind her head. "Yeah," I say. "She got that done when she was just about nineteen. She was performing in a *carpa* in those days."

"What's that?"

"It was a kind of traveling circus for poor Mexicans. She used to do some sort of acrobatics. No shit."

"Really. That sounds so different."

"Well, she did other things, too. I mean, she worked as a cotton-picker, and ever since I've known her, she's cleaned houses. She's tough."

"You love her a lot, don't you?" She sounds very sad for me. For some reason, it both thrills me and bothers me.

"Let's not even talk about it."

"Okay."

"Why does your dad hate me?"

"He's my stepdad. He's not my dad. He drinks."

"Was he drunk when I called?"

"No. Not yet. On his way."

"Is he a mean drunk?"

"He's a mean everything." She goes on to tell me how he's always waking up her and her little brother at night when he comes in fucked up, screaming and cursing. She tells me that last week he pushed her little brother against the wall, screaming right in his face because he said the kid left his shoes in the living room. Motherfucker.

"Is your real pops around?" I ask. Somebody should look after her.

"He lives in Chicago," she says. "I haven't talked to him since I was in the third grade." She's saying all of this like it doesn't really matter, like it doesn't really affect her anymore. Like she's gotten used to it.

"You want something to eat?" I say to change the subject. "I can make you something. A grilled cheese? If you're really hungry, I can make you French onion soup. Ever eaten that before?" She shakes her head. "I learned how to make it in French class. I took French when I was a freshman. I flunked it. Didn't learn a damned word except how to count to ten. But our teacher, Monsieur Borden, he was a nice guy and he tried to make the class interesting. It wasn't his fault that I didn't want to learn. But one of the things he did was have Culture Day. He'd bring in these terrible French movies. You ever watched a French movie?" Amelia shakes her head again. "Always, *always*, gotta be some kid discovering his penis for the first time in those flicks. Also, he'd give out recipes and everyone had to make something to bring to class and we'd eat all kinds of French things. He gave me the onion soup recipe. It's really easy to make, but it's good. Really good. You want me to make you some?"

She smiles at me. "Well, after a buildup like that, how can I refuse?"

"It's good. Trust me." We go into the kitchen and I open up a can of Campbell's onion soup. While I'm heating it up, I tear some french bread into two bowls and then shred some mozzarella cheese on top. Lots of it. When the soup is steaming, I pour it on top of the bread. "Taste that and tell me if it isn't good."

She gives it a taste. "That's good," she says. She tries to mean it, but I can tell she doesn't really like it all that much. She's cool, though, and she eats the whole thing. The two of us sit there at Grams's table and eat and talk. I feel almost happy for a while. I don't make any moves at all. I don't really feel like messing around anyway. It's enough to just have her company.

"Can I ask you something?" she says.

"Sure."

"What happened to your teeth? I mean, they don't look bad. But it looks like whatever happened must've hurt. Did you get in an accident?" I don't feel like going into my thuggish past.

"I told you I'm a vampire," I say jokingly. "I can only come out at night. Remember? You're my next victim." She smiles. She seems to get a kick out of me. She reaches over and puts her hand on my head and strokes my hair really quick. "You couldn't hurt anybody. You're about the farthest thing from a vampire I can think of." Ordinarily, I might get defensive about that kind of observation, but Amelia doesn't make me feel like I gotta prove shit.

"You want to meet her?" I say all of the sudden.

"Your grandmother?"

"Yeah. I want you to meet her." I do, too. It seems important. "I mean, I'd have to tell her about it first. She might not want to be seen in the hospital. My grams is proud. But if she wants to, do you?"

"Yes," she says. "That'd be nice." She reaches for my hand again. My fucking heart hurts when our hands touch. Crazy. But I don't mind this pain. It feels good and it drives the other one, the one that burns my stomach and keeps me up at night, out of sight for a while. At least until I drop her off around the corner from her house and I have to drive home to the house that now seems a lot darker and lonelier.

My pops comes over without warning the next morning just before I head off for work. I hear him pull into the driveway. He's got his girlfriend in the car waiting. "I went to see your grandmother last night. I'm just checking up on the house and how you're doing."

"I'm doing alright. How long are you going to stay?"

"I'm due back for some recording work next week, but I'm going to be gone as little as possible." It strikes me that my pops is hurting, too. I don't really want to admit it, but it's true. I can hear it in his voice. "You going to go see her later?"

"Yeah," I say. "As soon as I get out of work."

"She's not going to get well," he says all of the sudden. "You know that?"

I don't say anything.

"Robert?" he says like it's a question. "Do you know that?"

"Yeah," I say finally. I say it sharplike, as in, I don't want to talk about it with you, get it?

"She's going to come home. She wants to be here, not in a hospital. Are you going to be able to handle that?" Him asking *me* that question. "I can handle it," I say. "When?"

"Soon. Probably tomorrow or the day after."

"How long?"

"Not too long." He's about to cry and I'm embarrassed because I've never seen this from my pops before. He's always been so cool, so self-contained and smooth in front of me. The original nothing-gets-me-flustered-Mexican-macho man. But the words sink in. *Not too long*. And then there's that awful word again, *malignant*. It describes everything about this fucked-up universe. It's the perfect, most awful fucking word.

"I gotta go to work," I say.

"Well, I'll see you tonight at the hospital." I leave my pops in the house and head for my car. I don't bother to wave at his girlfriend, who's busy giving me a scowl because I hung up on her ass the last time I called looking for him. That almost cheers me up.

Nacho's waiting around for me when I get home from work. "Hey, man," he says. "When did you get back from Califas?"

I've been avoiding him for some reason. No, I know the reason. Nacho connects me back to Sunnydale and school, and also to the drugs and fighting, and I've been trying to be good, or at least better. But is anyone even watching? I guess I've decided that there isn't.

To tell the truth, I'm happy to see him. "Yeah, man. Got back a few weeks ago. When'd you get that bike?" He's on an old Nighthawk motorcycle. It's a little beat up, but it still looks sharp.

"Got it a couple of months ago. Had to do something with my money. Wanna ride?" he asks me. "Don't worry, man, no one's gonna think you're gay." He has a sly look on his face, which I take to be a dare. He only has one helmet and he puts that on himself. "I gotta wear it so I can see. I don't want bugs getting in my eyes," he says explaining. I sit behind him, and not wanting to look too much like a punk, I hold on to the little chrome rail designed to keep the rider's ass from sliding off the seat. He guns the motorcy-cle onto the street, deafening sound falling around me, vibrations running up my spine. The motorcycle doesn't have a muffler and it sounds like all hell crashing down. At first I think he's trying to show off, speeding around the neighborhood, taking hairpin turns, popping the gears to make the bike jerk. It's enough to make me start breathing all deep and everything. But then he turns his head a little and yells, "I'm gonna take you on this back road so we can open her up a little."

"I don't have a lot of time," I yell back, "I gotta go to the hospital," but I give up because either he can't hear me or he's pretending he can't hear me. Either way, I'm going on this trip with him. We ride out to this jerkwater road, half unpaved and bumpy, and then he opens the throttle. The bike keeps picking up speed and getting louder and louder until all I'm conscious of is the vibration and the deafening sound. The bastard has picked up so much speed that my eyelids are turning inside out. My chest feels like it's collapsing with a paralyzing fear that I'm gonna end up with a split head and an ass full of asphalt. Although I can't read the speedometer, he must be cranking at over one hundred miles an hour on this roadkill-littered back road. I got a mouthful of grit, I can't focus my eyes, and all I can think is that if this fucker hits one bump or crevice, it's *all* over. Every bit of it. The thing is that this fear, this adrenaline-pumping craze, makes me realize that I do not want to die. All of my sorrow and self-pity can't hold a candle to the power of my survival instinct. I don't want to go. Not fucking *ever*.

My legs are shaking when I get off the motorcycle. Nacho gives me an "everything's cool" look and shuts the thing down. "That thing moves, huh?" he says, barely containing his pride in scaring the dogshit out of me. "Yeah," I say. "It moves."

"Where's your grams? You got time to smoke one?" He's pulling out all the stops, God bless him.

"She's in the hospital," I tell him.

"Serious?"

"Yeah. Malignant."

"Fuck that shit, man. That sucks. Are you alright?"

"Yeah. I gotta go see her."

"Maybe you *should* smoke one then. If I had to deal with that, I'd be high all the time."

"You are high all the time."

"Yeah, but I'd be high *all* the time." The thing is that I've got my own weed. And I have been wanting to smoke it to distract me, but I've been thinking that I gotta stay straight. *Take it straight*, without any painkillers. Fuck my stomach, my grams is dying—that sort of thing. I've even felt guilty about Amelia because in a way, she lessens the pain, even for a while. Maybe if God's watching, if I can show that I'm willing to take my punishment straight, no excuses, no asking for mercy, then He won't take my punishment out on Grams. I tell Nacho this.

"Man, Robert. You're crazy. God ain't killing your grandmother. Cancer is."

"What's the difference?"

"There's a big difference. One way, it's God, the other way, it's just dumb, blind chance. The second way, you got nothing to do with it. Smoking a j ain't going to mean shit either way."

"Well, I'd almost rather it be God that's killing her. That way maybe He'll change His mind."

"God doesn't change His mind."

"How do you know that?

"Man, didn't they teach you anything up there at Sunnydale? If I've learned anything from Sister Mac, it's that. Anyway, God's just another word for 'chance' as far as I'm concerned. You better face that one."

He makes sense and we sit on the back porch and smoke one. There's always a moment, maybe the best moment when you smoke marijuana, that you first notice you're high. You're passing the joint, chitchatting, when *whooosh*, you feel the top of your head lift clear off and whoever you're smoking with suddenly seems to be chattering in another language. You have to re-orient your senses just to start listening again. It's the most pleasant feeling, like everything around you that just a second ago seemed normal, so normal that you've stopped noticing it, now seems different, foreign, worthy of new contemplation. That's when strange ideas begin to float through your mind and things, everyday normal things, take on a new significance. They seem to contain a hidden, secret meaning within them. Not just the meaning that people assign to them, but meaning that can't really be spoken. But you try anyway, and that's why stoners always sound so banal and stupid to people who aren't high.

"You know what I've started to do every morning?" I say. Nacho doesn't say anything. He's lost.

"Nacho," I say louder.

"Huh?" Nacho says.

"What I'm doing every morning?"

"What?" He's confused. He doesn't want to listen to my idea right now. He's got his own.

"Do you know what I do every morning now?"

"No, what?" He's back on the porch.

"I make my bed."

"Why?"

"It's the only thing I can do lately that makes me feel like I got something under control."

"Damn."

"Yeah. I get up and stare at the bed, all unmade, the sheets all crumpled, always, always at least one of the pillows thrown on the floor. I get this urge to make it all right. It makes me feel good to smooth out the sheets, spread out the comforter, make it even on each side. Then I plump up the pillows. I give them a little smack on their pillow-asses just to let 'em know it's all good."

"Gives you a sense of order."

"Yeah," I say. "That's it. Order."

"Gives you a sense of accomplishment."

"Yeah. No matter what else happens to me during the day, I can remember that at least I made my bed. It's waiting for me nice and neat."

"You're wrecked, man. You sound like one of those goddamn housewives, the ones that are all neurotic about stains and shit," he says. He thinks it's funny. I guess it is. "You need to smoke some more of this shit and stop thinking about everything so much."

"Your grandmother is sick," my pops says to me. "She's coming home, but she's not going to be the same. She's going to need your help."

"Where are you going to be?"

"I'm going to be around, but not always. I have to be back and forth between California. Your grandmother's cousin, Tonia, is coming to stay with her from Fredricksberg. You be a help to her." He's saying it serious. If it weren't so pathetic, it'd be funny. Him telling me to be a *help*? He doesn't have the first idea about help. He doesn't have the first idea about what Grams needs and he doesn't have the first idea about who I am. I hope he does go back to California and the sooner the fucking better. About the only thing *he's* good at is helping chicks in and out of the sack, and helping my moms go off the deep end. Fuck'im. I don't need anyone to tell me to help my grams.

She comes home that afternoon. She's been gone more than a week. She seems smaller in that house, like the hospital swallowed a big part of her. They didn't just take out a part of her liver, they took out her strength. Pops and me put Grams on a wheelchair and we roll her inside to her bedroom. It's tough moving her to the bed because she's got no power and she feels delicate, like any sharp or unexpected movement will break her. "You be careful there, boy," she says, but I'm not sure if she's talking to me or Pops. "You trying to kill me before the cancer?" She's *repelando*. A kind of funny complaining that old Mexican women do. It can get on your nerves, but to hear Grams doing it now, with all this, it makes me feel good, like even though she's dying, she's still Grams. I want her to be Grams until the end.

I saw a cousin die when I was a little kid. At the end, she wasn't herself anymore. She seemed more like a rag doll that people were using to mourn around. She just lay there and moaned and looked scared or confused, until finally she didn't do anything but become this thing that tubes ran in and out of. It was horrible.

That night, I hear Tonia whispering and Grams moaning quietly and then her breathing heavily. I get up so drowsy I bump into the fucking doorsill of my bedroom. "Can I help?" I ask, standing at the entrance. "Your grandma, she can't get up," Tonia says. She's practically an old woman herself, but she's nice. She hardly talks at all. My grams is next to the bed. She's slipped off and she can't raise herself up. Her white cotton nightdress is pale in the dark and rumpled around her legs. I don't turn on the light because I don't want her to be embarrassed. I have to go very slow because she's so fragile and everywhere I try to get a hold of her makes her cry. It takes more than an hour, the minutes dragging slowly, the moonlight making everything glow so that it almost seems like a bad dream. One of those where you're trying to do something, like run or lift an object, but your muscles won't work right so that any action seems hopeless and it frustrates you all the more. The whole time I'm trying to get her back on the bed, the horrible idea that I won't be able to keeps running through my head. I've never imagined that my grams would be this helpless. I guess she never imagined it either.

The next morning, I get up to take a shower. Just before I walk into the bathroom, I pass by Grams's door. Looking in her room, I can see her sitting down on her wooden rocker that I moved in there. Her long silver hair is hanging below her shoulders, not in its usual bun. I didn't know her hair was so long. "Robert," she calls to me. "Thank you." She says it quietly, not really like her at all. She is losing at something she never expected to lose at. "I don't mean to be so much trouble."

"You're no trouble," I say.

"I'm just trouble now. Look at my hair. I can't even comb it anymore." She starts to cry in front of me for the first time ever.

"You're no trouble," I keep on repeating because I don't know what else to say. Then, "I'm glad you're here." I walk in and put my arm around her. I hug her to comfort her. I want to *be a comfort* to her. As I sit there holding her frailty, I want to try to reach her strength because I know it's in there, that strength I've always depended on. But I've got to be strong now. Because I must be the comfort.

Comfort/Malignant. Those words clash. And for a split second, it makes sense to me. I gotta choose, *everybody's* got to choose what force they're going to give in to. What they themselves are going to be. It's an honest-to-God revelation.

Grams is a woman, and I've never seen her that way. She's a woman who still cares about her hair and who feels herself edging toward death. Facing it. Actually *facing* death. I feel her fear and her despair, and though I can't do anything about it, I sit there holding her, somehow trying to let her know that I'll be there as she has to do this awful, goddamned thing. When I come home from work that night, Grams is already asleep. Tonia is sitting talking with another relative, a cousin I hardly ever see. She looks at me and says, "Your grandmother kept telling everyone who came to see her today that you told her how she was no trouble and how much you wanted her here. You made her very happy."

The next morning, Saturday, I ask Grams if she'd like to meet Amelia. She says it's okay. I have to pick up Amelia at the mall because her miserable stepdad won't let her come over here. Grams is feeling really bad, so the visit is short. Amelia brings her some flowers, just a few pink carnations. Grams likes them and she tells her to be careful about me. "You have to watch him." But then she looks at me and says, "No, he's a good boy. A good boy." Amelia leaves. Her friend comes to pick her up. Grams wants to talk to me. "You like her a lot?"

I say, "Yeah, I guess I do."

"If you really like her, you be good to her, hear? I know a good spirit when I see one. She's got that walk. I know what that walk means. She's suffered. *Hay suffrido mucho esa muchacha.* Don't you add to it." I nod and neither of us says anything for a while. "Take one of these oranges," Grams says pointing to a basket of fruit my great-uncle dropped off for her. I take one and start to peel it. I peel oranges really well. One long strip, all the way around. I pride myself on it. Grams watches me. "Give me a piece." I hold it out for her and she takes it, her hands shaky. "I'm going be gone soon," she says. "You know that?" I put the orange down. "You know that, Robert?" She wants me to answer. I'm hoping I can keep her from giving me her deathbed speech through a combination of ignoring the question and feeding her more orange slices. I'm not ready for it.

"Answer me, Robert. You know that?" I nod my head.

"You've had a hard life," she says. "Too hard. You young in years, old in pain. That's why I love you the more. You know pain. We've both of us known lots of pain. You don't like pain?" It's a strange question, but I can tell she wants me to answer it.

"No," I say. "I'm sick of it."

She looks at me long and hard. "You better not get sick of it. It's going to be around you all your life. You better learn to appreciate the pain more than the joy. We're all born to pain. There ain't no way to 'scape it. Only way to 'scape it is to die. Nobody wants to die. I ain't never met anybody worth a damn that didn't suffer lots of pain in their lives. You know that?"

I don't say anything.

"My momma, she died when I was eight years old. I watch her die from pneumonia. I remember her telling me something, though; she say, 'Rosita, *nunca déjate de las cosas duras. Es la noche mas oscura que nos dice las cosas mas importantes.*' You know what that means?" My Spanish isn't that great and I shake my head. "It means 'Never keep yourself from those things that appear hard. It's the darkest night that shows us the most important things.' *Las cosas profunda.* What's that mean? I don't know the English for that."

"The most profound things," I say.

"*Sí.* You know what I knew when you was born?" I shake my head. "You was chosen. *Chosen.* Like King David." She's looking me straight in the eye, my grams, my old grams who never blinks when something's got to be said. I see her there, all there, for this minute. She is using all her strength to tell me something important. I understand the importance of it, for once, the importance of a moment that is happening now. I listen. "You ain't suffered all this misery, all this pain, for nothing. You going to use it, boy. You going to *use* it. You gotta make sure you use it for good, somewhere for someone. That cancer that's in my bones, in my organs, that ain't nothing compared to pain kept inside your heart. Ain't nobody can keep that kind of pain without it coming out. You either going to use it to kill yourself slow, and to give it to others that come after you, or you going to use it to understand other people's pain. *Lágrimas.* That makes you human. That makes you part of God. That's the spirit I'm talking about. *El espíritu santo.* You know what that is? The Great Comforter. Don't you wait for no sign from God, boy. Don't you wait for Him to come down and cure you or me or your neighbor. We here to do God's work. You know how?" She doesn't wait for me to answer. "Your dark night, your pain, is everyone's dark night, everyone's pain. You make it less. That's what you do. If you do that, you make something new. You make love. You'll be wiser than Solomon if you know that, stronger than David, closer to God than you ever imagined. Don't you doubt God. Don't spend your life blaming Him, or worrying yourself that He hasn't done anything. You do it, and you'll be answering that call like King David did. You hear?" She wants an answer, requires one, now.

"I will." I don't know what else to say.

Grams stays at the house for only about two more weeks. She gets worse and worse till the visiting nurse tells me and my pops that she's got to go back to the hospital. Grams can hardly talk now because they're giving her so many painkillers. But I know that she doesn't want to go back there. It's not that I can see the fear in her eyes, or some bullshit like that. I just know she wouldn't want to be there. But there's nothing I can do. My pops and the doctor decide to check her in again.

I go to see her as often as I can, but not enough really. Every time I go, she seems to be worse than the last time. After a couple of weeks and another unsuccessful operation, they put her on a morphine drip so that all she does is mumble or talk about things that don't seem to make any sense. She does a lot of apologizing, saying she's sorry about this or that, things that she's got no reason to regret, but that with the drugs and the pain seem somehow regrettable.

One day, I go in to see her. I've been working and the fiberglass is irritating me, and I stink. I don't have much time because I'm on lunch, but I want to check in on her. No one is with her. She's alone. I know that she hates that the most. The idea of dying alone. But that's what she's doing. I guess that's what everyone does. But that doesn't change anything. That's probably why she planned her own funeral, so that no one would have any excuse not to come. She wants to be seen off, and on this beautiful Saturday afternoon, everyone is outside enjoying the day, or trying to make the best of the weekend. I stand next to her bed and say hello. For a minute I don't think she recognizes me.

"I'm sorry I haven't given you your dollar," she says clearly. My allowance again. She used to give it to me on Saturdays, and today's Saturday. She knows intuitively that it's allowance day. "I don't want a dollar," I say to her. "I just came to see you, Grams." I should tell her that she can give it to me when she gets out or something like that. Make her feel needed. But instead I keep on telling her that it's alright, that I don't need it. "I'm sorry," she keeps repeating.

I try to reassure her, but it does no good. After about an hour or so, I have to leave. The fucking dirty insulation is waiting for me. I give her a kiss and stroke her now-white hair for a second and then I leave. She's fallen asleep by that time. She dies before I get a chance to see her again, just a couple of days later. Nobody's there when it happens, although my pops gets to the hospital only minutes after.

It's late, past one in the morning. I got out of work earlier, went home, took a shower, and then went to meet Amelia at the public library, where she'd told her old man she was going to study. Then I'd been sitting here drinking a Dr Pepper, not thinking about Grams or anything else really. Instead, I'd been almost enjoying the feeling of being really, physically tired. When the phone rang, I smiled thinking it was Amelia, but instead it was my pops. He didn't hem and haw. He gave it to me straight, no emotion, no nothing. "Your grandmother died tonight," he said. Just like that. He said it *just* like that, and *just* like that my grams was dead. "She's in heaven now, with your grandfather."

"Okay." That's the only thing I could say, and he said something about coming around tomorrow.

That was an hour ago. Now I'm slumped against the door in the front room, covering my head with my hands. I'm not really crying. Not yet. Instead, I just keep sitting there, not really knowing what to do. On the door, I watch my silhouette, dark, vaguely familiar, more real than the moment itself. It makes sense. A visual sense of all that I fear and feel. Just a big black shape, the me that's even more alone than a few minutes before, and the me that I'm stuck with. It's this image of death, that still, black shadow. And all I can seem to do is sit here and stare at it, my mourning staring back at me. It's myself looking back at me, knowing that this sadness will always be right there, just behind, sneaking up when it's darkest.

It's then that I look at Grams's little metal box where she keeps coupons. I think about how she's never going to use them and how sad it is that she had to clip them and that she took time to do that so that she could save a few cents, and that's when it really fucking hits me that she's gone. No, no. That's not it at all. She's not gone. She's *dead*. That's when I lose it. I get scared. More scared than I've ever been, so scared I can't even walk to my room to get some clothes. I just grab my keys, get in the car, and drive.

I think about going to Enrique's or Juan's, but I don't want to talk. I don't want to get Amelia in trouble. So I just drive till about three in the morning. Finally, I stop at a Denny's, but I can't go in. It reminds me too much of Grams. She didn't even like it that much, but remembering that she didn't like it that much, and remembering how she used to tell me that she made better pancakes than they did, makes me too fucking sad. So I keep driving till I can't keep my eyes open. Instead, I turn back and drive home, but I don't go in. I don't even put the car in the driveway. Instead, I park it on the street, so that it's next to but on the outside of Grams's fence. The house is dark and it already looks haunted. I lock the doors, not because I'm worried about ghosts, but because in this neighborhood there's a good chance some asshole junkie might try and smash the window and my head for seven dollars' worth of change. I lean back in the seat and recline. The next thing I know, my pops is knocking on the car window and it's morning. I wake up and the first thing that I remember is that Grams is dead.

CHAPTER 16

Grams's funeral is a sham. My pops rearranged the whole thing. He bought her an expensive copper coffin, not the cheap wooden one she wanted. She never was fancy about anything. I know everyone says that funerals are for the living, but as far as I'm concerned, they should be a little bit about the dead, too. Anyway, Grams was living when she told me about how she wanted her funeral.

That fucking funeral director was there, too, but when he saw my pops coming, he knew he had a big sale on his hands. I went with him mostly because I didn't want this kind of thing to happen. I wanted to jump in there if any funny business started to go down, but when that weasel started suggesting all this fancy shit to my pops, I didn't stand a chance. Pops spent a ton. Everything that lying thief rattled off, my pops was ready to sign off on. After a while, I was so sick I couldn't even listen anymore. I tried just once to keep Pops and that weasel director honest. I said, "Pops, you really think Grams would've wanted all this?" Before I could say anything else, that dude jumped in with his smooth voice, all oiled up in this fake-assed, soothing timbre. He said, "Oh, it will look wonderful. Such peace for the bereaved to see that their beloved is lying in comfort. It's your final chance to show how much you love her and how much she will be missed." He had my pops hook, line, and sinker. My grams would have looked that funeral guy in the eye and told him to go screw himself, although she wouldn't have used the word *screw*. But she would've meant it in just that way, and that weasel would have *known* that she meant it in just that way.

I haven't gone back to Grams's house. I can't do it. It's too dark. It's filled with pain, and not just mine. Grams didn't go in a way that I can feel good about. She went alone and hurting. It was too terrible and no matter who tells me what, I won't believe it. I won't give in to some punk fantasy about her going with a smile on her face and heaven in her heart. Nobody should go the way she did, drugged up so that she can't even tell what time it is; so that she doesn't even know where she is. Confused and alone. How fucked up is that? I'm not going back there to that house right now, and when I go to the funeral, I'm not going to bow my head and pray thanks to God for taking her. I'm not going to get up there and sing some phony song about sheep and shepherds and angels and clouds. No sweet by-and-by. If they ask me to say something, they'll be sorry because I'll tell them that Grams wouldn't have liked the way they set this thing up and I'll tell them that she never really liked them and that they never really knew her and that they left her alone too much and I'll tell them that I was an asshole to her and left her alone when I could've been there to help her and keep her company. I'll tell them how fucking rotten I feel, how my stomach bleeds for her now, and not for my own self-pitying bullshit. I'll tell them all that, and then I'll tell them that all I want to do is apologize, but not to them. To her. Only I can't and I'll never be able to. That I should've done it that day when she told me those things in her bedroom while I peeled an orange for her. I'll tell them that I wish it was true that I was chosen for something better than I am right now, than I've become, a little, punk-assed, snaggle-toothed vampire that creeps around trying to find ways of causing trouble. I'll tell them that my biggest fear is that Grams was just telling me that stuff because she wanted to feel some amount of hope or peace about me. That I was a disappointment to her and that she had to concoct some story about King David just so that she could die without going crazy with worry about me.

But they won't call me.

The funeral is at my uncle's church. Since I've been staying with him and Enrique, I drive there with them. When we get to the church, there are a lot of people already, old people I've never seen before, gray figures from my grams's past, a past that precedes me, that I don't have a clue about. It's a big church, rectangular, with dozens of heavy wooden pews divided in the middle by an aisle that leads up to the pulpit, which sits on a slightly raised platform. My grams's casket lies on a table. From the back of the church I can see the warm hue of the copper, its half-lid propped open. I can make out what looks like my grams's forehead, a shock of white hair brushed back. I stand back there. I don't want to walk any closer to the front.

So instead of moving, I scan the front pews looking for my old man. I see him hunched over, his head in his hands, transfixed by the sight of the copper coffin, probably looking at that shock of white hair and that pale forehead, too. Just then, one of my father's cousins comes back to get me. "Go to your father. He needs you." She leads me to the front pew and I sit next to my old man. I feel nauseated, my ulcer making my stomach roll around so that it feels like I'm on a damned boat at sea instead of in this church. I can't say good-bye to her here, not like this. My pops looks miserable but

I can't reach over to him. He doesn't really seem to need me, anyway. His girlfriend is next to him and she's holding both his hands now, rubbing them hard through her black cotton gloves. From behind, one of my grams's old friends, some woman that I don't know at all, reaches over and puts her hand on my shoulder. *"M'ijito,"* she starts out, her voice shaky and ready to bust a wail on me, "she love you very much. She look so peaceful. Have you gone up to see her?" I want her to take her mothball-smelling arm away from me. I want to give her hand a rap and tell her to leave me the fuck alone. How come she's alive? She's old, too, older than my grams ever was. But she's alive! Her breathing is an affront because by being old she both reminds me of my grams and yet is so grotesquely *not* my grams.

Finally, the service starts. After a musical number, where some old-timers get up on stage and play an instrumental, my uncle starts to preach. It's not a eulogy. He doesn't really talk about Grams as a person. Instead, he begins talking about death and why it happens and what it all means. He gets me there, my attention, that is.

"This woman, my father's sister, and my great-aunt, many will say, went in a horrible, painful way. They'll seize upon that to say that God is not good. That God is indifferent to our pain, to our fates. Perhaps they will even say worse. That God *causes* our pain and that thus God cannot be good, but that the case is that He is the very opposite of good. That He is evil.

"I want to tell you that this is not so. I want to tell you that our pain and our death, our misfortune, mean just as much, if not more, than our joy and our triumphs. Do you know why? Because they reveal a plan, a system, a *story*, that God is writing. It is a story that has been written to tell us of our frailty. It tells us of the brevity of life, of this earthly paradise, or rather what we humans often cling to as if it were a paradise.

"We are here only a minute, and for that minute, we experience a pain that is in reality a deeper longing for something that we are lacking, and which nothing, not even life itself, can fill. Too often, we cling to earthly love and delight for the wrong reasons—we think that love and delight will satiate the hunger we feel so deeply inside. Think on this, brethren: Earthly love and earthly pain are linked in our hearts because they have the same cause. They point to the same *lack*. Rosita Lomos no longer lacks. She no longer hungers. She is no longer thirsty." The people are all listening now, some of them beginning to say "Amen" and others to say "Hallelujah." It distracts and annoys me. I'm trying to listen.

"She has finally learned, in the language of the spirit—the language that God speaks—what it is that was at the root of her pain, and I'll tell you that it was not 'cancer.'
"If we listen with still spirits, with humble hearts, with a quiet that allows us to hear the whispering of the Spirit, we shall perhaps be able to make out the sound of God's answer. Listen!" And then he lowers his voice. "Your pain has been that interminable distance put there by the cares of the world, by that which you have loved so much that it separated you from Me: *life itself*." He gets louder. "Come to Me now, God has told Rosita Lomos, come to Me now and be filled with a love that spells not longing nor absence. Be filled by My fullness, My Being. Rosita Lomos heard that call and has been brought out of the desert, the Desert of Life, the Desert of Pain, the Desert which brings us to God."

I look over and my pops is crying. He has heard and believed. My uncle has spoken and everyone in the church seems to be seeing my grams's body in that copper coffin as the final paragraph in some eternal, universal, holy story.

Everyone except me. I don't feel it. I don't see it. All I feel and see is a pain tied straight to my grams and how much I miss her, not to anything else. I'm no David. I'm not chosen. Not even my grams, the best person I've ever known, seems chosen, even with my uncle's sermon still playing in my head. I can't believe any of it, although for a minute there, I wish I could more than anything else, because then Grams would be right, and all this would mean something more than it does. I could march right out of here, find that asshole Nacho, and tell him that his agnostic theory and pot-head philosophy are all wrong. That he better watch it. Then I could chill, feel peace. A peace that would let me think out my "purpose," the one Grams talked to me about.

The rest of the funeral is a blur, a long, terrible, blue blur. I wish that I would've brought Amelia, but I told her not to come. I told her that I didn't want her to skip out of school, but the real reason was that I didn't want her to see me all choked up and crazy. I didn't want her to see all the holy rollers so up-close and personal. To tell the truth, I was afraid that it would grab me and take me along and I didn't want her to see me like that. But as they're lowering Grams into the ground, I can't help but wish that Amelia was here. That somebody could be here just for me. I wouldn't have needed her to keep me from passing out or even for her to give me a shoulder to cry on. It would've been enough that someone next to me *knew* that I was feeling as empty as an old paper bag.

When she's in the ground and this thing finally breaks up, Pops asks me to ride back with him and his girlfriend to Grams's house. The "close" relatives are getting together there to eat and talk about Grams. A family memorial, my pops calls it. I tell him that I'll be there in a minute, after I pick up Amelia. I figure if I bring a girl into the equation, Pops will understand. He does, although I can tell he wishes I'd roll with him. I feel bad about that, at least for a second, but then I think about all those damned relatives sitting on my grams's couch and on her chair, using her bathroom, putting their grubby hands on her fridge and sink, and I can't do it.

I don't go anywhere near Amelia's. Instead, I just drive around till I get the bright idea of going by the job site. As I drive into the parking lot, though, I can't bear to do that either. I don't want to see those assholes right now. I don't want any company. I don't even want to be with myself, but that's a tough order. I have a joint in my ashtray and as I sit in the parking lot, I smoke it till I feel a buzz creeping in. It isn't much of a solution to how I'm feeling, I know that, but it's the only option I feel up to choosing. After a while, some of the guys start to filter out of the building. It's quitting time and I split before anyone sees me.

I drive past Grams's, not because I have any intention of getting out, but just because. Just because I feel like driving down that familiar street, and seeing that familiar house, and being close to about the only comfort I've had but now've lost forever. The yard is filled with strange cars and on the porch I see a couple of shit cousins, young punks. I drive by slowly, but they don't notice me. They're just kids, playing around. They don't know nothing about anything. I drive off to find a hotel.

I hole up at the Motel 6, my home away from home. It dawns on me that I could star in a fucking commercial for them. "Got nowhere to go, got not much moola? Are you a lonely, pathetic, forlorn loser? There's always room at the Six, the deep Six. Tell 'em Robert sent you." I smile at the camera with my chiseled vampire teeth.

Two days later, I finally call Amelia. She's been worried, but she's cool. She doesn't sweat me. Instead she asks me how I'm feeling and how I've been doing. I feel bad about that. "Why don't I pick you up?" I say. She's all for it. "We have to be careful though. Well, I do, anyway. My stepfather found out I'm still seeing you, and he gave my mother a real bad time about it."

"How bad?"

"Bad." And I know that she's not bullshitting.

"I'll pick you up at the library."

"I don't think that's going to work anymore."

"Well, where then?"

"I'll have to sneak out. You'll have to wait till three o'clock in the morning, when everyone's asleep. Can you do that?"

I pick her up at the usual spot, just around the corner. I recognize her shape, walking slow, her small limp becoming more pronounced as she gets closer to my car. She gets in and she smiles, her brown eyes so welcome. She reaches over and hugs me and for a minute, I shit you not, I feel like I'm going to just put my head on her shoulder and either start bawling or fall asleep, but I resist and instead, I give her a little kiss and say, "You hungry?"

She nods. "Sure."

"Where?"

"Denny's?" I point the car in that direction.

Once we're at the restaurant, she wants to know about the funeral. I tell her about how phony the whole thing was and how I didn't stop at Grams's house afterward. "Why didn't you go in?" she asks me.

"I just didn't want to be around them," I say.

"Who, your father? Why not?"

"No, I mean yes, that's part of it. But that's not all of it. It's hard to explain, but I knew what they'd be doing. They'd be sitting around talking about her, telling each other stories and shit like that. I didn't want to hear that stuff. Not from them."

"What's wrong with them telling stories? It'd be because they loved your grandmother, too," Amelia says. She's not being stubborn, I can tell that. She's just trying to figure out why I'm being so bad about this. I know it doesn't really make sense, but I want to explain it to her. To myself.

"I don't want them to act like they had a piece of her, like she belonged to them. She didn't at all. She didn't even like them."

"Not even your father?"

"She loved my father. I don't know if she liked him much."

"I wish I would've been there." She says it like she means it.

"Why?" I ask her.

"Because I didn't really know her at all. Just the once that I met her and that's it. I would've liked to have known a lot more about her. I would've wanted to hear those stories."

"Why?" I ask again. "You don't even know your own grandmother that well. Didn't you tell me that?"

"Because she was so important to you, Robert."

"Oh," I say because that catches me by surprise, that this girl could want to know a dead woman just because she meant something to *me*.

"Why don't you tell me something about her, a story, anyway."

I think about it for a second. "I could tell you one right now," I say. "One that wouldn't make me too damned sad, though."

"A happy one then," she says. "Not at all sentimental." So I think about it, and the perfect one comes to mind right there in a Denny's of all places.

I'd been faking being sick so I wouldn't have to go to school. I hated going to school. My moms told my grams and so she took me to go see a shoe cobbler one day. She told me she had to drop off some shoes to be fixed, you know, just an errand. I was only six so I was just along for the ride as far as I knew. It was just some little shop where the guy probably lived, right there in the neighborhood. The shop was shabby and plain, with an unvarnished floor made out of old dull wood. There were two or three chairs with his workbench in the middle of the room. He was an old guy, and when we walked in, he said hello to my grams by first name, "Rosita," he said, a few crooked teeth poking from his wrinkly brown lips. I could tell he was a nice old coot offering his hospitality to my grams. "Got some shoes for you today, Lencho." She held out a pair of old-lady shoes for him to take. He grabbed them, happy-like, a regular businessman. He walked immediately to his bench and began to reheel my grams's gray shoes. "This boy, he looks like a good boy," he said as he tap-tapped with his little hammer, like some elf from a fairy story. "Oh, he's okay, but he's gonna be a *burro*." The old man stopped tapping for a second to peer over at me with a serious look. "You don't wanta be no *burro*, boy." He started tapping again, but kept talking, too. "I'm a *burro*." I looked over at my grams because I wanted to crack up at the old man who'd just called himself a *burro*, but she was listening to Lencho and so I stifled the laugh and looked back at him. "Yeah, I never wanted to go to school. My momma, she needed me to work anyway, so she didn't care if I stopped going to school. Now all I do is fix these shoes, *when* I get shoes." Then Grams started talking to him. She pretended to ignore me like I wasn't even there. "I'm a *burra*, too, Lencho. I have to clean houses for those old, rich, white ladies over on the north side of town." She shook her head slowly. "'magine that. Me, an old lady, cleaning houses for ladies the same age." Lencho brought over the shoes that he'd just reheeled. "Look at us," he said, looking at me, "a couple of *burros*, and you with the chance to go to school." He shook his head sadly, like I'd disappointed him in a big way. "He's gonna be a *burro*, too," Grams said matter-of-factly, "I know it. That's what he wants, all the time pretending to be sick, coming home crying early from school because he don't like it." The two *burros* looked at me so sad-like. Grams gave him a couple of bucks and he took it and put it in his apron. The cool part was that just as we hit the door, I heard the old guy go "Heeehaaaw!" just like a burro. I still faked being sick the next day, but I knew that I wouldn't be a *burro*. That always stayed in my head. Always. My grams was always good that way.

I look over at Amelia, and that crazy girl is wiping away a tear. "That wasn't supposed to be a sad story," I say. "Why are you crying?"

She's staring right at me and she says, "Why are you crying?" and just like that, she wipes a goddamn tear away from my eye. And that's the way I say good-bye to Grams.

My grams's relatives found a way of saying good-bye to her, too. They've stolen all her stuff. After a week or so, I finally decide that I gotta go back to Grams's house. At least to check on it. The house is locked up, but inside it's empty so that it's like when Grams left, everything left with her. I'm confused for a second. "Maybe I walked into the wrong house," I keep thinking as I walk from room to room. In the front, everything is gone except for her writing desk. They've even taken her portrait. They left the TV because it's a piece of shit. I guess the desk was too heavy. My room is still together, but the kitchen table, the chairs, even Grams's bed is gone. In her room, only the old metal fan is there. They probably thought it was broken. I look in her closet. Her clothes are still there. So are her shoes. Who would want old-lady shoes? They also left my old encyclopedia set and a few books I'd put in my room. A 1946 Britannica isn't very useful, I guess. Grams's secret closet is empty, too. All the pictures and my granpa's funeral flag, the one that was folded military style and given to Grams—gone.

It's not that much of a shock really. Grams always told me that people would take everything when she died. Her warning plays in my head, "They'll come quick with a truck or two and they'll clean my house out. You better get what you want first. That's what they did to the old man who lives across the street. His body not even in the ground, and I seen 'em, people who hardly even spoke to that *viejito*, taking his furniture." Even dead, Grams is still getting it right. And it almost makes me happy to have her prediction come through, her wisdom proving right one more time. Could it be possible that if she was this right about those vultures, that she might've been right about me being chosen?

The phone rings. It's my pops. "Where have you been?" he asks me, pissed off. "You just disappeared." It's ironic: *him* telling *me* that I disappeared. I'm about to tell him that when he tells me he's going back to California. "I won't be back for a few months, so you're going to have to watch that house."

"Too late," I say.

"What do you mean?"

"Motherfuckers already took everything, just like the Grinch."

"Don't talk like that," he says. "I told people at the wake that they could take mementos if they wanted."

"What? You did *what*? Did you forget I live here?" I say. "Did you forget that me and Grams lived here and that she wouldn't have wanted those motherfuckers taking all her stuff?" He's about to go off on me, but before he can do it, I hang up. It doesn't really matter. I mean it does, because I don't have a chair for my ass, or a pot to piss in. But I know that it's not really that that's bothering me. It's that the stuff I was counting on to remember her is gone. The light spots that jump from the empty walls where pictures hung are the exclamation marks to her dying. But that's what I get for being a punk and staying away. If I'd been here, I would've worn out my sneaks on anyone's ass, including my pops, who tried to walk off with my grams's stuff. She tried to warn me, but I didn't listen.

I head off for True Value and buy some new locks and put them on the front and back doors. The little girls next door are watching me do it. "What are you doing, Robert?" Tina asks me.

"Changing the locks."

"Why? Because they stole your stuff?" I put the screwdriver down and walk to the fence.

"Did you see people taking stuff from here?" They both nod big, eyes wide open.

"Yup, we sure did," says Ruthie. "We told 'em, 'what are you doing?'"

"They didn't listen," says Tina.

"Yeah, well, thanks for trying," I say. "They should've known better. But I'm making sure they can't get in anymore."

"Didn't they already take everything?" asks Ruthie.

"They haven't taken the house," I say. "I'm not going to let them do that." I'm not, either.

Two days later, I get a letter from some small-time Mexican lawyer named Ray Candelaria. He writes that he put together my grams's will, and that I should contact him soon. His office isn't very far. He's strictly a westside chiseler, with an office full of people who are getting fucked by some monster because they can't afford car insurance or because they got fired by some jerk-off middle-manager who thinks all Mexicans steal or are lazy, or because they got hurt on the job and now they're getting screwed.

Candelaria's secretary tells me to wait, but I don't have to wait that long. The lawyer, this short, dark man with white hair and a cheap suit, is sitting behind a desk. "Sit down, Mr. Lomos. Sit down." I do. "I don't have a lot of time, but we can settle this fairly quickly. Your grandmother has made some provisions for you in her will. Basically, she's left you everything: her car, her house, her savings account, and her insurance policies. She was quite a hard worker. But I'm sure you know that. The savings account has almost eleven thousand dollars in it, and the insurance policies are worth just over twenty-five thousand." I don't say anything. "There are some conditions, though. First, you can't touch the savings until you turn eighteen, and your grandmother wanted me to read you this note. 'Roberto, you use this money to go to college. That is what it's for. But if you decide to be a *burro,* you use it for your kid's college. Live in this house, make it your home. Always be the good man that you are and remember I love you. Your Grams.' Now, according to this document, you aren't yet quite seventeen."

"No," I say. "A few days."

"Very well. I'll probate the will. Your grandmother already paid for my services. You should be receiving checks from the insurance companies very soon. I advise that you put them in a savings account as soon as you get them. It seems like a lot, but it's not really. It's a nice little sum. If you take care of it, you'll find that it can help you through college. Where are you thinking of going?" I scan the wall above his head. His law degree is from St. Mary's University.

"St. Mary's," I say.

He smiles. "Very good. A very solid place. What is it you want to do?"

I have no idea but I say the first thing that comes to mind: "Be a lawyer."

"I don't need the competition," he says, laughing a little bit fakey. "Maybe you can come work for me. Your grandmother said you were a bright boy."

"She did? When did she come to you?"

"Oh," he says, looking at his file, "just about four months ago."

"Did she know she was sick?"

"I don't know. I think maybe she suspected, but I don't remember talking about her health. She did tell me that you were smart and that she'd been saving a long time for you to go to college." I thank the guy and I walk out in a daze. Four months ago I'd been in California playing the fool. *Grams had known it all along, that all that shit with Moms would blow up, and that I'd come back.* She'd had a backup for me. A plan she thought would work. A plan she must've thought I could see through. I get in my Mustang and drive back to her house, *my* house. I stand on the front yard and look at it. It looks different to me. Nobody can kick me out. My grams made sure of that. I don't have to run anywhere, because I'd only be running away from myself, from my home. But maybe that's always been the case, and I feel Grams's death deeper and harder than the day she died. The next day I go back to work. Brace and Phil are already putting up ceiling tiles. When Brace sees me, he gives me the hold-up sign. He hustles down the scaffold, almost falling on his ass. "Sum'bitch," he says grabbing on to a pile of tiles to keep from splitting his forehead. "You don't work here anymore."

"What?"

"Yeah, man. Nothing personal. P.J.'s laying everybody off. Only me and Phil working now. The summer's almost over. Remember, 'shit labor'? Don't feel bad, kid. You don't belong here anyway. Your grandmother just died. You should take it easy right now." I just nod. "You can pick up your last check from the office. If you got nothing else going on next summer, I'm sure P.J.'ll hire you back then. Take'r easy." He scrambles back up the scaffold, only he's more careful this time.

Next summer? There will be a next summer. What will I be doing next summer? It hits me. I *don't* belong here, and not just because my grams died. Fuck if I'll be *here* next summer. I might not be a college boy, but I'm not going to be washing fiberglass from underneath my balls this time next year, that's for sure.

I go to Target and buy some cheap pans with that nonstick surface on them so that I can burn stuff without worrying too much about it. I gotta learn to cook something besides French onion soup. I gotta learn to do a lot of things.

CHAPTER 17

What will I do? Amelia keeps asking me. She's the only one that seems interested. I tell her that I don't know, and I don't. I'm not sure that I can be a college boy. I'm a dropout after all. But the real truth is that I don't trust myself not to fuck up. I don't trust myself to do the things I have to do to make it. There's a lot of shit I'd have to do just to get in. Stuff I have to figure out, fill in, send off. Then there's school itself. But I do like to read. That I know I can do. So there's always next summer and what I'm going to find myself doing. Sometimes I get these momentary fantasies where I run off to Mexico with the money and just live on the beach, smoking weed all the time, watching the ocean come in and go out. Maybe I leave my whereabouts for Nacho and Juan and Enrique so they can come kick it with me whenever they want to. In one version, I take Amelia with me. In another one, I tell her she can live in Grams's house so that she can get away from her stepfather. Lots of stuff crosses my mind, but I stay home every night and stare at the TV that sits on my grams's writing desk because there's nowhere to put it.

Tonight, I get this idea. I take the set off the desk and put it on the floor. I face the TV toward the wall and leave it unplugged. I bought this white plastic lawn chair from the grocery store for four bucks and I put it in front of the desk. I sit down. I pull out some typing paper from one of the drawers and I grab a pen from the coffee cup that sits on the top. With Grams dying and my moms and Antony being so far away, and me about to turn seventeen, I've been thinking about how things change all the time. I want to write some things down before I forget. People always forget. They forget the most important things. That's why they spend so much time writing little stupid lists of things they need to do. But I don't want to forget, and I don't want to use this paper and pen to write down a list of piddly-assed things I need to do. I want to write about my grams. I want to write about some of the things that I don't ever want to forget, because Amelia made me realize that night in the Denny's that to forget something is how you *really* lose it. Maybe if you protect it, your memory, then no one can steal anything from you.

I've been thinking that it might work that way with Antony, even my moms. It works like this: Maybe we're more than just our experiences. We're what we learn from those experiences, and what we remember about those experiences, and in that way maybe we can choose what we become, at least a little. Maybe, then, it's possible I'm more than a fuck-up? What else I am, I don't know, but it seems like it might be important for me to send Antony these memories, all these stories I've got, to let him know that part of him, of who he is, is back here. Because I'm back here and Grams is here. This house is here. A kid should know that. Maybe that's why I went to California, at least part of the reason: to help him to learn to read and to put a face to them so that when he reads these stories, he won't have to lose them or me. So I sit there all through the night, threading together what I can, for myself and my brother, and for Grams. And this is what I write:

GRAMS'S PHOTO ALBUM

When she died, besides her house, she left me a five-pound coffee can filled with silver dimes and quarters that she collected all her life. "Silver and gold, that's always worth something," she used to say. She was always ready for the next Great Depression. She taught me to be ready for anything.

Living with her when our parents split, I would get stomachaches in the middle of the night, and she would go outside in the dark and pick a few yerba buena leaves and make me a hot tea that always calmed my stomach.

She had a little treasure box that had a tiny padlock that me and Juan were always curious about when we were little kids. She told us that we were not to touch it. One day, while she was at work, we broke it open. Just a bunch of scraps of paper inside. I still wonder what they were, although I understand why she wouldn't speak to us the rest of the day.

Outside of the living room window, on top of some gray cinder blocks, rested the largest air conditioner in San Antonio. God alone knows how old it was. Dull gray, four feet high, three feet across, it cooled using water. Grams would tell me and Juan to "put water in the 'fan.'" It had three detachable walls, vented filters made of some sort of absorbent straw. We'd pull them off the unit, lay them on the grass, and turn the hose on them, soaking those vented panels thoroughly. Then we'd turn the hose on the inside of that machine and we'd soak it. Then me and Juan would put those panels back on and race into the living room to turn it on full blast. It always smelled like a rainstorm was coming out of that machine after we wet it down. The air would come streaming out of the vents with little droplets of cold water, smelling so fresh. Grams had a double bed in the living room for me and Juan and it was just within range of that air conditioner. We'd lay there, little kids in little-kid underwear, nice and cool even on a hot South Texas day.

Grams had a garage with a bedroom and small bath attached to it. In the garage and the room were old boxes that she would let me and Juan look around in whenever we wanted. Once we found a couple of straw hats and straw canes, the kind vaudevillians used. We put on a show for Grams and charged her a dollar to watch.

She made the best apple empanadas I ever tasted. Every Thanksgiving I would watch her make them at my house. She always let me have the first one.

I have a picture of her making tamales. She would take over the kitchen, and Moms and me would spread the masa on the cornstalk leaves. Together with those empanadas, Grams gave us autumn to taste and smell.

I remember her sleeping over one night after Pops had left and I was still living with Moms and you. Grams was moaning in pain. I got up and took her outside, where I told her about the house improvements I wanted to make. I pointed to houses and told her, "I like those shutters. And this is the kind of grass I want to put on the lawn. I like this color to paint the front." I thought I was the man of the house all of the sudden, and she didn't step in and tell me I was just a kid. She understood that I wanted to be a man. She wanted me to be one, too. So she stood outside with me, and her pain seemed to go away. Later she claimed that it was calambres, terrible cramps in her legs that had kept her up that night, but I know now that she needed comforting same as me.

She was an acrobatic performer in the carpas, the traveling Mejicano tent shows. She didn't like to talk about it. It seemed sinful to her now that she was a "Cristiana" and an old woman, too.

At her house she had a small gas heater in each room. It was connected to small gas faucets on the floor. The heater used a blue flame to heat up these ceramic bricks. They worked very well, but I had to be careful getting up in the middle of the night to go to the bathroom because if you rubbed against the heater, you'd give yourself an awful burn. She was like that, too. Comforting, but don't make her mad.

On my birthdays, when I was a kid, Grams always handed me a penny for every year of my life, and I'd take it to the front of church on Sunday morning and put it in the offering plate, and she'd ask everyone in the church to join in a birthday prayer for me.

Every night, I write one of these memories down. Tonight is my birthday. This last one I put down as a way of letting her know I'm not forgetting and that I know that she's left me with something once again.

Amelia is coming over to be with me. I don't know yet if I "love" her. But one thing I do know is that I want her to hear what I've written about Grams. She's the only person who I want listening. I don't know what that means. Maybe it *is* love.

She says she's made me a cake. She even asked me what kind I wanted. I told her chocolate with cream cheese frosting and maraschino cherries on top. She said that was strange, but she made it, anyway.

The day started out alright. I even got a card from my moms. It didn't say much. Antony wrote his name in it. I won't go into it. But it was cool to get it.

After a while, I hear Amelia at the door. She's holding my cake in this big, round plastic deal. She says "Happy birthday!" and she brings in the cake and sets it on the table. I lift the lid and it's just what I'd imagined. Cream cheese frosting with cherries and in the middle it says "For Robert."

"I couldn't fit 'Happy Birthday' on it," she explains. I hug her tight. After we eat, I ask her if she wants to hear what I've written. She does, and she actually listens carefully. She tells me that it's beautiful, and I don't mind her using that word because it seems right. It describes not what I've written so much as it describes my grams and her.

We're sitting on my bed because there's no couch in the front and she says, "So how are you feeling now?" I tell her that I'm okay. "I've got what I need. At least it feels like it. Everyone took what they wanted, but somehow I still have what I need." I point at the fan. "Helps me get to sleep, and if I can't, I go out and write a few things down on the desk in the front. I had this strange dream a couple of nights ago, where I was somewhere else. Just gone, you know, not living here. And I drove by the house and I saw something in the window so I got out of the car and went in. It wasn't so much scary, but more sad than anything else, the feeling of the dream, that is.

"Grams was sitting on her rocking chair knitting something like she always used to do when I was a kid. So I'm standing there feeling completely confused and guilty at the same time. I say, 'Grams. I didn't know you were alive. Why didn't you tell me? I would've come back here.' She looks at me, not creepy like in a horror flick, just calm-like. She says, 'I was just waiting for you to realize it. I knew you'd come when you were ready. You know I'm never going to die, Robert.' And I sit down across from her and watch her for a while, just knitting and not really paying much attention to me. But I'm happy because I know it's alright and that I can go ahead and stay there. Then I woke up, and I didn't feel scared, the way you usually do when you have a dream about a dead person. It was weird, you know?"

"Maybe that was her telling you something to make you feel better."

"Comfort me," I say.

"Yeah," she says. "You should write that dream down."

"Maybe I should." She puts her arms around me and I settle my head down on her lap. She runs her fingers through my hair and it occurs to me to ask her. "Are you okay? What about your stepfather and your moms?"

She sighs and smiles at the same time and I feel bad for her because I know what's inside her. I pull her hand from my head for a second and I hold it. I don't really say anything because there's nothing really to say. I just want to try and let her know that I'm here with her right now. That this very second, I know how she feels and that she's not alone. Tonight we are together and we're safe. You can't really say that with words and so I just hold her hand.

After a few minutes, she goes back to running her fingers through my hair and I begin to think about what I'm going to do now, and to tell the truth, I'm not really sure. Maybe I'll do the college thing. Maybe I'll just work. But I won't be a *burro,* and I will be a man. From above my head, I hear Amelia start to sing, not loud, but almost like she's humming, and I stop thinking about all that shit.

She's singing so pretty that it doesn't really matter that I can't make out the words, because she's not just singing for me, she's singing *to* me. I can feel my body sinking into something I haven't felt in a long time. I guess you could call it peace. I'd forgotten it, it's been so long. My eyes close and I feel her fingers on my head, still stroking, making me feel heavy. But I'm not going to go to sleep, not yet. I know now how important it is to stay awake for all this and that I need to listen to every note of her sweet, sad, brief song. Amelia sings and I listen, and the funny thing, *the really great thing*, is that somewhere in there I stop thinking about tomorrow and find that I've let myself slip into the embrace of this day.